GREY MOTIVE

Lissa Oliver

maverick HOUSE

Grey Motive
Published in 2023 by Maverick House Publishers.
Maverick House, Unit 33,
The Business Centre, Stadium Business Park,
Ballycoolin, Dublin 11, Ireland.

info@maverickhouse.com
http://www.maverickhouse.com

ISBN 978-1-908518-73-6 (Print)
ISBN 978-1-908518-74-3 (Epub)

The paper used in this book comes from wood pulp of managed forests. For every tree felled, at least one tree is planted, thereby renewing natural resources.

A CIP catalogue record for this book is available from the British Library.

Dear Michael,

For Rory, a shining example of racing's real future.

Thank you for all your patience and friendship,

Lisa

CHAPTER 1

Year One, October

'We've got a problem.'

Jack looked through an intentionally long and unkempt fringe at the disinterested expression of the Deputy Head, which so perfectly matched the man's tone of voice. The old bloke was probably aiming for calm, with the lure of confidante; the good cop without the bad cop, but acting wasn't his forte. He couldn't disguise the boredom.

Which made two of them. Reprimands were just as tedious from the receiving end. Jack was only fourteen, but he'd already had more than his fair share and usually undeservedly, he felt.

'Your parents can't pay the fines. It's school or care, Jack; school or care.'

Jack had already been threatened with being put into care. Mainly by his parents.

Mandy was far worse than him and they'd not got shot of her yet. But he didn't want to call their bluff and find out the hard way.

He said nothing, a shrug enough to acknowledge he'd heard, but maybe his expression betrayed him because there was a sudden change in the Deputy Head's demeanour.

'There is a third choice.'

This time the tone sounded like grasping at straws, as though the suggestion would be way worse than the other two options.

A thousand kids before him had scorned Plan C, that much Jack decided. He looked into the eyes of an already defeated man, fully prepared to be his saviour. A thousand kids hadn't wanted to be saved. A thousand kids had been happy to hang out with the kind of kids Mandy called friends and he skipped school to avoid. Jack knew he wasn't one of them, even if no one else did. He waited.

'Have any of your teachers ever mentioned the Racing Futures Programme?'

Possibly, but as he was so rarely in school he wouldn't have known. He shook his head.

'There's a stable not too far from here in Lambourn, part of the programme, willing to take applicants.' The Deputy Head suspected he saw a spark of interest in the eyes hidden beneath the mop of hair.

'A stable? Like horses, you mean?'

'Racehorses in fact, Jack. You work with them, learn a trade within the racing industry, and continue your education alongside, at a dedicated facility. Not like school at all. Call it a work placement, if you like.' Mucking out stables. As far as he could tell, that was the upshot of it. If the kids didn't shoot him down, the parents always did. He could never quite sell it the way the brochure had.

He stood up and sorted through the papers on his desk, finding one of the folders the racing crowd had left in with him. He'd considered their visit to a Reading comprehensive school a waste of time, most of his pupils had never seen a horse, although they all knew how to pick them down the bookies.

'Take this home and have a look through it, have a chat with your parents, see what they think.'

'Thanks, Sir.'

Jack snatched eagerly at the glossy brochure, his ticket out of here. He wasn't at all concerned about convincing his parents. For all her faults, Mandy had at least done a good job at breaking them.

A horrible thought hit him. 'It doesn't cost anything, does it, Sir?'

'Not at all. They pay you; a bit of an allowance, not a lot. It's work, Jack, make no mistake, not a free pass from school.'

Jack beamed brightly. The very words "the Headmaster says I have to" saved any need of argument, but at least he had one, already embellished to ensure victory.

'Thanks, Sir, bye, Sir.'

'Bye?'

But it was too late, the boy was already gone and there was little likelihood it was to his next class. Why break the habit of a lifetime?

* * *

'We've got a problem.'

Terry jumped down from the small grey thoroughbred colt and stood at its shoulder, gently rubbing its neck as it picked at the grass, on a loose rein.

'There's a reason why all the lads want to get on him every morning,' he said, with an air of excitement.

Chris hadn't seen Terry look this animated since he'd told him he was going to propose to Su – and that had been thirty years ago. It wasn't that his friend and business partner was never happy; just possessed of an unfortunate face that looked in perpetual audition for the definitive pictorial dictionary entry for sombre. Today's audition was a positive fail.

'He's good, is he?' Chris surmised.

'Remember sitting on Salvinius for the first time when we were boys?'

Chris nodded. He did remember, even now. It had been that good. The only Derby winner they had ever ridden, but unfortunately not on the racecourse.

Terry's smile broadened. 'Well, you take him out in the morning and you'll feel it again. This lad's special. We've got a Derby colt, Chris. Guineas, Derby, no reason he won't stay the Leger trip. We've got a Triple Crown horse!'

It was the Holy Grail of racing. Limited to three-year-olds, a colt only got one shot at each of the three Classic races, and very few were good enough to contest all three. Winning all three was even rarer and had only been achieved fifteen times in its two-hundred-and-fifty year history. Dreams of the Triple Crown had faded into history.

Chris leaned over and gave the yearling colt a hearty pat. 'Should've guessed as much when they all wanted to get up on him.'

'He's an easy ride with a Ferrari engine. And we can't keep him.'

'We can't sell him!' Chris protested. His normally cheerful, elfin features were beginning to match Terry's usual severity. 'We'll get our money back if we're lucky and no more, and he'll end up getting over-raced at two and won't even get a Classic entry!'

'Well we can't keep him. Just about breaking even is one thing, but not making anything on him? We're just a small yard. Nothing good enough to work him with, for a start.'

'Any of the big yards would let us work him with theirs. Someone would lend us a lead horse, even.'

'And sub us the entry fees?'

Chris winced mentally. Terry had a point.

'First Derby entry stage is the first week of December, six hundred quid. I'll have to look up how much it is to keep him in at the next stage, it gets dearer each time.'

'He'll be three by then! If he hasn't won his entry fees already we can put him in one of the "win and you're in" races.'

Terry's face returned to its more natural sombre state. 'He's a horse, Chris. He'll find every way he can to injure himself or run a temperature, or get short-headed if he does make it to the races. Nine grand to keep him entered in The Derby by April, plus the rest. And about three grand to enter him in the Guineas, as well. He probably won't have even run yet, never mind earn twelve grand.'

'Twelve grand's nothing, Terry. We pay three times that on one at the sales.'

'To get upwards of four times that at the next sales,' Terry pointed out realistically.

'So we don't turn a profit on him? He's a Derby colt!'

'We owe forty grand on him, Chris. We've to pay it off by April, not the summer after next. Plus the couple of hundred he's costing us every week we keep him. And the same amount we'll be losing from a paying punter when he moves into one of the boxes for horses in training.'

'We gamble every time we go to the sales!' Chris argued. 'We gambled on him and it looked like we'd lost. Now he's offering us double or nothing – we should go for it.'

It was tempting, even for Terry. 'He's grey,' he pointed out, 'there hasn't been a grey Derby winner since 1946.'

'Then it's long overdue. We'll speak to the girls, see what they think.'

'Bloody hell, Chris, three to one! That's not democracy!'

'If he's as good as you say, he'll pay his way. Hell, if he's as good as you say, he'll win the Triple Crown! We're bloodstock investors, it's what we do. And he's an investment.'

'A forty grand one, and stabling and feed. And the bank to convince.'

'And the chance to train. Real trainers, not just pinhookers trying to get back some money from the horses we couldn't sell. Trainers of the first Triple Crown winner in seventy-odd years. Think about that, Terry.'

* * *

'We've got a problem.'

Around her, Joy noticed, no one was paying much heed to the relief manager. Maud was slowly checking her till, Rhys making a start on last night's betting slips. But the words stopped Joy in her tracks. She froze momentarily, then pushed the last drawing pin home through The Racing Post page, the day's race-cards by now on full display throughout the betting shop.

'How much should there be in the floor safe?' Gareth asked.

'Forty thou,' stated Maud, not bothering to look up.

Joy wondered if she was the only one aware of the devastation behind his words? "Should there be"? You don't count the shop's money and announce a problem. However calm and quiet his voice, Gareth was about to destroy their comfortable existence. If there was forty thousand pounds in the floor safe he wouldn't need to ask.

'And who checked it last night?' He looked down through the paperwork as he spoke. 'Anita signed it off. Did she check it herself?'

Rhys barely looked up. 'Huh!' he said in response.

'Oh shit,' Joy said softly.

'Why? What's wrong?' Maud sat back, giving Gareth her full attention at last.

'It's not there, is it?' Joy asked resignedly.

The relief manager exhaled slowly as the full enormity hit him. 'No,' he said, 'it's not. You've not unlocked yet, Joy, have you?'

'Nope.'

'Good. We'd best stay closed for the minute while I ring the police.' He took in a deep breath and exhaled slowly once more, as though taking time over something as mundane as breathing might postpone the inevitable. 'And Head Office.'

* * *

'You're home early, love.' Paul put down his half-eaten cheese sandwich and rose from the kitchen chair just enough to kiss Joy on the cheek, before plopping down in his seat once more and resuming his snack. 'Everything alright?'

Joy dropped her bag down on the table and slumped into the chair opposite him. She unzipped the bag and pulled out the household telephone that had got her no end of stick when she'd first started unplugging it and bringing it to work. She stared at it coldly, considering, too late, whether it would have been better left in her bag.

'So what's up? Any problem?' Paul pressed.

'I don't know, you tell me? What are you doing home? Not on strike again are you? They never mentioned it on the news.'

He smiled, without concern. Even the major problems couldn't straighten his laughter lines, Joy noted. The cheeky grin had got him into habitual trouble at school; no teacher had ever been convinced he was taking things seriously. The kids still walked all over him now, ignoring his threats and outrage. Well, Mandy did. Jack was just another regular chip off the old block. It all came down to her, in the end, to sort it all out, whatever life threw at them.

'Na, gotta do an extra evening shift, so they let me off a bit early for a break. And you?'

'I wasn't due in 'til seven, you weren't gonna leave the kids home alone, was you?'

He reached across the table and took both her hands in his. 'No. I wasn't. Now take a deep breath and tell me what's wrong.'

She leaned back in her chair. 'I'm suspended, on full pay, aren't I?'

'You're what?'

'Suspended. We all are. The whole bloody shop.'

'Why? They're not gonna close it, are they? They're not laying you off?'

'Oh, Jesus, Paul, I've no idea. No bloody idea. Someone's done a bunk with forty grand out the floor safe and until they find out who, we're all under investigation, suspended on full pay and up the bloody creek without a paddle.'

'But with full pay?'

'Yes with full pay. But that's not the bloody point, is it? I might not have a job next week or next month or tomorrow, even. I could go to prison.'

'Go to prison? How could you? You didn't take it! I wish you had, how much was it, anyway?'

'Forty grand, I told you. And who will they think did take it? The merry widow or airs and graces madam? Or the stupid bitch who has to bring her phone to work cos she can't afford the bill her bloody daughter's crank calls run up?' She sighed wearily. 'They'll be hard pressed to find the right forty grand among Maud's millions, won't they? Or trace it getting spent down Anita's tennis club, that's probably forty grand a year membership, the way she swanks it up. And what would young Rhys want with it, he can just get Mummy and Daddy to pay for it all, can't he? No; it's me they're gonna look straight at. The only bloody one of us who needs it.' She looked at him sternly. 'And what the bloody hell are you so happy about?'

'Anyone ever tell you you're dead gorgeous when you're angry?'

She allowed herself a smile. 'I haven't got it, if that's what you're thinking, you can stop buttering me up for that Emirates season ticket!'

'I'd settle for just a sports channel.' He took a bite of sandwich. 'Who'd you reckon took it, anyway? Inside job? No one should even know there is a floor safe, that's the whole point, isn't it?'

'None of us! How should I know? But it's the end to a cushy number, that's for sure. They won't let us back in there again. Spread us round the other shops.'

'At least you'll be shot of madam.'

Sometimes she looked all of her forty years and plus some, usually if Mandy was within screeching distance, Paul felt. Right then, resigned, vulnerable, a little lost, she looked as young as the day he'd met her, her short hair sprayed stiffly into place, her make-up simple, none of the Barbie Doll plasticity of so many of the other wives and women on the estate. She deserved better than what they had and certainly didn't deserve to lose it.

She smiled at him; a gentle, concerned smile, completely unselfish. 'She's not so bad, poor bitch. That shop's her whole life. She only takes a day off because they force her to. It'll kill her, when she finds out.' She was lost in her own thoughts for a few moments, then her smile broadened. 'I tell you what will kill her, having to tell them down the tennis club!'

Paul grinned. 'I'd best make a move, the buses won't drive themselves.'

'Where're the kids, anyway?'

'Mandy's at her mate's – Trish? Treena? I don't know, the orange one with the hair.'

'Tisha.'

'Bless you! Yeah, that one. Jack's gone down the library, looking up horsey stuff for some project for school. They're sending him somewhere for work placement or whatever, he's fetched some stuff home, in the living room on the side. I told him you'd look at it.'

'Christ! And how much is that gonna cost us?'

'Nothing! It's all free, some education programme or something.' He smiled reassuringly. 'I'm glad I was here. Don't be fretting about it, eh? I won't be that late, one-ish. We'll talk about it, if you're still up.'

'Still up? How can I even think about sleep? Anyway, I'll still be waiting up for that little bitch, won't I?'

'I told her eleven.'

Joy gave him a rueful smile. 'And Tisha said they'd be having tea at her mum's, I s'pose?' He was putty in their hands, but she wouldn't have him any other way. 'Go on, get on with you, I'll be fine.'

* * *

Inspector de Freitas flicked through the brown file on the top of his in-tray ready for the morning. He may have been nearing retirement, but he still relished a challenge and the thin file appeared to be anything but.

'Employee taking the takings? A bit trivial for us, Will, don't you think?' he complained lightly. 'Go palm it off on Hector.'

Sergeant McCulloch smiled. 'It's a bit juicier than it looks, Les. Not just an employee. Any one of seven employees and at any time between this morning and three weeks ago.'

De Freitas raised an eyebrow. 'A bookies? Do they not have some way of checking and storing their cash? Don't tell me they really have satchels still!'

His young colleague grinned.

'Worse than that. A fool-proof system and a bunch of long-in-the-tooth complacent staff taking shortcuts. And what with your in-depth knowledge of the sporting world...'

De Freitas smiled ruefully. 'A couple of jockeys' inquests twenty years ago?'

'You'd be typecast for less as an actor!'

'You've read the entire file, then, I take it?'

'There was an obvious flaw in the way the shop was run, a theft simply crying out to happen. It took them ten years to spot it and three weeks to realise someone had.'

'A fair bit of unravelling to be done, then. We'll leave Hector to missing cats and add it to our To Do list, shall we? Which I see has coffee at the top, so sort that out first, Will, and I'll treat you to a day out tomorrow. I might even let you drive, if you're good.'

* * *

It was nearer two in the morning than one when Paul got in. Jack listened to him making a hash of creeping up the stairs, the carefully-opened cupboards and silent making of tea noisier than the normal process, the doors squeaking more the slower they were moved. Mandy could glide in and out in the small hours, and knock her friends up some pizzas and make a dent in the drinks cabinet, as noiselessly as a ninja.

Not that his dad had disturbed him; he'd been awake anyway, thinking about his interview for the stable placement. There'd be one, it said so in the brochure. Carefully vetted and suitable candidates and all that crap. Basically them taking whoever they could get and the school offloading him wherever it could, but he was taking no chances and had studied for the first time in his life, looking up and memorising what he hoped would get him through the interview.

He could hear the low mumble of his parents talking and climbed out of bed, creeping in silent Ninja Mandy fashion to their bedroom door. Dad had said show Mum and Mum had said she'd talk to Dad, but she'd been pretty much all over the idea, impressed that the Head Master had singled him out for a career, a scholarship as she viewed it. And mind you don't let us down, was the only stipulation.

He listened now in case Dad had something else to say on the matter, but the few words he could pick out didn't seem to involve him. They seemed to be prepared for a visit from the police, which was typically over the top of Mum, she over-reacted about everything, even work placements. Scholarship!

That was only for the benefit of that stuck up cow at the shop, he knew.

Someone brushed by him on the landing, her jacket still damp from the cold night air.

'Move, freak!' Mandy hissed under her breath.

'You're so for it!' he hissed back in response, moving out of her way sharply, nevertheless. 'The pigs are coming round about you tomorrow. Mum said.'

She held up a finger in reply as she slipped into her bedroom.

Jack returned to bed, content that no hopes would be crushed come the morning. He couldn't help but admire his sister's skill, coming in at half eleven just late enough for a half-hearted reprimand that saw her storm off grouchily to bed. Mum hadn't even bothered to check on her after that. Pure genius. He couldn't imagine what she'd been up to, to involve the police. Just Mum going on an endless rant again, most likely. Just as well she didn't know what Mandy really got up to.

He didn't mind her latest boyfriend. He'd seen him about at school, overheard him occasionally if they were queuing at the chip van at lunchtime. Unlike most of the others, this one didn't refer to her as "this girl I was with last night". And unlike the others he never went into the details, either, which had cost Jack his place in the queue more than once in the past.

As he drifted off to sleep, he wondered if racehorses could bite and kick or if they were domesticated like dogs?

CHAPTER 2

'There's no question,' Anne agreed with Su, as they watched Chris pull up on the little grey yearling. 'If he says he's as good as you think, Terry, we have to keep him.'

Terry shook his head doubtfully as he tried to force his head to overrule his heart. It wasn't easy. Animals could always find a way into the heart; and racehorses could always find a way to break it.

'You're in the office, Anne, you know our profit margins. Keeping him will hammer us.'

'True, but we can afford to get hammered for a year. Worse case scenario, we sell him this time next year.'

'If we've won with him it will be ten times what we get for him in April,' Su pointed out enthusiastically.

'If we win with him, we won't need to sell him!' Anne reminded her.

Terry pulled a face. 'Unless it's an eight-hundred pound novice race on the all-weather.'

They looked up at Chris expectantly as he walked the colt past them.

'The Triple Crown's a done deal,' he called out, 'if we can keep him fit and happy for the next two years.'

Terry, already admitting personal defeat in his inner battle, waved the white flag. 'Best think of a decent name for him, then.'

Back in the yard, after the final horse had been bedded down for the afternoon, they regrouped in the office. Buying horses to sell was their living and never done lightly. Buying horses to keep was never intentionally done at all and another matter altogether. The training licence couldn't pay for itself without the education allowance and the immediate selling on of winners.

The grey's "page" was uninspiring and unlikely to make them the money they had expected come the sales in April. Every horse in a sale had an assigned page in the catalogue, upon which appeared its date of birth, pedigree and the all-important successes of its immediate family. Very good races were highlighted in bold, the so-called black type races. Buyers liked to see plenty of black type on a page and, at the very least, plenty of minor successes. A weak page was of little interest and a physically weak individual of no interest at all.

Which was how Terry and Chris had picked him up for far less than his predicted value in the first place. They had known his mother, had ridden her at work and in her races. She was the type of horse they were currently dreaming about, an unfashionable stamina-laden pedigree, but blessed with a sharp turn of foot and speed that made the spine of a jockey tingle. More importantly, she was willing; a feisty little battler who hated to give best, even to a better horse. She would dig deep and find a bit more, while her unnerved rivals caved in.

But luck had never been on her side, a virus keeping her off the track as a two-year-old, lack of experience and injury keeping her out of the major winner's circles at three and four. Nevertheless, they'd not been able to afford her first foal when it appeared at the sales. For whatever reason, it had never appeared on the racecourse. Her second foal had been beyond their budget, too, though they'd tried hard and only just lost out to a higher bid. They had regretted that a few months later, when he'd blasted his way up the local gallops and raised the hopes and temperature of his trainer. "Bloody hell I've got a live one here" was the Royal Ascot-bound report. A few coughs and sneezes later and the trainer wasn't the only one with a high temperature. The colt was still a Classic hope, but had yet to appear in public and, crucially, wouldn't do so before the April sales.

They'd bought its full-brother at an open sale back in February, in the hope of later selling a full-brother to a coveted Royal Ascot winner, a champion two-year-old maybe. Something to bring lustre to an otherwise lacklustre page and make their bargain buy look like an inspired purchase. Instead, yet another "unraced" to devalue the page still further.

The off-putting family history of promise snuffed out by ill-luck hung over them now as they once again pinned their dreams and finances on luck. The age-old honey trap had sucked them in against all logic, but that was racing, no place for logic, just the lure of The Dream. Even horse traders dreamed; it was what kept them in the game.

'So, then, we need a name registration form and a Derby entry form,' Anne said, settling at her desk. 'And one less sales entry to pay for – he's nearly covering his losses already!'

'Best get out there and start earning.' Chris stood up, his and Terry's place out in the yard, preparing the horses for their future sales dates.

'Yep, me too,' Su said, the practical work of stable duties of more appeal to her than the office. 'What about you, what's on the agenda?'

Anne pulled a face. 'Interviews. I hate interviews.'

* * *

'What's first on the agenda?'

'Interviews.' Detective Inspector de Freitas slipped his notebook into his coat pocket. 'I love interviews, don't you, Will?'

'Sifting out the straight edges of the jigsaw to start building a picture.'

'You're one of those, are you? Mrs de Freitas always starts with a feature.'

Detective Sergeant McCulloch shook his head. 'Couldn't work like that. Corners first, then the edges.'

'So who's our first corner, Will?'

The sergeant tapped open his notebook and came to a quick choice. 'Anita Wallis. Top left.'

'To the bat mobile, then.'

* * *

'Nice of you to turn up, Reid.' The form teacher glanced at her watch. 'And nearly on time, too. Wonders never cease.'

Jack sneered his disdain, he hoped. Sneers could be a bit hit and miss. Mandy had offered to call the stroke response unit when he'd wordlessly acknowledged her last snide remark.

'Where am I first, Miss?' he asked, not generally in need of a timetable and therefore not possessing one.

'Mr Sayers' office.'

'But Miss! I've not done anything! I'm on time and everything!'

'Interviews, Reid. Seems you turned up just long enough to put your name down for something. And if you fancy fitting more into your hectic schedule, Science Lab Two whenever he's finished with you.'

Interviews. Already? Jack dragged his heels through the empty corridors, stamping noisily up the stairs to the Deputy Head's office. Good job he'd prepared right away; although now they'd forced it onto him when he wasn't ready. Through force of habit, he tapped so quietly at the office door that he was unlikely to be heard. Hours could be wasted, waiting outside the Deputy Head's for punishment. Remembering that he'd rather get this over with, though, he knocked again, more firmly.

'Alright, alright! No need to hammer the bloody door down, boy!'

'Sorry, Sir. Miss said I was to–'

'Oh, yes, the interview. Have you the consent form signed?'

Jack produced the much-folded paper from his back pocket.

The Deputy Head checked it over with care. 'Perfect. They only interview one day a month, so they said we could go today if you were keen. No time like the present.' He sounded almost enthusiastic.

Successful placements probably looked good on his record, Jack thought uncharitably. And one less exam failure to bring down the school's rating next summer. At this rate the interview would be a breeze.

'Anyone else applying, Sir?'

'Not from here, no.'

Jack allowed himself a subtle knowing smile.

'Stop smirking, Reid, what's the matter with you?'

Together they walked down to the teachers' parking area, where a minibus and bored driver awaited them. The driver informed the Deputy Head that he had to take Four-C swimming at two, in such a way that it was clear he wasn't happy about it, and the Deputy Head didn't seem happy about that and Jack again got pulled up for smirking, as if it were a crime.

He sat in the furthest rear seat, chin resting on fist resting against the window, noting how the teacher sat the way they always did, sideways in the aisle seat immediately behind the driver, so that they didn't have to look at the driver or the passengers and could brazenly flout the seatbelt laws, needing to jump up and sort out Four-C and their ilk at the drop of a hat. It vindicated Jack's view that he was personally regarded as of that ilk and that the interview would be a formality. A programme designed for bad kids. It made him all the happier to be escaping, before he fell into the trap of believing them.

It seemed a lot further than just the half-hour away old Sayers had said, especially with the driver reminding them both of the fact every few minutes, which the Deputy Head clearly found just as irritating, but dared not remark upon. The adults always had to stick together in front of the kids. This time Jack deliberately smirked. Like the kids didn't know when the substitute had lost it and got discreetly called out into the corridor! A nice rule to have for yourself, when you could call a kid up to the front of the class and tear them off a strip, to the amusement of their classmates. Huh!

'What are you grinning about this time?' The Deputy Head demanded, as the bus finally scrunched over gravel to a standstill. 'Come on, get a move on, you don't want to be late, now, do you?'

Jack stared up at him. He'd been delivered by school bus, yet could still get into trouble for being late, like it was his own fault! No wonder Mandy had learnt the one finger salute in primary school. He tried to convey the salutation in his expression, but the Deputy Head was already off the minibus and greeting the welcome party.

Jack followed him off and briefly took in the couple now chatting with Sayers. They looked alike enough to be brother and sister, with their black hair and dark eyes; but hers looked like it came out of a bottle and she was twice the height of him and all over him, more like his girlfriend than a sister. Jack looked down at the ground as they turned their attention to him, never quite sure where to look or what to say.

'I'm Terry, this is my wife, Su, and you'll be meeting Anne, she's doing the interviews across in the office.'

Jack merely nodded, looking around him properly for the first time as Terry gestured toward the office. There was a massive old brick archway leading into a courtyard lined with stables and one or two horses peering out over the top half of their stable door.

'Can I stroke one?' he asked at once.

'Work away.'

'Be careful, horses bite,' Sayers warned, as Jack hurried his step toward the nearest horse.

'You're fine,' Terry called after the boy, 'ours don't.' He smiled at Sayers. 'Treat them with respect and kindness and they don't need to.'

Sayers wasn't quite sure how to take that and merely nodded a cagey acknowledgement, suspecting a jibe had just skimmed his bows; but that was what teaching the Mandy Reids of this world did to you.

Terry kept an eye on the boy, watching the horses duck away from the raised untrained hand that moved too quickly for their liking. He would learn, like they did, by reward and there was no better reward than the warm gentle softness of an equine muzzle. Until then, he couldn't get close enough to be bitten.

'You can go through to the office now,' he called to the teenager, saving the kid further disappointment and frustration.

Jack gave up on the horses and did as he'd been told, entering the bright and airy stable conversion that had been filled almost beyond capacity by shelves, filing cabinets and a desk and chairs. There were only two this side of the desk and he took the empty one, a girl maybe a bit older than him giving him a sideways glance as he sat beside her.

'Don't panic,' the woman sitting opposite them said pleasantly, 'this isn't really an interview as such, just a chance to explain what the programme is about and for you to ask me questions.' She smiled just as pleasantly, without a hint of the boredom of a teacher, Jack noted. She reminded him of his mum, though he wasn't sure why. Maybe the short brown hair and lack of make-up.

He sat through her presentation in virtual silence, her concise explanations well practised. Where there may have been cause for a question, Mai, as it turned out his companion was called, was quick to speak up, leaving him with little more to do than digest the barrage of information. He figured they'd show him what to do step by step when he actually started, so didn't do a great deal of digesting, instead wondering more about Mai's determined line of questioning. Half of what she asked had never occurred to him and the other half singled her out as the type of fairly interesting person he'd like to have had in his class. She would keep old Sayers on his toes, anyway.

'Any questions, Jack?'

The direct question caught him off guard, his mind already straying as it often did in class. He was too easily bored, and equally bored teachers gave up on him just as easily.

'Er, not really, Miss, except when can I start?'

'Anne, please; the one thing you'll find is it's not school. And you can start as soon as the paperwork has gone through. I'll give you a call, probably Thursday or Friday. Does that suit you, too, Mai?'

Mai, it seemed, was in Jack's camp of "the sooner the better" and Anne let them go, both sides of the table delighted by the enthusiasm shown.

'It went OK then?' Sayers guessed as he walked Jack back to the minibus.

It wasn't quite a shrug, nor quite a grunt, but as positive a response as he ever received from his students and enough to satisfy him into silence.

* * *

'That went OK, wouldn't you say?'

The two detectives had pulled into a convenient space outside a coffee shop, largely convenient for their ability to pull rank and ignore the parking restrictions.

McCulloch placed the two cups carefully into the cup holders. 'A not so typical innocent, but I wouldn't call her guilty. Not our top left corner, anyway.'

'Not so typical…' de Freitas mused.

He lifted out his cup, raised the lid and cautiously sipped at the too-hot-to-drink coffee. The innocent ones, he'd come to learn over the years, sweated and squirmed with their perceived guilt while the guilty sat quietly confident within their fabricated alibis. Anita Wallis had done neither; seemingly oblivious to the threat of prison, or even arrest, but acutely afraid of Head Office and aggressively defensive when it came to her perceived alibi.

'You've got to feel sorry for her staff,' McCulloch observed. 'I wonder what it is she actually does all day?'

'Delegates, Will; and particularly well, at that.'

The woman had, in fact, delegated to the point of handing almost full control of her shop to her staff, although she had indignantly refuted any such notion. Her job as manager, she'd fiercely pointed out, was to check that the day's opening balance matched the previous evening's closing balance and that there was sufficient to pay out any larger bets not yet collected. This she personally did by having trusted and dependable cashiers provide her with the amounts. That was their job, after all. Hers was to sign off the shop accounts and settle the bets and ensure her shop ran smoothly and profitably.

De Freitas got the impression he and young Will were being used as a sounding board and dry run in preparation for the more important date with Head Office. Anita Wallis was someone so anxious about losing her job that the thought of actually being accused of theft had yet to dawn on her; and Will had carefully recorded that observation in his notebook.

'Where to next?'

De Freitas considered it. 'Who was your bottom left, Will?'

'The regular relief manager, Lee Baxter, but according to the surveillance team he's away.'

'And convenient for us if he doesn't come back.'

'And not have the thrill of the chase? I didn't become a detective just to have them hand themselves in.'

'It is Friday, though. Next suspect, then?'

McCulloch had a quick look at his notebook. 'Joy Reid, one of the cashiers.'

'To Mrs Reid's it is then.'

'Delegation?'

'I prefer to call it on the job training.'

* * *

Joy anxiously watched the rather ordinary car pull up directly outside the house. It was not so ordinary, parked in her street – a mite too new and too executive-model. It had probably raised similar alarm bells outside Anita's, albeit for being a might too old and not quite top of the range. She watched with a growing sense of dread as two ordinary guys in suits got out.

At least they didn't look like police, insofar they weren't wearing uniforms. But they never wore uniforms on TV either. Maybe just Jehovah's Witnesses, which she hoped for now as a welcome blessing. They looked pleasant enough and mild enough. The young one looked like what Rhys at work might grow up into in another ten years, less eager ambition but still a posh kid going places. He carried himself like Rhys. It was probably confidence. The older one had no discernible demeanour that made him memorable, he could be a Jehovah. Or an insurance salesman. Or another bloke from the School Board. He had a comfortable face, not stern or blank, which was a good thing if her first guess turned out to be right.

They knocked at the door, knuckles against wood in the absence of any door-knocker or working doorbell. Joy expected the worst as she opened the door, but still their words sent her stomach plunging to her ankles.

'Detective Inspector Les de Freitas and my colleague DS Will McCulloch, may we come in?'

'Yes, of course.'

She tried to combine her best telephone voice with a breezy hostess' welcome; pretending to look with care at the two ID badges proffered, even though she wouldn't know a toyshop fake from the real thing. Was it good manners to study the ID or better manners to trust them? All that neighbourhood watch stuff, they probably preferred conscientious citizens… Should she write their numbers down, like they told you on the ads? Ring it in… where?

She felt her cheeks redden, suddenly conscious they were waiting patiently for her to finish her detailed inspection. She'd been too distracted to actually see the written details anyway, genuine or otherwise, but nodded acceptingly as though satisfied.

'Come through to the lounge,' she said as brightly as she could, 'will I put the kettle on?'

'We shouldn't really,' de Freitas admitted conspiringly, 'but it would be much appreciated, thank you. Would you like a hand?'

'Not at all; sit yourselves down,' Joy insisted.

McCulloch sat; and learned and marvelled, as he always did, at his Inspector's uncanny ability to put interviewees at their ease, as beverages and their sugar and milk content were finalised. At Anita Wallis' the offer of tea had come late, almost as an afterthought, and politely refused. Wallis was not adjudged to find the domestic process soothing, focused or distracting. De Freitas always had an unerring knack of recognising which purpose a cup of coffee would serve, whether he wanted one or not.

'There you are,' Joy said, a few minutes later, 'we're all out of biscuits, I'd meant to go out in my lunch break, but… well…' Not that she'd intended any such thing, but she was never going to admit to them that since the kids had found the secret stash she couldn't keep a packet for longer than two seconds. Mandy seemed to think it her duty to eat them all before Jack got at them and Jack believed himself morally bound to deny his sister any. She'd kept a packet of chocolate digestives in the washing machine in case of visitors and couldn't imagine how either child had discovered them.

'The policeman who came to the shop said we shouldn't go anywhere,' she pointed out, the inability to offer biscuits worrying her, 'and he said our bank accounts would be frozen.'

De Freitas smiled reassuringly. 'More a case of not leaving the country.' They could go where they liked, they'd all been under surveillance since the report of the theft. 'And your accounts are being monitored, that's all. We appreciate you have a home to run, Mrs Reid, so try not to let this get in the way too much.'

Though she was still sitting too stiffly to the front of her chair, her relief was palpable.

'If we could pin-point when the theft occurred it would be a great help,' de Freitas said, in a tone that suggested he needed her help and not the other way round. 'Could you talk me through a normal routine?'

Joy sat back a little. 'Anita unlocks; usually me and Maud are there waiting, Rhys not far behind us. Anita unlocks the safe and gets to work on the previous night's bets. Being in the precinct we close earlier than our other shops, so we've the evening matches and dogs to catch up on.' She relaxed as the confidence in her role and routine flooded back. 'Maud and me check the cash while Anita and Rhys settle the bets. It never takes long, so one of us'll start knocking out the losing slips and passing back the winning slips to Rhys and Anita while the other puts up the papers and special offers. Depends what we feel like, we just volunteer for one or the other. Whoever finishes first puts the kettle on.'

'So what does checking the cash involve?'

'We check the tills. Just the change, left in them overnight. Should match the opening figures on the sheet, carried forward from the day before. The rest is in the safe, we check that. Anita would have banked most of it the night before and just left a small float for the tills.'

'And the floor safe?'

'That gets the actual float left in it, the actual amount needed to pay out any outstanding big bets. Some punters only come in once a week and it'll be too big an amount to guarantee taking in a day. We've a couple of blokes who come in at lunch time, big bettors, but they tend to only get their own money back if they win, but we still have to be ready in case they only collect and don't punt.'

It was, in consequence, generally the same amount left in the floor safe and neither she nor Maud ever bothered to physically check it. But she wasn't about to admit that to the police.

De Freitas had been looking at the copies of the account sheets as she spoke, flicking back through to find one with something other than forty thousand in the floor safe. It was clear that the tens of thousands were grouped in the floor safe and the remainder in the shop safe, visible to all. There was no mention on the sheets themselves of safes or whereabouts of cash, merely the cash total; added up from the tills, the safe and the rounded-up lump sum hidden beneath a carpet tile in the kitchen. It had been three weeks ago that the amount had altered, from thirty thousand to forty.

'And on Anita's day off?' he asked.

'I take the keys on her day off and usually it's young Lee on relief.'

The popular, likeable Lee, de Freitas read from her expression and tone.

'Maud and me have it all checked and ready to open for him,' she continued. 'I get the sheet filled in, he just has to settle the bets. It's tough on the relief blokes, never in the one shop, so we do what we can for him; he's such a lovely young kid.'

And a looker, no doubt, de Freitas surmised. The lookers always won the popularity stakes and had the mother-types like Joy and Maud willingly running around for them. The grudge in her tone had been noticeable to his finely-tuned ear as she'd described her same duties for Anita. Lee, it was a safe guess, appreciated what Anita took for granted.

'And the other cashier, Tracey Pattinson?'

'Our Saturday girl,' Joy told him. 'She's a student at the Uni', she just does her till, nothing else. We always need one extra on a Saturday. Rhys just covers for me and Maud on our days off.'

'So she'd never be involved in the sheets or checking cash or handling the keys?'

Joy shook her head. 'She just takes bets. Doesn't even knock out the losing slips. Maud and me'll often knock out the losers if it's quiet on the tills, but no point teaching a Saturday girl, she'll be gone when she graduates.'

De Freitas put away the sheets and passed the file back to McCulloch.

'You've been an enormous help, thank you, Mrs Reid.'

'Just glad not to be arrested,' she quipped, with more lightness than she felt and definitely more sudden frankness than she would have liked.

Both detectives reached for their coffee at once.

'I see you were saving up for something,' de Freitas said conversationally, 'anything nice?' He looked across at an aged family photo on a shelf, the children much younger than he'd been told. 'Daughter getting married?'

'Huh! Not for a few years yet, I hope! No; a caravan in Tenby, just a pipe dream. We were doing OK for a while, 'til we had to dip into it. Kids needing stuff; Paul out on strike.'

'Holiday home?'

She gave a half-muttered tut. Holidays were a push, never mind holiday homes! What world was he from?

'Retirement home. You don't think I want to stay in this place all my life?' But she already sounded resigned to it.

'You've a long way to go yet, Mrs Reid; we never know what's around the corner,' he reassured her.

'Usually more trouble!'

The mugs of coffee were returned to the coffee table, still full, Joy noted uncomfortably. Her guests stood up and thanked her for her time and she felt tempted to stand at the door and wave them off, as she would for family. It hadn't felt like an official visit at all.

Instead, she watched warily through the net curtain as they sat in the car, probably comparing notes before pulling away. She'd been a bloody fool to mention the caravan. They only had to search the internet to find forty grand would cover one. It had been twenty-five when they'd first started saving. The depressing thing was, it would always get further out of reach, the more they saved.

Maud and Anita had never had to save up for anything in their lives. Lee had promised them all a postcard from Portugal. Rhys had asked him whereabouts, like he knew the whole country. Whatever notes the police were comparing, they could only point to one suspect. Pity; she'd liked the older one.

Outside, in the car, de Freitas compared notes with McCulloch.

'How much would a caravan in Tenby set you back, Will?'

The sergeant consulted his notebook, the compact tablet barely bigger than the paper versions of old, but so much more versatile.

'Between thirty-five and fifty grand, as it happens.'

'Would you bother your arse to lift out and count cash that sits untouched for weeks at a time in a kitchen floor safe?'

'I wouldn't see the point, to be honest, Les. Count the safe, count the tills and add on forty grand and tick the balance as correct. Simples. Unless it's your shop, you're responsible for the cash and you're handing it over to a relief manager tomorrow. Damn right I'd count it, if I were Anita Wallis. And that Lee Baxter wasn't too clever about it, either.'

'If Maud Simmons is half as pleasant and efficient as Joy Reid, I'd be a little too trusting myself. We all want an easy life, after all. At least Joy has made it pretty clear who didn't take it, don't you think?'

'Lee Baxter and the Saturday girl? She'd only know the kitchen contained the kettle and I doubt he even knows they've got a kitchen!'

'How much for a fortnight in the Algarve?'

'A budget package booked at the last minute,' McCulloch remembered, without the need to consult his files on Baxter, 'second week free, two-eighty a person.'

'Nice. Might check it out myself, Mrs de Freitas and I are getting bored with Devon.'

McCulloch slipped his notebook back into his pocket and turned the ignition.

'Where to next, then?'

'The merry widow Maud Simmons. The lady who apparently works for the sheer fun of it.'

'Don't we all, Les?'

CHAPTER 3

'What the bloody hell are you doing up so early? It's not Christmas, you know?'

Joy watched Jack examine the contents of the fridge as she sat at the kitchen table, mulling over her tea. It wasn't the sort of table anyone used, more a collecting point for grabbing last minute snacks before heading out the door, or a dumping ground for whatever they'd walked in the door with. That morning, she'd got as far as the table before wondering what else to do with her day.

'Well? Anything planned?' she quizzed.

He seemed to hear her for the first time. 'What? No. Why should I? It's Saturday, I can do what I want, can't I?'

'All right, keep your hair on, I was only asking!'

He tipped the contents of a box of cereals into a bowl and sloshed in some milk, grabbing a spoon on his way through to the living room.

'What about this mess?!' Joy called after him.

'What mess?'

She tutted loud enough for him to hear, not that it had any effect, and stood up to get a cloth and wipe the table. She selectively cleared the spilt cereals and milk, wiping round the plate left out earlier by Paul, cleaning up the butter and toast crumbs as she did so. Maybe she'd clear the table a little later and wash up. Or just wait 'til after Mandy had breakfasted at lunchtime and save herself the wasted effort.

It was so much easier when she had her normal routine. A hurried dash about, leaving the place clean and tidy as she headed out the door to work. Repeating the process when she came back in. How they ever managed to get it in the state it was in in the meantime was beyond her. Paul always cleared up after dinner. That was Their Time then, if he wasn't on a late shift; snuggled up on the sofa watching rubbish on the TV, while the kids tutted about "get a room, for God's sake!" and complained about not being able to watch whatever was on the other channel.

There hadn't been many late shifts lately; not many shifts at all.

It seemed Jack wasn't the only early bird out that morning. She'd always imagined the house remaining silent, and briefly tidy, between her departure and at least after lunchtime on a non-school day. But her daughter was further proof of her misconception.

'What are you doing here?' Mandy demanded, just as surprised to find the kitchen occupied.

'Sitting minding me own business.'

Mandy gave her a typically dirty look. 'I didn't think Madam granted Saturdays off.'

'Expecting the house to yourself, was you?'

'Just on my way out, actually.'

'And what were you doing creeping in at two o'clock this morning? D'ya think I never hear you?'

'For God's sake! I'm sixteen, not twelve!'

'You're not eighteen, either, so stop acting like it!'

'Grow up, act your age – I wish you'd make your mind up! It's him you should be having a go at.'

'Why? What's he done?'

'The little freak has gone through every drawer in my room! And he said you'd called the cops on me! I was only at Tisha's watching a film.'

Joy's tone mellowed somewhat, not in the mood for a fight. 'Boys, eh? I'll have a few choice words with him. Where are you off to today, then?'

'Nowhere. We might hang in the park, if it stops raining.'

'What, dressed like that?! You'll freeze!'

'God, you sound just like Dad. Where is he, anyway? D'you think he could pick us up if we went into town tonight?'

'No chance, he's on a double shift today, trying to make up for last month.'

'So why did you take the day off? We could've hung out here 'stead of Tisha's.'

'It's just the way it worked out.'

'You should be able to choose your days off, when it suits you.'

'Shop steward now, are you?'

'God, I'm just being helpful.'

Joy smiled. 'Midnight. And no later, you hear me?'

Mandy made a sound that Joy took for acknowledgement, at least, and headed off to meet her friend; leaving her mother to dwell on some of the closing remarks. There were a couple of points Joy could have brought up, given the perfect opening, but she wasn't yet sure if she should. Did the kids really need the grown-up anxiety of wondering whether their mum was a thief and that their life could face a dramatic, irreparable change?

Jack flopped onto the sofa and switched on the TV, flicking through to the horseracing programme that he'd got up early especially to see. He tucked into his breakfast, balanced on his lap, as he struggled to make sense of a sport previously overlooked in favour of football and music.

The hour-long programme did little to enlighten him. Pundits debated which horse would win which race, without ever reaching a unanimous conclusion, and the betting guides were equally non-committal. The favourite was likely to win, but wasn't good value at its restrictive odds, while a horse less likely to win represented great value at longer odds. Jack was no maths expert, but suspected winning very little was better than not winning at all. It reminded him of his dippy sister, buying stuff she didn't need because it was a bargain.

He also learned that a collection of industry experts – betting gurus, trainers, jockeys and broadcasting journalists – had made this their life's work and were unable to confidently predict a winner from any of the seven races to be televised later that afternoon. Horses were unpredictable and he was about to start working with them. That raised more than one doubt within him, but the one thing he was sure about was that he wasn't ever about to start gambling on them; the experts had just taught him that much.

He switched off the TV and considered what else they had taught him. Preferred distances, preferred ground conditions, preferred tracks, even preferred jockeys. Horses, it seemed, had their own agenda and no one could do a great deal to alter that. Much like in the rest of his life, it seemed his safest course of action was to simply humour any horse in his care.

Doubts quashed, he turned his mind to other questions. Such as why Mum was home on a Saturday, which he'd not considered until overhearing Mandy pointing it out? And why Mum had been going through their things? Mandy could accuse him all she liked, but Mum hadn't immediately yelled for his guilty presence. And someone had clearly been through all his drawers and record collection and wardrobe, too.

He'd assumed it had been Mandy, looking for one of his console games or pocket money. She'd been careful enough to put everything back almost exactly as it had been, even in its state of disarray, which, thinking about it, was well out of character. She had never shown any respect for him or his stuff.

So what did Mum suspect them of having, that she wanted to find?

He knew he had nothing, but whatever Mandy had he could be sure he wanted it. Blackmail and ransom were always useful weapons against his big sister.

'Mum!' he complained, taking his empty bowl out to the kitchen, the spoon forgotten on the sofa, 'She's got my PSP again!'

'Well go and get it back then, and mind you don't make a mess looking for it.'

Duly licensed to raid, he entered Mandy's room unhindered by fear of getting caught and stood in the doorway, contemplating where to look. Nowhere Mum would think to look. He lay on the floor and reached an exploratory arm under the bed to peel back the carpet from the far corner. He always hid things there, in his own room, but the carpet refused to budge, never disturbed by Mandy. There was no easily-lifted base in her wardrobe, either, a fact he only discovered after having to move piles of magazines.

He tried every pocket in the garments hanging up and felt inside any sleeve ending in a ski-cuff, without success. None of the drawers had a false back, either. His own were equally lacking, but he'd seen it on some movie on TV once and considered it worth a try. She'd had enough boyfriends, maybe one of them had been a DIY buff.

There was no false back, but her underwear drawer did have a false bottom, as it turned out. He lifted the piece of hardboard expectantly and discovered a crack and small hole in the hardboard base beneath it. Dad was no DIY expert, either.

Disappointed, he picked up an exercise book from her dressing table, hoping to read her embarrassingly intimate secrets, but it contained only summaries of the recent films she'd seen, for some sort of homework. It was so unfair that she got to watch films and write reports on them and all he ever got was algorithms.

He read her report of some movie with a foreign title, but she clearly hadn't bothered to watch it, prattling on instead about the "cinematography" and "camera angles" and "directional shots" and even "natural lighting". He had to hand it to her, a bit of fancy wording and she'd be getting an eight out of ten without wasting an hour and a half reading subtitles.

Mum, he decided, was going more off her trolley than ever. No cops had turned up to arrest Mandy and there was no drug cache in her room. And he'd "won a scholarship". Nothing was ever just normal from Mum's point of view; he probably never really had been in danger of being shipped off to a care home, just for bunking off school a few times. He was relieved now that he hadn't told her why he skipped school; she would have over-reacted and who knew how screwed up she could have made it all?

He needed a pee and went into the bathroom, his gaze focusing on nothing in particular as he relieved himself. He'd stared down at the corner of the bath panel a million times before, but he'd never before noticed it was bowed slightly away from the skirting. Someone had prised it away.

For all her faults, Mandy had always been brighter than him, labelling him stupid because invariably he was slow to catch on to her latest trick or react to her jibes. He kicked himself now for not being the one to think of such a brilliant hiding place, in the one room that guaranteed privacy.

It was probably a stash of pregnancy testers, he bet with himself as he pushed the flimsy plastic panel inward. It pressed up against something, the bath itself or a frame, and he changed tactic to pull at it instead of push. It slipped out quite neatly, to reveal little more exciting than copper pipes and cobwebs.

At first glance the thin plastic zipped folder wasn't exciting either, other than the fact it didn't belong under a bathtub. Jack lifted it out with more interest than he usually reserved for paperwork and carefully unzipped it, looking through its contents without removing any. The few sheets of paper and collection of receipts hardly seemed worth the effort of hiding, yet their importance warranted secretiveness.

He carefully removed a receipt, noting where it had been. It was written in German, though the seller's name and address was local, and someone had paid two-hundred pounds for whatever "exacta mount zeiss jena flektogon 35mm" translated to. The one part he could understand worried him.

The price tag ruled out anyone in his family. Maybe the people who'd lived here before had tucked it away, or whoever had put the bath in. It wasn't Mandy's drug or pregnancy tester stash, anyway. He slipped it back in its correct place and pulled out the next one. A "16mm C mount Kern Paillard Switar" didn't need as much translating, but just us much money. He didn't bother looking at the others, his interest quelled.

The bath panel failed to go back quite as neatly, but he'd stopped caring, the disappointment at failing to find incriminating evidence killing any enthusiasm, until it occurred to him there was nothing to find because Mum had already found it. Ha! Mandy was for it now, big time. Mum would wait 'til Dad got in and then there'd be trouble. He looked forward to eavesdropping later.

* * *

'How's the spying going, Will?'

De Freitas paused to look over McCulloch's shoulder, on the way back to his own desk. Bank statements and credit card bills made the surveillance team virtually redundant, consumers recording a convenient diary with every swipe.

'Look at this,' McCulloch replied, without looking up, 'his whole day detailed to the exact time and place. I always wonder who's tracing me when I go on a spending spree. Some bored Mastercard clerk telling a colleague "he's been on Ticketmaster again".'

'Bored, are you, Will?'

'Fascinated, actually. He might not be splashing our missing forty K around, but he's having a good holiday. A restaurant last night. An excursion company yesterday morning, thirty quid. One of those all you can eat and drink boat trips, do you think?'

'I wouldn't know; Mrs de Freitas and I tend not to go in for anything more exciting than the pedalos, and we pack our own lunch. If he's with a group of friends it would be tempting to splash out a bit, wouldn't you think?'

'Not a splash in sight so far.'

'No, not even a ripple here, either. If we could all be as content as Maud Simmons what a pleasant world it would be.' De Freitas sighed and sat back in his chair, briefly easing stiffened muscles. 'Have you been involved in this type of case before?'

McCulloch nodded. 'Last year. Only one suspect, who fully denied it, of course. He couldn't go the week without dipping into it.'

'They don't usually manage to sit tight for longer than a fortnight.' De Freitas considered their lack of evidence. 'Why would you steal, Will?'

'To obtain something I couldn't otherwise have.'

De Freitas nodded. 'They've had the opportunity for years, so why only now? What is it that's so urgent; and yet allowing them to sit tight still?' He sat forward again and returned to the unrevealing bank statements. 'I've an idea this particular thief will keep us hanging much longer.'

'Oh, I don't know, Les – another one of the Wallis' credit card bills will be dropping through their letterbox next week. Keep paying the interest? Or just pay it all off?'

'It's greed that triggers theft, after all,' de Freitas agreed. 'But is interest tempting enough for a quick dip? And is Anita Wallis our top corner?'

There were never any foregone conclusions in his work, but de Freitas had enough experience to usually draw the correct conclusion. They hadn't yet ruled anyone out, but between them had refined their focus. Tracey Pattinson, the Saturday girl, had no access to the floor safe. Lee Baxter, the usual relief manager, currently sunning himself on the Algarve without undue stress on his credit card, had been given no access either. Theoretically he should have had every opportunity, but over-efficient cashiers denied him the chance. Like regular manager, Anita Wallis, he had never needed to pick up a key or physically count cash.

Relief manager Gareth Rogers, stepping in at short notice for Baxter, who normally covered Anita's days off, had done things by the book, as did all other managers in the nationwide chain. An established team of over ten years in the one shop was a rarity and Rogers had simply done his job, checking the cash himself. It had never occurred to him to do otherwise.

Which left the trainee manager, Rhys Fordham, and the cashiers. Fordham, as interviewees had verified, sat straight down at his desk every morning and settled bets alongside Anita. His banking habits were just as innocent, so far.

And that was the biggest problem. The cash could have been in any one of their possession for three weeks already and no one had yet spent a penny out of place. Not even a credit card accruing interest had tempted a discreet dip into carefully hidden funds.

Maud Simmons, christened by all, including herself, as the merry widow, rarely seemed to spend anything and had accumulated a substantial bank balance as a result. Inheritance, a well-pensioned and insured deceased husband and a new husband who had sold his own house in order to share her home, had simply added to the fortune.

'I love my job, I love watching the races, I love gossiping with the customers and I love going home in the evening and telling Cardi all about my day,' she enthused, when they had tactfully enquired why she continued to work. Cardi, her devoted house-husband, loved to cook and keep house and disliked going out. Twice a year they holidayed for two weeks in Barbados, visiting Cardi's extended family in Bridgetown. Their credit card was used only to book their flights, and her wages were retained each week, short of the standing orders for utility bills and a little-fluctuating weekly cash withdrawal, which suggested an unimaginative grocery shop.

In stark contrast, Anita Wallis only just managed to live within her means. Her husband "in construction management" was in fact a bricklayer, but well paid. A tennis club and three holidays a year on various Greek islands maxed out all of their credit cards at one stage or another throughout the year, the overdraft cleared on payday gradually re-accumulating in the four weeks that followed. It was all carefully managed and well-planned, the childless couple not quite in debt and not likely to become so. The credit and debit cards revealed they shopped frugally in a budget grocery store, but invested heavily in their more visible trappings, the BMW repayments taking the bulk of their income, designer fashion discount outlets accounting for much of the remainder.

The bulk of Joy Reid's household income had, until four years ago, gone on child maintenance; a mistake Paul Reid had made twenty-three years ago costing him dear for the next eighteen years. Other than a monthly standing order that had matched the BMW repayments of the Wallises there appeared no other involvement; a one-night stand followed by a Child Support Agency letter nine months later.

The Reids had made the most of their new-found disposable income, gradually paying off credit card debt and overdrafts and even building up savings for a couple of years, but their own children had taken them back to square one; teenagers demanding on resources, and second-hand cars even more so. Garage bills and car loans on two cheap cars in four years had sapped the savings more than the recent public transport strikes. The credit card was held in reserve only for Christmas, which took until April to pay off, and the annual week's holiday fluctuated between May and September, when it could be paid for in cash. They camped in Wales, but dreamed of a caravan to retire to.

De Freitas closed the file and reflected on the contrasting social statements disclosed by the financial statements, that of the Wallises as sad as that of the Reids, he couldn't help but feel.

'I wonder what Maud and Cardi Simmons did in a previous life?' he mused out loud, dropping the files back into the filing cabinet.

'It wasn't burning down orphanages, that's for sure,' McCulloch agreed.

* * *

'We must have outdone Genghis Khan in a previous life,' Chris cursed, without humour, cradling the head of the yearling colt while Terry rang the vet.

In the hour since turning the horses out into the paddocks, their world had turned upside down. The usual winter cash-flow difficulties had suddenly grown into a financial crisis.

Chris picked a handful of grass and the colt accepted it happily, showing no sign of distress and content to have his forehead gently rubbed, as he held his near-hind leg awkwardly off the ground. Nature had a way of protecting her injured and her cortisol currently pumped through his bloodstream, until the vet could arrive with artificial pain relief.

Chris and Terry were not so blessed, although Terry kept his distress under control as he gave the vet concise details.

'An ambulance will be here in fifteen minutes,' he told Chris as he hung up. 'Poor little bugger, what did you do, eh?'

'Go in and put the kettle on, and make that coffee Irish,' Chris said, and Terry needed no second bidding. He'd never been good around hopelessly injured animals, holding it together only long enough to speak to a vet. Now he needed to get away before he set Chris off, too.

Chris passed the time by chatting to the peculiarly relaxed horse. 'You've no idea, have you, little mate? Never mind, we'll get you sorted before it even hits you.' If they could... 'What did you do, eh?'

That, they would never know. The colt had been grazing contentedly in a paddock with two of his unflustered buddies when last checked. He may have slipped, or stepped awkwardly or just given a playful buck and a kick of exuberance and struck the gate. Speculation mattered little; only the hard facts were now visible.

The striking bay was bred to be a good two-year-old and it already showed in his looks. Only a fortnight ago he'd set them back more than they usually preferred to speculate, when the hammer fell to them at eighty-five-thousand pounds, but it had been easy to see him making upwards of a hundred-and-fifty-thousand next April.

It was a numbers game, investing in maybe ten yearlings in the hope that at least two would turn a big enough profit at the following year's spring sales to cover the two or three who inevitably showed a loss.

Theirs was a jobman's yard, scraping a living in the historic stable that had long since become too big to pay its way simply as a racing establishment. Its days as a home to Classic winners had appeared to be past when ex-jockeys Chris and Terry had taken up the condition-riddled lease.

They had five loyal owners who had backed them up with horses when they'd retired from the saddle four years earlier, but a dozen racehorses wouldn't keep them in business for long. The racehorses who won even minor races early in their career were immediately sold on for a profit, but that left them without potential stars to put them on the map as a racing yard. That had never been the full intention anyway; they were realistic about their future.

Pinhooking was their real livelihood, a term once coined by tobacco buyers who would stake the next year's profits on a pin-sized shoot if they had the eye to recognise a good crop at that early stage. It seemed an appropriate term for those who saw the future potential in a gangling foal or tubby little yearling. The thoroughbred pinhookers bought foals in November to sell as yearlings the following October, and bought yearlings in October to sell as "breeze-up" horses in April, ready-to-race two-year-olds who were ridden to breeze up the gallops at their fastest pace before potential buyers started bidding. The high-stakes gambling on racehorses started long before they ever reached a racecourse.

For Chris and Terry, the gamble had already been lost. The bay colt was insured, of course, but at his current value, not the final amount on which a hammer might have fallen in six months' time. And the equine hospital was about to make a significant dent in that. Modern equine science meant that horses no longer needed to be euthanised for a mere broken leg, but a complicated fracture was a different story, not always guaranteed a happy ending. Best case scenario also happened to be worst case scenario; if the colt survived, there'd be no insurance pay-out and a hefty vet bill, for a horse they couldn't sell.

All of which kept Chris mentally occupied until the colt was eventually loaded into the horse ambulance and Chris was assured of the best possible care and outcome; for the yearling, at least. He patted the now sweat-soaked neck and wished the colt well.

'If we get to keep you, I know one of your little pals we won't be keeping,' he told the sedated colt in parting. 'Christ, I need that coffee.'

* * *

'I thought that coffee was never coming,' de Freitas teased, as McCulloch set a mug down on his desk.

'I ran into Guy from Surveillance. Nothing to report, he says, but he's given me a big enough written report on it.'

'Suspect seen leaving house at six fourteen,' de Freitas mocked. 'Always sounds more efficient in court than quarter past. Nine minutes past – now that's the stuff of promotions.'

McCulloch grinned and settled down with his coffee and reading matter. He scanned the pages, satisfied there was indeed nothing to report, and then returned for a more thorough perusal, something within the report catching his attention.

'Do they have auction houses for racehorses?' he enquired of de Freitas. 'We checked the usual art and stamps and comic books.'

'Who's been buying racehorses, then?'

McCulloch was already tapping away on his notebook. 'Joy Reid's son has just joined some form of special education scheme at a horseracing stable.' He took a sharp intake of breath as his notebook educated him. 'Recent sale results, Tattersalls. Established 1766, so it says. Average price, three-hundred thousand. Top price, four million. Every buyer is named and our suspects are around a zero or two short of featuring on the list. These racehorses are dearer than Ferraris! Still, it was an interesting development, while it lasted.'

'The only development. Let me see?' De Freitas took the page. 'Sainte Bastien.' He stared at the paper thoughtfully.

'You've heard of it? It's the stables the Reid boy is going to.'

'I've been in it. About twenty years ago. Not a very happy memory, I must say.'

McCulloch nodded. 'Ah, yes – those jockey inquests. Not the same meat on the bone as you've grown accustomed to.'

'I wouldn't say that, Will. If you're going to use that analogy, then I wouldn't have been able to clear my plate. More meat than I needed, to be honest. A basic suicide at first glance escalated into two more deaths within a month. Had the perpetrator not been among the casualties, they wouldn't have been written off as death by misadventure.'

'Death by misadventure,' McCulloch mused, 'when will people learn that standing on a dodgy stool with only a rope about your neck for balance is not the safest way to change a light bulb?'

'When it is no longer taboo, Will. There are times when we're faced with a very grey area between victim and villain, and they were all victims on that occasion, if my own opinion counts for anything.' He sighed theatrically. 'Which, thankfully, it doesn't; our job is simply to uphold the law.'

'And be grateful for grey areas?'

'Small mercies are still mercy, Will. The courts dispense the justice, but we still have to sleep at night. Let's hope there's only a villain in this one, eh?'

Recalling the Sainte Bastien deaths made de Freitas grateful that the multitude of victims, even the guilty ones, had only served to increase his compassion. He had seen plenty of others become disillusioned and cynical. He cast a sideways glance at McCulloch, who pretended not to notice, and allowed himself a satisfied smile. Will would grow into the compassion he wasn't yet old enough to fully possess, de Freitas felt confident of that.

He handed the page back.

'Look into it, Will – find out if this scheme costs money or requires any specialist equipment; anything that might be hanging over Mrs Reid when an eager kid fetches home be-all-and-end-all forms. I wonder when he was offered the place?'

'I'll find out.' McCulloch shook his head at more information passed on by his notebook. 'Seems racehorses drink more than a Ferrari, too. Four hundred a week to feed and keep one. That's twenty-thousand a year and the good ones race for two years.'

'Forty-thousand. Yet another coincidence.'

'Hmm, that's what I thought. If it didn't cost a few hundred thousand to buy one.'

'If you can buy one, Will, then someone can sell one. Which usually means they got the original product for a good deal less than they sold it for. Make enquiries.'

CHAPTER 4

Jack plugged the headphone socket into the record player and carefully removed an LP from its cover and inner sleeve, handling it with the reverence he reserved for all his records. The faint hissing and crackling as the vinyl spun into action were due to his Grandad's lack of diligence in needle replacement and handling, not his own. Nevertheless, he liked the sound of age, even if he took great care not to add to it, and could even identify a song before it had actually started, simply from the unique crackle between each track.

As the only member of the family who had never complained and asked for "that old crap" to be turned off when visiting Nan and Grandad – Nan included – Jack had been gifted the record collection one afternoon during a grand tidy-up and clear-out. The more he heard on the radio and his friends' downloads, the more his passion for his Grandad's collection increased.

He settled back on the bed and let the classic rhythm and blues accompany his favourite role play game on his handheld console, most worldly cares banished; only the occasional niggling annoyance of why some of his records had been removed from their sleeves disturbing his concentration.

Maybe they'd all been messed with? Certainly some had been put back in their covers wrongly, the B-side face up instead of the A-side. And Mum had no idea of his filing system, either. The bands might be in alphabetical order, but he kept their albums in chronological order, which had betrayed someone snooping.

And why was his birthday money still safe inside one of them? What had she been looking for?

The Big Boss suddenly demanded his full attention once more and by the time the battle had been won and the next level reached he had forgotten the snooping. He snapped the game shut and turned the album over, his thoughts straying this time to the horses he'd be meeting in the morning.

And Mai.

Not that she was pretty or anything. She was alright, mind.

He knew he was what some of the Sixth Form girls at school described as "ahh, cute" and what some of the First Year girls described, with giggles and blushes, as "cute", and he would have preferred the latter description from the former group, but saw that kind of cute as unattainable. He was ordinary, and in spite of hiding it beneath his hair he was never going to be boyband cute or emo cute or bad boy cute.

He returned the completed record to its sleeve, the girls of bygone eras just as out of reach as the modern ones, if the songs were anything to go by. He slipped off the headphones and settled into bed, listening out for Mandy and scandal and checking once again that the alarm on his phone had been set.

* * *

'Any word yet, love?' It had been a long shift, yet Paul found Joy still awake as he tried to slip quietly into bed beside her. It wasn't hard to guess what was keeping her from sleep.

'No. Still suspended. Still a suspect.'

'Not you, though; you're not a suspect. How can you be? They've searched the house and everything.'

Joy smiled. 'Doesn't mean we've not got it though, does it? They're just waiting for one of us to slip up and buy a Ferrari.'

'Not with forty-thousand you can't!'

'Check then, did you?' She smiled and snuggled up to him. 'I've not got it, you know, so you can put the Argos catalogue away!'

They lay in silence for a while as she dwelt on his words, her guilt bothering her.

'The kids know their rooms were searched. Well, Mandy does, at least, and Jack's sharper than her. Mandy blamed him and he'll blame her. D'ya think we should tell them? I feel lousy, keeping it secret.'

'Maybe we'll sit them down tomorrow, have a talk,' Paul suggested, tiredness overtaking him.

'It's Jack's first day on the scheme. We can't ruin that for him. Next day, though.'

'Yeah,' he agreed, already half asleep, 'next day.'

* * *

Chris and Terry could still remember a time when the Sainte Bastien yard had always been this chaotic. The old boss had been loud and reliant on staff knowing what they were up to, with scolded grooms running around in panic and fresh instructions barked out whenever that theory collapsed.

These days it had become a serene bastion of routine; raised voices discouraged, tempers rarely given cause to fray, everyone knowing their role and patiently shown or reshown any task not correctly completed. But this morning the calm atmosphere had been upset by one too many disturbances, the arrival of the police the least of their concerns.

Chris looked hurriedly at the ID held out by what he'd assumed to be salesmen. It halted him only briefly.

'Yeah, look, could you just wait in the office a minute.'

'We only need a–' McCulloch began, but Chris was gone.

'Inopportune moment?' de Freitas surmised.

McCulloch shrugged. 'Better do as we're told and wait in the office.'

Their wait proved a lengthy one and hardly taxed their detecting skills to surmise there was a secretary missing.

'Sorry about that,' Chris apologised when he eventually reappeared, 'you've just caught us at an awkward time, I'm afraid.'

'You may want to check your answer phone,' de Freitas suggested, 'the phone was hopping somewhat.'

Chris grimaced. 'Sorry. Thought I'd diverted it. My wife's usually here, but she's stuck on the Downs at the moment trying to catch a loose horse. My partner's gone to A and E with his wife, I'm two staff short, a horse has just arrived back home from the equine hospital and we've a bus load of kids arriving at ten,' he glanced up at the wall clock and his two visitors followed his gaze, noting they had fifteen minutes to spare. 'Anyway – how can I help?'

'We're really only looking for some technical information,' de Freitas said apologetically. 'We can come back at another time?'

'Now's as good or bad as any, work away.'

McCulloch took out his notebook and de Freitas settled back more comfortably.

'We were wondering about horse ownership. Can it be done on a limited budget and could I keep my investment private?'

Chris hoped he didn't look quite as horrified as he felt. 'I'm so sorry; I assumed you were here about the break-ins at some of the yards in the village.'

His mind raced through the infinite apologies and excuses he could make, but none seemed enough to placate potential owners who had been kept waiting for too long while their yard of choice exposed every crack and weakness.

'Can I get you a cup of tea or coffee?' he asked instead, the disaster too far gone to salvage. 'We'll go through to the house, it's more comfortable. How much were you looking to spend?'

De Freitas smiled and signalled for him to remain seated. 'Unfortunately, it's purely hypothetical. We're investigating some missing money and wondered how easy it might be to invest in a racehorse? But clearly it's a bad time for you.'

Relief and disappointment were quickly displaced by a willingness to help. He'd only been running an education facility for four years, but it was already impossible for Chris to ignore his inner teacher, as Anne had jokingly dubbed their newfound vocation.

'Very easy to lose money in a horse,' he assured the Inspector. 'If you were a genuine owner, I'd have something here for you no matter what your budget. And I'm only one of thirty yards in this village. The BHA has an ownership department, you might find them useful.'

'We found the BHA a little too technical,' de Freitas lied, 'it helps to sit down with someone like yourself. So, had I forty-thousand pounds to invest?'

'It's not an investment, you need to know that before anything else,' Chris warned. 'You invest in a racehorse in the same way you invest in a top of the range home cinema system. It's something you want and get pleasure from, but you don't expect it to pay its way or make you a profit.'

'But there's some resell value?' McCulloch asked, not yet needing to take notes.

'I can't guarantee that, either,' Chris told him truthfully. 'We just welcomed back a horse from the hospital. He cost twice what you're looking to spend and at the moment he might make someone a nice riding horse for a thousand pounds. We wouldn't let one go for less, it's the best way to vet if it's a genuine offer of a good home. But he's not actually worth the thousand pounds.'

He looked at them carefully. 'You've got forty-thousand pounds of stolen money that can't be used, so you'd be happy to exchange it for a thousand pounds of spending money, is that it? Can't you just spend it anywhere? A car boot sale or a few safe bets in the bookies?'

'Our man needs to be far more discreet than that,' de Freitas explained.

'Well, yeah, we can sort him out. We can sell him a nice horse for that, which might be in with a chance of winning and maybe even turning a profit. And we can sell a share in maybe four horses, spreading the risk and the purchase price. Or it could be a tenth share in a four-hundred-thousand pound horse, getting you more quality and more chance of a winner. But until they run, there's no guarantee whatsoever. If you're not in it for the enjoyment alone, it's better to sit on your money until you lot have given up looking for it.'

'Unfortunately, we never give up,' de Freitas pointed out.

'Can't I buy a horse that's already raced?' McCulloch asked. 'Take out some of the guess work?'

'You can, but they're cheaper with the guess work still left in! And there's one thing you're forgetting – unless you've also got four-hundred a week for his training fees, that will have to come out of your budget as well. Basically, you've only got twenty-thousand to spend and he's going to eat the other half for the rest of the year. No luck in the world will get you any of that back.' Chris grinned. 'In fact, we even have to pay to get rid of manure!'

'And keeping my investment private?' de Freitas checked.

Chris shook his head. 'The BHA has a list of registered owners, so you'll be on that. And your name will be published every time the horse runs and in all form guides. If you join a syndicate or racing club, where ownership is shared between lots of people, the BHA will have a list of all those individuals. They each have to sign a registration form.'

'So the buyer listed at the sales might not be the sole owner?' McCulloch asked.

'Usually not the owner at all, full stop. Most owners have a trainer or a bloodstock agent buy one for them.'

McCulloch considered an alternative route around the many dead-ends. 'It can't actually cost four-hundred quid to feed a horse, though? What if I asked you for a cheap mate's rate?'

'I might be able to knock a tenner off, and that's the truth, Officer. The food and the bedding and the veterinary and hoof care, that's some of the fee. We probably take out about a tenner for our salary. The overheads are in there, but mainly it's the staff wages. It's a highly skilled job, caring for a racehorse, and we reflect that in their pay. The industry minimum wage is a lot higher than the national minimum. They can only look after five horses each, so you've to pay a fifth of that, no avoiding it.'

'OK then, so where do racehorses come from? Who produces them for the sales? Any chance I can go direct?'

Chris shook his head. 'Whatever makes you think your man is getting into horses, I think you're way off track. Breeders produce the horses. They pay around thirty or forty grand on average to have a good stallion mate with their mare. Some stallion fees are up to half a million a pop. A year later a foal arrives. Nature decides whether it's a decent looking horse or not and if it's not, they won't get back the breeding costs when they sell it a year later. You might get lucky and get a bargain at the sales, but you'll never get a bargain going direct to the breeder. Until it walks out unsold from a sales ring, they'll want its full value. After that, you're buying a cheap horse and getting exactly what you pay for. I'm sorry, but there's no secret budget way in.'

McCulloch returned his unused notebook to his pocket. 'A sport for rich men, not crooks.'

'You could say that,' Chris agreed. 'Although some might say you'd only be half right! You're welcome to a tea or coffee? The kids aren't due in for a few more minutes.'

De Freitas shook his head. 'No, thank you, we've already taken up enough of your time.'

'Come by anyway, when you're passing or off duty. We won't be able to find your missing money, but we can show you the horses and what we do here.' Chris sifted through a drawer and handed de Freitas a brochure on the Racing Futures Programme.

'Thank you. I may take you up on that.'

Back in the car, de Freitas took a moment to take in the busy stable-yard and the grand house, before turning the ignition. He'd met Chris Marsh before, he now knew, a jockey back then and helping him with inquest investigations. The memories rekindled, for all their sorrow, were fond ones. He glanced across at the brochure McCulloch had on his lap, ready to thumb through. The irony of its glossy promises was known only to him.

Twenty years ago there had been a horse looking out at him over every stable door and forty employees to interview. Now he'd noted empty stables and just two couples running it, apparently dependent on paying students.

'Not so much a dead-end as the wrong route,' McCulloch observed as they finally pulled away.

'I wouldn't say that yet, Will. Over the years I've learned never to accept a coincidence.'

'They happen.'

'Oh, they happen. But not nearly as often as you'd think.'

He flashed to allow a minibus to pull into the drive, before pulling out and heading back to the station.

'Cop car,' said Grant, looking out at the car that had just flashed to let them go. 'Fraud or paedos, what d'you reckon? Gotta be a con job, getting government grants to train us, but then again, busloads of kids?'

Jack shrugged. 'How d'you know it's a cop car?'

'Usually they drive Skodas, but my dad sold them the new fleet last summer. Same make, model and colour. That or a coincidence.'

'He must have sold them to normal people as well?'

'People don't buy V-forties, you can get a Beemer for the same price, and deffo not in Misty Blue! That was last year's colour three years ago!'

Jack snorted a disparaging agreement.

'What's your dad drive?'

'Merc,' Jack answered at once without lying.

'Yeah?' Grant sounded suitably impressed. 'Which model?'

'I dunno, I'm not interested in cars. A dirty great purple one.'

Grant laughed. 'Sounds more like a bus!'

The minibus pulled up as close to the yard as it could get and the driver ended any further discussion by asking them, not so politely, to disembark.

'I'll be leaving at four o'clock whether you're all back on or not,' she warned.

Jack had been first on and was now last off in consequence, eternally grateful to the angel behind the wheel for choosing to pick up from his estate before the surprisingly smarter homes of the others. He hadn't been so lucky when Grant had chosen the seat he'd hoped might remain free until Mai got on. She had, however, acknowledged him with a brief smile as she'd sat elsewhere and Grant, as it had turned out, had proved a surprising mine of useful information.

The welcoming party had changed and he didn't recognise the short thin guy who was ushering everyone into the centre of the yard; not that it made any difference, as he'd already forgotten the names of the dark-haired couple from last time.

He watched two Jack Russell terriers sniffing around a laden wheelbarrow and hoped they might come over, grateful for any canine distraction from the predictable welcoming speech. Although, as only he and Mai were new, maybe it would just be a predictable introduction speech. Grant the car expert had started the previous month and, according to him, most of the others had been there since September.

'Before we crack on, I'd just like to welcome Mai and Jack,' the little guy announced, bang on cue, pointing them out; Mai responding with a confident wave to her new comrades. Jack tried to take in the faces without making eye contact.

'Usually you team up with one of the staff or Terry and myself, but we're banjaxed this morning, so just muck in where you can and if someone screams for help and you think you can, jump in; if not, keep well away. We've already lost Terry to A and E, I don't want to be calling out another ambulance! We've had loose horses and Terry got kicked and Danno and Greta are off sick, so just try and struggle through to lunch as best you can,' he advised the group, before turning to individuals.

'Mai and Jack, you can come along with me. Grant – are you okay mucking in or do you want to give me a hand?'

'I'll be fine with the others, Chris.'

Chris nodded and smiled and led his two new trainees to the house. It was where every induction began; not just a run through of the basic health and safety rules and the other induction formalities that Anne usually dealt with so efficiently, but an introduction of a different sort, a passion only the old house itself could convey.

The BHA, the British Horseracing Authority that had replaced the Jockey Club of old, had allowed a few pieces to remain in the house when it had been bequeathed to the

Authority and the more valuable and historic contents had been dispersed to BHA-owned museums and offices.

'Terry and I first arrived here a bit older than you, sixteen,' Chris told them, as they stood together in the entrance hall. 'We weren't allowed in here, it was the family home, private. It's a bit more than just a future job, this. Either you're interested and it sucks you in, or you're not and you walk away from it. See those curtains through there?'

He picked up a cushion from a hall chair, made of the same fabric, and pointed to one of the horses embroidered in the design. 'This horse is Sainte Bastien, a Derby winner. Her success built this house and the place is named after her. Each of these other horses won a Derby as well and you'll see the original brass plaques on their stable doors when you go out into the yard. There'll be a few more plaques, because there's been a few other Derby winners since then, plus other champions, and they all get a plaque. Most of them will be on the same door, because when you get one you think is a bit special you put him in the box used in the past by the very best.

'Our whole future and all our dreams are built on the past.' He pointed up at the oil paintings gracing the wall ascending with the stairs. 'Each of those horses were trained here. Have a minute, wander around, look at the trophies and the pictures. Read the inscriptions. Ask whatever questions you want. The trophies those horses won are still there to be won now. Every horse down in the yard shares most of these as ancestors and is dreaming of winning the same races. If you choose to make racing your vocation, you're becoming part of the history.'

Mai was already lost in reading the inscription beneath the nearest picture, Jack noticed, but he simply took in his surroundings. Like a stately home, only lived in and a bit short of dusting and polishing. He could sense the passion in Chris' words and understood it. He felt the same about his record collection. The names and inscriptions meant nothing to him and he didn't bother to read any, but he knew within a few weeks they probably would become heroes, like when Dad had first shown him all his old football programmes and had got excited over players he'd never heard of. They'd become his heroes, too, in the end, along with Grandad's pop stars. People long since dead and buried, but still alive in spirit.

'Did you come here on a scheme, too?' Jack asked Chris.

'No, we left school and got an apprenticeship here, as jockeys. There weren't any schemes back then.'

'So are you in any of the pictures, then?'

'I never rode a horse on the racecourse good enough to get his portrait done. But I did ride that one, through there.' Chris led them through to the portrait above the fireplace of a gleaming chestnut. 'Salvinius. Me and Terry, we both got to ride him, in the mornings when he was being exercised. We were still just kids fresh out of school, but I won't ever forget that feeling.'

Chris knew the memory had begun to fade and maybe would have been lost, but for the grey yearling rekindling it. He stared up at the portrait, hardly daring to hope they really did have another standing in his same box outside, just as good.

'He looks a lot like that other one,' Mai observed, going over for a closer look at another painting of a chestnut and reading aloud the inscription, 'Quartzite.'

'Yeah, their trainer always said they were alike. Salvinius was Quartzite's grandsire. Grandfather. We call the mother and father the dam and the sire, you'll get used to that. You'll see all our horses have the same families, the same sires or the same names cropping up in their pedigree, which is their family tree. Familiarise yourselves with the cards on their doors, see if you can't start to see the same likenesses or personalities in horses with the same sire. Just feel your way, keep your ears and eyes open, ask all the questions you want and don't be in a hurry. You're a lifetime learning in this game.'

He left them to browse while he hurried off to take calls and check outside.

The respect and equality, not to mention trust in being simply abandoned, had no little effect on Jack. His interviewer had been right; this wasn't school. It wasn't his place in life yet, either; but already he wanted it to be.

'That's vile, don't you think?' Mai remarked, as they came to a stop in front of a Victorian whip, a tapered solid wooden stick given added viciousness by a silver tip. It was in a broken wooden case, the glass missing, an engraved card stating the past owner and victories.

'Pretty nasty,' Chris agreed, returning beside them, 'it gives me and Terry the shudders, but Anne found it in a box with some of the old guv'nor's personal bits and put it back in its case. It belongs in a museum, but they missed it when they were clearing the house.' He considered that a pity. There had always been something uncomfortable about it and Terry, he knew, felt the same.

He took them through to the hall and pulled a modern whip out of the otherwise unused umbrella stand.

'This is what we use these days. Knock yourselves out.'

Mai took him at his word and gave her palm a heavy slap. 'Hold your hand out,' she demanded of Jack, who could only do as told.

The air-cushioned padded leather thudded down without mercy, but also without discomfort. It felt like being hit by a pillow. He grinned and tried to grab it off her to retaliate.

'Knock yourself out, I said, not each other!' Chris reprimanded.

'What's the point of it, if it doesn't hurt?' Jack asked.

'It's not meant to be a punishment. Mainly it's just for steering, but also encouragement in a finish. My arm's not long enough to reach back and slap them on the bum, like you'd slap a runner on the back to urge them on, so it's basically an extension of my hand.

'Anyway, things are pretty quiet outside now, so I'll take you round to meet the horses, show you the basics. Then Anne will get you sorted with the daily routine and do's and don'ts. We've two really nice horses for you to meet, actually. One of them will have his portrait up on the wall in two year's time, all going well.'

'What's his name?' Mai asked.

'He hasn't got one yet, he's just the grey Lei Motif. We just call them by their sire. They're usually sold in the spring, so their new owner gets to name them. But we're keeping him and a bay Quartzite colt.'

He grimaced inwardly to himself. Each time he voiced those words their enormity sunk in a little further. It wasn't great for business financially and he certainly hadn't intended to be keeping the injured colt, whose sale had potentially guaranteed their security for the year ahead. But his pulse raced that bit quicker at the thought, as it hadn't done since his days as a jockey. The discussion with the bank manager would come in April and, until then, he could dream.

CHAPTER 5

Jack had predictably faced the Spanish Inquisition when he got home later that day; except no one famously ever expected the Spanish Inquisition. Mum's interrogations were far more dependable and delving. She'd even asked what the two dogs were called.

He was sparing with his information, knowing what was likely to please and what wasn't. The fact that he'd be learning French and Japanese and Business Studies was first to be mentioned. The bit about Terry getting kicked and needing stitches was one of the more interesting aspects of the day to be omitted. He also took care not to mention Mai's name, suspecting the teasing it would lead to.

'So you look after the horses all morning and do your lessons in the afternoon?'

'Sometimes a bit of both. We're going to do Equine Anatomy and Physiology out in the stables with real horses.'

'Bloody hell, that sounds dangerous! You mind you don't get kicked or bitten! Remember to keep your hand flat if you're feeding them and never stand behind them. Did they teach you that yet?'

He rolled his eyes to Heaven. Chris had actually shown Mai how to let one of the horses take a tiny Polo mint out of her lips. 'Yes. They did,' he assured her.

He left her studying his timetable for the week and disappeared up to his room without need of explanation. Instead of his own room, however, he cautiously pushed open the door to Mandy's room.

'Piss off, freak!'

'Did Mum go through your stuff?' he asked, ignoring her as he walked in and flopped down on her bed.

'Someone did and we all know who, you little freak! Have fun in my underwear drawer, did you? It's the only bra you'll ever get to see, loser.'

'It was the police. And they went through my stuff, too.'

She took a sudden interest, as he had suspected she might.

'How do you know?'

'Amad saw their car parked outside.'

Of course, Amad hadn't known it was a cop car, only that it was last year's Volvo. A proper petrol-head was Amad next door, gushing about the capabilities of the V-Forty that made it better than the comparable BMW Five-whatever. Any nearly-new car in their street made Amad wet his knickers. Jack couldn't have cared less, until Grant had jogged his memory with alphabets and numbers. Not to mention last year's colour. 'Who buys a metallic blue car these days?' Amad had asked him scornfully.

'Shit.'

Jack smirked. Whatever she'd been up to, she was done for now.

'And they went through your stuff, too?' Mandy double-checked.

'Yup. You're for it.'

'We're all for it, you stupid little freak. What the fuck did you think they were looking for?'

'Evidence. Shoplifting and stuff.'

'Thanks for your faith in me! Like they don't pull you over on the spot, Einstein! When has Mum ever been called to pick me up from the police or a store detective?' She shook her head at his ignorance. 'You don't get arrested for hopping off school or giving teachers an earful. Whatever the search warrant was for, it's Mum or Dad they're after, not me, you dumbass.'

Jack sat up sharply, enough truth in some of her words to upset him.

'It's not Mum and Dad, it can't be! I bet it's whoever used to live here. This used to be an arms house.'

'A what? You are such a dumbass! Do you even know the difference between a council house and an alms house?'

'You know, gun runners. Arms dealers. Selling sniper rifles to gangs. Amad said.' Amad had known less about guns than cars, but had confirmed his suspicions about the receipts.

She smiled. Both types were so wide of the mark. 'So, right, Amad knows this how, exactly? He only moved in last year! Wake up to yourself, we got this place when you were born; the only useful thing you've ever done for me since. If you'd been a girl I might still be stuck sharing a room with you in a poxy flat. The police don't go searching houses for fourteen-year-old evidence!'

He considered her words. 'Then what were they searching for?'

'I don't know; but it can't be good. Mum hasn't been going to work.'

'Why?'

'How should I know? I only noticed Saturday. But this one time last week, we hung out at the precinct and heard a punter coming out moaning about the new girl. The only time they'd have someone new is if someone left, and Mum would've been full of it, wouldn't she?'

'Not if someone's just on holiday.'

'With Mum off at the same time? On a Saturday?'

'She would've told us,' Jack said doubtfully, but he knew in his heart his sister was right.

'So why hasn't she?'

Neither voiced their fear, but Jack was aware of the volumes of cash Mum handled daily. Enough for a search warrant if a till came up short one day.

'She's not a thief,' he said quietly.

'We were struggling when Dad was out.'

'She's not a thief!' He was silent for a moment. 'What can we do?'

Mandy reached over and messed up his hair, with less vigour and more affection than usual.

'Nothing. We can't know 'til she tells us. There might be nothing in it, like; just a couple of days off in a row and routine searches down the whole street.'

They both knew how improbable that was, but Jack nodded and took comfort in her words anyway. Days off were random, why couldn't it be Saturday one week and Monday the next? Until tomorrow proved them wrong…

He left Mandy in peace and stretched out on his own bed, trying to lose himself in carefully chosen music. His favourite songs didn't quite have the desired effect and his mind continued to turn over the possibility that Mum had been sacked. Not for theft; the police would have arrested her. Or they would have all uprooted and moved to Spain or somewhere before she got caught, which would've been pretty sweet. But suspicion of theft was just as bad. It hurt to be thought of as a bad kid; he knew.

He wondered what had earned Mai and Grant a place on Racing Futures. They didn't seem like "disadvantaged" kids. Not that the programme brochure had mentioned the word; but kids like him didn't get offered opportunities otherwise. Futures were only offered to those who faced none.

* * *

'We need a solid plan for the future,' Chris said, as they sat together in the living room of Sainte Bastien House, a rare takeaway meal finished and Terry and Su's usual departure for home deferred for an hour or so.

They were all in agreement they'd so far been working on a wing and a prayer, but were all short on ideas how to take the new venture forward. And it was a new venture. As Chris had pointed out, they were horse dealers, playing at training kids and a dozen horses. The potential Triple Crown winner out in the yard had skewed the balance.

'Not just a new financial plan for the bank,' he warned them. 'Something ambitious, to match our dreams, and concrete; to stop us falling on our arses like we did today.'

'Disasters like today are always going to happen, whether you plan to avoid them or not!' Su pointed out realistically. Terry and Anne were the worriers and planners within the partnership and she wasn't at all happy at losing Chris to the dark side as well.

'We can worry about a financial plan when the debts don't get paid off next year,' Anne said reasonably. She had no idea how to make a plan for the unpredictable and unforeseen.

'I just want to be able to cover our arses when they do happen,' Chris insisted. 'We're about to become bona fide full-time trainers and that could have been a real potential owner sat there in an empty office until I got back in and made it even worse! The old Guv'nor would have strung us up for the way we're running this place!'

'What are we doing that the old Guv'nor would be proud of, though?' Anne reminded him. 'Until we took possession of an unsaleable colt and a not-for-sale colt, we weren't trying to be the Guv'nor. We were trying to fulfil his dream and give a future to kids and make the yard pay. We might not be trainers first and foremost, but the yard and boxes are always kept fit for a Derby winner and the kids are learning why, and how to keep it that way. Now we've made that decision to train as our number one priority, the foundation is already there.'

Right now they were doing too many things at once and messing up, Chris knew. 'Yes, the yard looks great and the kids are passionate about what they're doing,' he agreed, 'but half the boxes are empty. You need at least thirty horses to make it pay, not twelve. The staff we have are excellent but we can't afford as many as we really need. Look what happens when we lose someone for the morning.'

They'd all been looking at it for most of the evening, an ugly stitched gash that ran from just above Terry's left eye to just above his left ear. A narrow miss on both counts. Simply because the two best riders in the yard were husband and wife and stricken with the same stomach bug. Pushing its luck, a colt partnered by a less experienced rider had backed into a skittish colt, who promptly caught an unsuspecting Terry with a fore hoof as it reared in readiness for flight. Nerves on edge, the skittish colt had later parted company with its rider on the Downs, dodging all until finally succumbing to Anne's patience.

In fairness, that was a bit of a one-off. But it had highlighted the need to make sure anyone in the yard could step in and fill other roles. If they were to be trainers, the office could never be unattended and an owner never left unentertained.

Switching the business from selling unraced horses to training racehorses, however, brought with it larger issues. Or one larger issue. Money. They were set up for paying off overdrafts in April, not adding to them. The only two horses likely to cover the year were no longer for sale; and instead of generating income they were going to run-up costs.

'At the moment,' Terry said emphatically, 'we're juggling too many different things and mistakes are happening. But, like Anne says, once we concentrate on training winners, the foundation's there and there's no reason we can't make a go of it.'

Su looked at him and grinned. 'You're meant to be the bad cop, remember?' She ran a hand across his chest. 'I could get used to this new reckless side!'

He squeezed her hand. 'Best not. You know it'll end in tears. But, hey, until it does, I may as well get swept along with the rest of you!'

'The Quartzite and the Lei Motif are going to put us on the map,' she reassured him. 'Even if people don't send us horses to train, they'll buy from us when we go to the sales. Tears of joy, good cop, tears of joy.'

'The sales will have to take a back seat,' Chris reminded them. 'We can't be trying to do two things at once. And anyway, if we don't turn a profit in the spring, we can't go on a spending spree in the autumn.'

He caught Su's mischievous glance and grinned. 'Yeah, I know, but it really is a complete reversal. The minute we register those colts as in-training, we're heading down the opposite path. A good one.' He winked. 'Paved with gold!'

'Or disappointment. There's a half-brother down the road who was going to Royal Ascot six months ago.' Terry gave an exaggerated wink in reply.

* * *

DS Will McCulloch considered the dead-end of the current case. It wasn't so much the wrong path as no current path at all. They were lost, with nothing to go on. He wasn't in the habit of taking work home with him, though it regularly hijacked his thoughts outside working hours, but he generally did his best to switch off. Wasting time perusing social media didn't really count as work, he reasoned, even if it happened to be the profiles of his latest suspects.

A suspect would have to be stupid to post incriminating evidence, but people were careless and it was more a case of someone else being clever, spotting the mistakes within the comments, the barely noticeable give-away lurking in the background. The antique silver carriage clock on the mantelpiece before they remembered to hide it away, the auto check-in they'd forgotten about at the rare coins and stamps shop.

Lee Baxter wasn't stupid. None of his social media friends would even guess that he was currently away on holiday. It was more likely he hid from burglars, not police. Neither Anita Wallis nor her husband used social media. Joy Reid didn't, either, but her husband and children did. One to follow a football team and news, one to follow an obscure music genre, and one to keep up with school gossip and collect Californian men.

The Americans weren't the usual Christian ex-military widowers seeking to scam the infatuated, but were in keeping with the girl's interests and friend-base. McCulloch marvelled at her depth of knowledge of her subject and wondered what had sparked such an unusual interest. Unusual, at least, for a council estate in the worst part of Reading; although, as he knew from her hidden receipts pre-dating the theft, an interest shared by enough others to enable her acquisition of fairly high-calibre stock.

The boy, in contrast, had few friends beyond the closed groups he'd joined and none whatsoever from school. He had a couple of friend-requests pending, linked to the Racing Futures programme; no doubt reluctant to allow them a glimpse into his private life. There was certainly nothing average about the Reid kids.

Quickly tiring of the Simmons' endless posts of every meal Maud's husband had ever cooked, McCulloch strayed to other links and couldn't help but focus on the recurring names within the friends and followers. He'd had no intention of bringing his work home with him, but he owed it to Les to take note of a few points of interest. His DI liked coincidences, after all.

* * *

DI Les de Freitas had learned to be wary of coincidences. They happened elsewhere in life, but in his line of business they invariably turned out to be contrived. Sometimes the jigsaw had been almost complete but for a single missing piece. And there it would be, in the exact location and on the exact date as the rest of the puzzle, long before it had started to be assembled, nothing more than that connecting them... until it fell perfectly into place to complete the picture.

Often, the pictures remained incomplete, the missing piece undetected. De Freitas preferred to collect up every random piece he chanced upon, filing them away in case the right space should one day open up. He looked at the paperwork Chris Marsh had kindly given him and carefully filed away the apparent coincidences that might one day become that single missing piece.

He hadn't intended to work on his evening off, but it wasn't really work as such, after all. The stable visit had been more of a social call than official business, as was this, he reasoned, picking up the phone.

Chris sat quietly in the office, contemplating the day; and new career path. The transition from jockey to horse-trader had been hard, but this next move was more worrying. He'd safely switched from riding horses to managing horses; the connection, the environment, the people were all still here. But what if this failed?

He'd seen failure, way too up close and personal. The failure in colleagues to adapt to career change. His own failure to make the correct split-second decision in a race he wished he'd never ridden.

It may have just been coincidence, the same mild manner and calming authority adopted by every detective who ever walked the earth, but yesterday's police visit took him back twenty years. He remembered the event vividly, but not those investigating it. Everything had been blurred for the few days after. An accident, a death by misadventure; they'd all known it to be suicide. The statistics warned him that one in every three retired jockeys would fall victim. It made him anxious for others. But not himself.

He didn't want to brood on the memories dredged up by the police, or on the leap into the unknown. A leap pinned on a single horse, as fragile as the dream it engendered. It wasn't really the horse; it was the realisation that they wanted more. Small-time dealers, small-time trainers who might have been content with their lot had the little grey colt not offered them a vision of something bigger.

His thoughts were rudely disturbed and he picked up the phone without thinking, the insistent ringing usually ignored at this late hour. The horses were bedded down for the night and so should he be, after the final check on them.

'Hello?'

De Freitas didn't apologise, unaware of the time or its significance on those who began work at six a.m. He merely reintroduced himself and enquired whether the offer of a stable tour still stood.

'Sure,' Chris agreed, 'it's open house here always, but if you really want to get a feel for it, come for seven and stay for the morning.'

'Maybe just an hour; I'll be on duty.'

'From seven? Can't you defer your work for a bit? I can promise you, Officer, you'll learn a lot from your line of enquiry – that's what you call it, don't you? It won't be social; unless you take me up on the offer of tea!'

'Oh, I think I may be allowed a tea break,' de Freitas conceded. 'Seven it is, then.'

Chris hung up and smiled. 'Speak of the devil,' he acknowledged quietly to no one but himself, mulling it over. It was Fate, he decided cheerfully, as he locked up the office for the night and went out for a final check on the horses.

'The two coppers dropping by, it was Fate,' he told Anne, back indoors.

'How so?'

'They're convinced some local bank-robbing racing fanatic is looking to hide his money in a horse – and we've got two.'

'Aha...' Anne agreed. 'And?'

'When we show them how, the entire Reading squad social club will be avid racehorse owners!'

* * *

'You may want to see this, Les.'

McCulloch had been waiting all morning for the belated arrival of his Inspector and handed him the printout of a social media screenshot before he had even sat down at his desk. De Freitas studied it momentarily, as he took his seat.

'Interesting.' He removed a folded sheet of paper from his suit pocket and passed it to McCulloch. 'Snap?'

The sergeant nodded slowly. 'I was only just thinking about your theory on coincidences; and now here they all are, like a row of London buses. What are the odds?'

'Still stacked against us, Will, but every little helps.'

McCulloch read through the invitation again, which more or less matched the social media posts. 'Is this what held you up this morning? Buying Mrs de Freitas a hat for Ascot?'

'Chris Marsh made it abundantly clear there's no guarantee of the horse even having a race.' De Freitas smiled inwardly at the small-print-style declaration that had been so at odds with the excitement and confidence behind every other mention of the horse. That morning, the stable-yard had reminded him of an incident room after the discovery of breakthrough evidence; the buzz of inexorable success had been palpable.

'I took him up on his offer of a tour of the stable this morning,' he explained. 'A spur of the moment grasping at straws, but no more than interesting. So far.'

'And will you take him up on this particular offer?'

'A free gift horse? What could possibly go wrong! It can do no harm, whatever their motive.'

McCulloch laughed. 'The coincidences keep on coming! According to social media, this dream horse of a lifetime is called Grey Motive!'

De Freitas smiled. 'I found that rather amusing, too. I'm afraid we're buggered, Will, we're not trained for grey motives, we need clear-cut black and white! Do you think Marsh and Jones are in on it and pulling our string?'

McCulloch considered it, but shook his head. 'He seemed a genuine bloke. And he genuinely seemed to have no idea what we were doing there. Jones, on the other hand, I have yet to meet. Did you?'

'I met him this morning. Ruthlessly honest, I'd say, the sort who'd turn his own mother in for a parking ticket.' De Freitas pictured the empty stables and lack of staff. 'The motive for the gift horse, at least, seems pretty transparent. Go and pin that up on the social noticeboard, Will. We mistakenly think the horsey set are loaded, while they just as erroneously assume detectives have twenty-thousand to throw on a horse. Perhaps I should give the advert to my dentist. Or Mrs de Freitas' hairdresser...'

McCulloch laughed and glanced back over the printed page offering ten shares in a possible future Derby winner, at twenty-thousand pounds each including all expenses. Or, for the same level of investment, a potential champion two-year-old. He could only assume this also to be a horse and not the immoral trading of a child prodigy.

'Forty grand for the set. Has a ring to it, wouldn't you say?'

'That did cross my mind,' de Freitas agreed.

'What's this other horse called? Honey Trap?'

'We can but hope.'

As McCulloch left on his errand, de Freitas read back through the paperwork Chris Marsh had kindly given him. The document, typed up by Mrs Marsh in the office as they chatted amiably, was quite specific on the terms of ownership. Not quite the expensive gift his young colleague imagined.

The stable tour had indeed been no more than interesting, and certainly not directly helpful to the investigation. He had been unable to mask his concern for the young people being introduced to what he considered to be a precarious future. Marsh had set his mind at rest; and in so doing had realised they had met before, in sadder circumstances.

'Look, you're not really here to buy a horse and I can't really help you trace your crook,' Marsh had accepted, after they'd watched horses gallop past them on the Downs, 'but I can help you out, get you behind the scenes, if your guy does get tempted. It's a small world. And the racing community is even smaller. You might get lucky, you never know.'

The five percent share in two of the stable's horses, given to de Freitas as a gift, did not include any percentage of their career earnings or subsequent profits from their sale or stallion career. Nor could it be transferred. An owner in name only, they'd agreed. But, crucially, he would get the legal documentation and access to the details of all other shareholders.

'You can bring your wife racing and enjoy the day as an owner, get wined and dined by the racecourse, be there on the podium when one of the Royals hands over the trophy, if we get lucky. You can't buy moments like that, believe me,' Marsh had promised.

De Freitas had been given a choice of horse, as they'd watched totally dissimilar horses gallop by; their hooves pounding out a rhythmic tattoo, the loud equally rhythmic breaths forming the harmonious backing track. It was easy to see why all those present shared such a passion, and how difficult such a choice could be.

He had been unhesitating in his choice. He knew Mrs de Freitas would think the horse pretty, resembling as it did a rocking horse, the grey coat conspicuous in an otherwise sea of brown. And de Freitas knew confidence and honesty when he saw it, though he was surprised to see it shining from an equine eye. He'd looked into the eyes of some of the other horses, later on in the yard, finding the usual number of dubious characters and innocence and arrogance he was accustomed to seeing among his human contacts.

As it turned out, for the sake of their past acquaintanceship, Marsh had split the offered share between the only two horses in the yard currently for sale. Half the share, but twice the fun and doubling the chances, as he'd pointed out. All Things Pass was the given name of the second lure, as McCulloch viewed it; but someone had felt the need for forty-thousand pounds long before there had been a horse to spend it on.

It was hard to establish a suspect without first establishing a motive. However amusing the name, de Freitas readily conceded it was unlikely that Grey Motive could provide any clue to the grey motive for this particular theft.

CHAPTER 6

January, Year Two

Grey Motive gave no clue to the brilliance just seen out on the Downs, as he was led off to the walker by Jack. The little grey colt looked unremarkable alongside the showy swagger of his work-mate, yet it wasn't the latter's rider who was now grinning inanely as though Christmas had just come straight back round.

'Jack's come along well, they make a good pairing, don't they?' Anne observed, as the young boy calmly released Grey Motive into the automatic walking machine that would allow the colt another twenty minutes of unsupervised exercise before being turned out in the paddock. Both boy and horse hinted of rich potential; a shared burning desire to succeed, hidden beneath a mild facade.

It hadn't been quite so well hidden that morning, Jack's ease among fractious horses noticeable as he settled them into their boxes, no more the uncertain young trainee. And as for the horse he had been assigned to look after... Grey Motive had cruised effortlessly alongside a horse who was physically his superior. The precocity of the work companion, a breeze-up horse destined for an early racing career, should have overwhelmed the weak and backward grey, who wouldn't be at his best for another year or two.

'It's like stealing candy from a baby,' Chris said, his wife's comment unnoticed as he still savoured the unleashed power he'd felt oozing from the colt that morning on the Downs. 'He was just cruising, we could have gone past Greta without even quickening. Sitting on him is like...' he couldn't actually think of a comparison, '...special.'

'But our breezer struggled,' Anne cautioned with a teasing grin, 'the one we intend to sell.'

'Greta said he worked lovely. But our boy's just better!'

They both knew it was early days, too soon for excitement and still plenty of time for disaster. Reality didn't quench the fire, though.

'Feet back on the ground and hands back on a yard brush?' Anne suggested. 'Terry's taking a few for riding lessons, Su's got a couple for practical classes in the yard and I've got two in the office. Which leaves you on chores!'

'I'll crack on with the yard work, then. Will I send Jack up to you? He's not done much in the office yet.'

Anne shook her head. Ordinarily she would have insisted, but she felt the horses were providing a welcome distraction to possible problems at home. He hadn't said as much, but Jack's demeanour on arrival each day was a great deal chirpier than on departure. 'I'll call him in when we start doing the sales and race entries.'

They went their separate ways, Chris falling into step alongside Jack as the boy came back from the walker.

'You're doing well with the horses,' he said amiably. 'There's a good future for you, if this is what you want.'

Jack said nothing, though he felt the strong glow of pride, hoping it wouldn't reach his cheeks. 'Could I stay here, for good?' he asked, after a moment.

'After the year is up? Don't see why not. But when you leave school you might want to apply to a better yard,' with more opportunities. Don't tie yourself down too soon.' He grinned. 'You might find out this was a crappy place to work!'

Jack smiled. 'Why did my school get chosen?'

It had been bugging him since he'd noticed those around him were far from disadvantaged, or troublemakers. Had he known it was a genuine open programme he might not have considered himself worthy of applying. And yet, here he was, on a par with them and singled out for praise.

'It was a bit far out of the travel zone,' Chris conceded, 'although they left in some brochures in case anyone was particularly interested. We didn't fill all our places, so when you and Mai applied we were happy to take you.'

It wasn't quite the answer he'd sought, though it underlined his suspicion that the Whitley Wood Secondary's reputation wasn't the prerequisite for a place on the programme.

'The whole idea of this is to give everyone a chance to get a foot in the door,' Chris continued. 'I know you don't want to sit on a bus for an hour to get here, but if you do, we won't stop you.

'You know, all that history in the house was just one family; handed to each generation on a plate. When the old Guv'nor was terminally ill, he had no heir, so he left it to the BHA for those who aren't born into it. Terry and me were given the first lease because we were apprenticed here, and among his conditions for the BHA was providing a new career for retiring jockeys, which we were.

'We're feeling our way with this, the same as you, so we won't let the rules stand in the way of ambition. If you want to stay, stay.'

His mobile phone halted any further conversation and he answered cheerily, glad to see the caller's name and buoyed by the morning's work.

'This morning? Of course, it's always open house. Pity you weren't here an hour ago! See you in a bit, then.'

He returned the phone to his pocket and his attention back to Jack.

'The trickiest part of this is that you're here to learn and technically you're not allowed to work. But, if you'd like to learn how to show a horse to a visiting owner, I'm happy to teach you!' Chris winked.

The first part of the lesson, Jack found, was having the yard presentable. Even though a few of the boxes were still being mucked out and horses were back and forth to the walker and paddocks, he and Chris swept up stray bedding, manure and hay, as he'd been taught from day one. He took pride in the spotless yard, enjoying the task that the next passing horse would render pointless. That didn't matter, somehow. There was always someone at the ready with a targeted broom or shovel.

If it looks fit for a Derby winner, someone will trust us with a Derby winner, was the mantra Jack repeatedly quoted in his head. And if he looked after "Mo" as a Derby winner, he might be entrusted permanently with the potential Derby winner.

He was sent to fetch Grey Motive from the walker and led him back to the freshly prepared box, apologising to him along the way for the delay in being turned out for a pick of grass.

'Stand, Mo,' he told the obliging grey, tethering him in the box, to be groomed.

He'd already learnt that it was hard to make the grey coat shine the way the glossy bays and chestnuts did, but the sheen on the colt's skin still shone through. He fussed over the immaculate mane and tail and cleaned the colt's feet until the horse was fit for a sales ring. It was easy with experience, like any skilled job.

'OK,' Chris approved, 'now to teach you both how to stand – he's new to this, too.'

As it was, the horse had been well-taught in preparation for the yearling sales and correctly stood naturally without any prompting on their part, his forelegs neatly together, his head up.

'This one's a born pro,' Chris pointed out, instead moving Jack along to a less experienced filly.

Teaching her where to place her feet was much harder; and keeping her there more so. Jack succeeded eventually, his patience and respect, the two essential tools of the trade, as Chris and Terry referred to them, finally rewarded.

Chris had warned him that horses were born to make fools of men, 'we make it easy for them!', but the expected tantrum never surfaced. When the time came to fetch out Grey Motive and have him stand for inspection, the colt remained as well-behaved as when practising.

'Our two star pupils!' Chris introduced the visiting shareholder. 'Grey Motive and Jack Reid. Jack, this is Les de Freitas, his part-owner.'

Jack shook the proffered hand and returned his grip to the slack lead rein.

'I can't pretend to know what I'm looking at,' de Freitas admitted, 'but he looks relaxed and happy, so I imagine that's half the battle.'

Chris grinned. 'Pretty much. The other half is still wrapped round his middle, but we'll get some of that off by summer!'

De Freitas put a hand to his own midriff. 'Perhaps you'll let me know the secret, when you do!'

'Take a photo,' Chris suggested. 'You'll see a big difference every time you visit him.'

Photos done, Jack took the colt out to the paddock, while Chris walked de Freitas back to his car.

'Just passing?'

'Yes and no,' De Freitas conceded. 'It didn't warrant a special trip out, but as I did happen to be passing, I wondered if you could clarify the new shareholder – Heidi Jones. We were struck by her age and profession; would you know her?'

'Not as well as Terry – Heidi's his daughter! I've known her from the cradle. What did she put down for profession, she's still at uni'?'

'Exactly. We were wondering how a nineteen-year-old student could invest in a racehorse?'

'You'd be surprised what they spend their student loans on! Her friend bought a boat. A proper little river cruiser! Her boyfriend's mad into the horses as well, so it was an easy sell. I wish we could get rid of the other couple of remaining shares so easy. There's no sign of your bank-robber so far; Terry and I know everyone who's bought in.'

'Is there any reason why All Things Pass has totally sold and not Grey Motive? You did describe him as a Derby horse.'

'And that's one reason right there. People don't want to wait 'til next summer for a return on their investment, or the autumn to have a runner. The other horse will be ready to run in the summer and one win or a decent placing behind a good horse and we can sell him on for a very good profit. Not everyone can afford to get into horses just for fun.'

De Freitas thanked him and pondered the many variables of racehorse ownership. A quick return within the year, a two-year plan, or an injury or simple case of misjudgement and no return at all. It wasn't exactly what you'd rob a bank for...

'May I just go and take a photo of him in his field, for Mrs de Freitas?'

'He's your horse, Les, work away.'

De Freitas headed in the direction he'd seen Joy Reid's boy disappear, a path behind the round horse-walker turning out to lead into a vast open area of pasture, divided into small square paddocks.

'Why is that horse in a cage?' he asked Jack, as the boy leant on the wooden rail of the nearest paddock, in which Grey Motive and another horse tore at mouthfuls of grass.

Jack glanced at the adjacent paddock. 'That's All Things Pass, he broke his leg really badly last year so he's not allowed to run around too much 'til it's properly healed, so we put him in a playpen. He can walk around and eat the grass and everything and have a roll, but he's not enough room to run about.'

'I thought perhaps he might be dangerous!'

Jack shook his head. 'He does give you a nip sometimes, if he's cross about something. Now his leg's better he hardly gets cross at all. I think he was just bored, having to stay in for ages.'

De Freitas raised his phone and took sufficient photos to keep his wife happy; although in truth he got more pleasure from seeing the horses than she did. He admired the assured composure of Grey Motive and the confident swagger of the caged horse. It was easy to imagine them as proud stallions, standing over their harem of mares. It wasn't so much their physique, the grey lean and lanky, the bay small and muscular, but more the bold eye through which they viewed him.

As he returned the phone to his pocket, he was conscious of another set of eyes burning into him. He ignored Jack's gaze and began to walk leisurely back to his car.

'Are you a policeman?' Jack asked, having walked in silence beside him for much of the way.

The question took de Freitas aback somewhat. Only on TV was it possible to "spot a copper a mile off"; he personally found that most strangers took him for an insurance salesman.

'I am, indeed. What gave it away, the flat feet?'

Jack's expression suggested he'd never heard of that particular misnomer. 'My friend Grant's dad sold a fleet of those cars to the police,' he explained.

'I see,' de Freitas nodded. 'Not so unmarked as we'd imagined.'

'How long does it take you to solve crimes? Is there a time limit? Do you have to stop and investigate a new crime?'

'We quite often investigate several crimes at once. My department has about twenty we're currently working on. And, no, we don't have a time limit; some investigations can rumble on for years.'

This clearly disappointed Jack, understandably as de Freitas knew.

'The longer we take, the better the outcome,' he reassured the boy. 'We wouldn't want to mistakenly target an innocent person; and the guilty are very careful about covering their tracks.'

'Do you ever solve crimes in your spare time, like helping people investigate stuff?'

De Freitas paused as they reached his tell-tale car.

'I prefer just to have a day off, don't you?'

Jack considered it, as he watched de Freitas drive away. He and Mai were in agreement they'd be happy never to leave the yard. But they weren't policemen. Still, it might have been useful to have someone on the inside to help Mum. The muppets investigating the shop robbery were a useless shower, he and his family had concluded.

It was as well he and Mandy had had a fair idea of the trouble ahead, when Mum had finally sat them down and told them she'd been accused of stealing a stack of money. Enough to change their lives, like winning the lottery, but instead it had had the opposite effect. Mum had been so upset, convinced she was destined for prison despite being innocent. He knew she was no thief, but the police were taking their time catching the real culprit.

Which left Mum doing her utmost to avoid pointing fingers. Christmas had been a total washout, the usual treats and extravagance given a wide berth to avoid any further suspicion.

The much-anticipated annual family trip to the supermarket had seen her throwing out of the trolley everything he, Dad and Mandy put in. 'Wha'd'ya think'll happen when they see us buying that lot?' she'd warned. The present wish-list had been cruelly assaulted by the same frugality, the credit card and pay-later catalogue options declared out of bounds in case the police questioned how the debts got paid off.

The police hadn't seemed to be doing any questioning and here they were nearly three months later still in limbo and prison still a real threat. At the rate Mum was saving money they'd nearly have the forty grand saved up. It wouldn't surprise him if she simply handed it over, just to get them off her back and have a normal life back.

Still, having her at home every day wasn't all bad. A bit of a nuisance and he missed the ready meals, but he secretly quite liked them all having a proper breakfast together and trying Mum's new recipes for dinner. Her cakes and puddings were better than the shop-bought ones they used to get and weren't rationed, either; there seemed to be a limitless supply. He figured the police only watched the shopping receipts for brand names and ignored stuff like flour. But he hated to see her so worried all the time. Even Mandy was being sympathetic, which was creeping him out.

'Plod?' asked Grant, back in the yard, as they gathered at what was once a hostel for stable staff and was now a block of classrooms and study hall.

Jack nodded.

'They must be on some whack to be able to own a racehorse. Unless it's part of a pay-off for the tax dodge and kiddy fiddling!'

'Both is it now?' Mai retorted archly.

'Worth considering as an alternative career,' Grant pointed out, ignoring her, 'unless you happen to be the next Marcel Dessaint, like Mai – you're going to be minted!'

She aimed a kick at his backside designed to fall short, but grinned amiably.

'What about you?' she asked Jack as they sat down together for Business Studies. 'Do you have a greater plan yet?'

He shrugged. There were loads of things you could do in racing, but he was happy where he was, looking after the horses. It didn't seem ambitious enough to admit to Mai, though. She was already planning where to put her Champion Jockey trophy.

'You are sooo good with the horses I wouldn't want to do anything but be a groom if I were you,' she said, pronouncing every superfluous "O" the way his sister did, usually in reference to some boy's looks.

'I'd be happy if that's all I did forever,' he agreed.

'Me too. Until Terry told me I could ride well, that was all I'd ever wanted. That's why I insisted on coming on this programme, never mind the arguments. My mum thought this was "demeaning". She said I could do so much better for myself.'

Jack said nothing, hoping his nod would be taken as knowing agreement. He didn't dare say his mum had been thrilled for him, achieving so much more than she'd thought him capable of. She would have even bragged about it at work... if there'd been any.

'Have you any older brothers or sisters setting impossible standards to live up to?' Mai asked.

Jack considered it. Mandy had set a standard his parents and teachers had considered impossible for him not to match; which wasn't quite the same.

'Yeah,' he admitted ruefully.

'I've an older brother who's an arsehole.'

'Same here, an older sister, total arsehole.'

'What is it with being born first? Did we come along and steal their thunder or what?' Mai complained lightly. 'Where do they get off telling us what to do? Just because they're older, right, and they think they know it all. Do you know what he told me? His golden advice? If I want to work with horses become a trainer and let someone else do all the work! Yeah, right! If I want to work with horses that's what I want to do – work with horses! Why would I want someone else to do the work?! And he's so smart, he doesn't know anything! A trainer does more work than the staff! When we've finished for the day, Chris and Terry have to make a start on the shitty management stuff that Arsehole thinks is so wonderful! Like I'd ever want to do that!'

Jack had only ever heard his parents complaining about bosses, so not having one might not be so bad. Then again, Business Studies sucked.

'Business Studies suck,' he agreed. 'Like, it's interesting enough, but you wouldn't want to sit and do it every day forever.'

'True, right?' Mai looked at him earnestly. 'He's only training for management and already he's talking about his own team next year, own area the following year, own company the year after that and he thinks I live in daydream land!'

Jack wasn't so sure he could see a problem with having an ambition, but he could agree that it wasn't one either of them shared.

'I don't want to manage other people, I want to manage me,' Mai insisted. 'I want to do what I want, not worry about someone else. Does that sound selfish? I bet it sounds selfish? But why should I want to be bossing anyone else around? Chris and Terry don't. The horses manage us, we just work around their needs and their routine. And anyway, my arse-hole brother is forever moaning about his boss, his supposed role model. Madam sits on her arse all day calling the shots, he complains, even though he's planning to do the same.'

Jack grinned. 'My mum calls her boss Madam. They must all be the same, right? Her boss does bugger all, she says.'

'Exactly! And that's what Arsehole aspires to and good luck to him. But really? He thinks I should, too? What an arse!'

'Is that his name? Arsehole?'

She giggled. 'Yeah. Too right it is. Arsehole. I hereby officially christen him.'

'Amen to that.'

They worked away in silence for a while, concentrating on the task set by the tutor, until Mai quietly revealed Arsehole's greatest failing.

'He loves all this rubbish,' she reflected, as Jack helped her with a ledger sheet she'd messed up. 'But he's so smart with figures he can't see the obvious. He's only had a bet on Grey Motive to win the Triple Crown, can you believe that?! He says it's a smart return, two-thousand to one or something, but he's so blinded by the maths and return, he can't see that it's two years away and probably won't happen!'

Jack hadn't thought his opinion of gambling could sink any lower. The televised racing he'd now become a fan of simply confirmed everything Mum had ever told him about the betting shop. Her punters only ever got their own money back. Minus a large chunk. And the experts knew precious little. Mai's brother was typical of the type who got suckered in.

'You told him about Mo?'

'Mo's a star! And all Arsehole can think about is a profit margin.'

'Still, two-thousand pounds is worth risking a pound for, I s'pose. And it could happen, Chris and Terry think he's really special.'

Mai laughed scornfully. 'More like two-hundred-thousand. He's greedy as well as stupid!'

Jack did the maths and double-checked the zeroes. A pound was disposable, but a hundred quid something to look after a lot more carefully. He could get a lot of vinyl LPs with that.

'Dumbass!' he agreed.

Later that evening, as he sat listening to records and playing his games console, Jack considered the zeroes and risks, meeting somewhere in the middle. A hundred pounds was rash, a pound wouldn't be missed, but ten pounds... for the lure of twenty-thousand? Or twenty pounds? If next September wasn't too late, forty-thousand could be Mum's get-out-of-jail card; the policeman had said crimes could take years to solve...

He knocked at Mandy's door, pushing it open at the same time. She was on the phone and waved a hand at him to get out. He ignored her and sat quietly on the edge of the bed.

'Look, my poxy kid brother's ear-wigging, see you down Shinfield Park first light for a practise shoot and we'll talk then, gotta go, see ya.' She glared at him. 'Ever heard of knocking?'

'I did knock!'

'So wha'd'ya want? It better be important.'

'I want you to put a bet on for me. For Mum.'

She laughed scornfully. 'For Mum? Who thinks it's pathetic and can't ask me herself? Dumbass!'

'For me, so I can give Mum her caravan money.'

Mandy's expression softened somewhat. 'You really are a dumbass. A nice thought, but someone should lock you up for your own safety.'

'No, seriously, that horse I told you about I look after, he's two-thousand to one for a race next year, so if I could put on twenty pounds we might get enough for Mum's caravan.' He didn't dare say what he was thinking, or pay off the shop.

Mandy smiled sympathetically. 'Where to even begin. Horses that are two-thousand to one don't win. And your horse hasn't even raced yet. And it's looked after by a dumbass, dumbass!' But she tussled his hair fondly.

'I don't care what you think,' Jack said defiantly, 'I have faith in him and so does Chris and Terry. I won't miss twenty pounds next year, but I'll cry forever if I miss out on forty-thousand pounds. And I can't pass for eighteen.'

'And I can?'

'You'll do it, then?'

'Maybe. If I can.' She shrugged. 'It's your money. You're a total dumbass, though.'

He smiled and released a well-folded set of five-pound notes from his grip, overseeing her zealously as she wrote down the details.

'If I was any sort of sister I'd hang on to it and give it back to you next year when you think it's lost forever,' she teased.

'Or just keep it and say nothing. But you'd better have my forty-thousand pounds, because he will win.'

'Yeah, right, of course he will.' She made a show of waving goodbye to the notes as she folded them into her purse.

He didn't immediately return to his room; locking the bathroom door with care as he re-examined the folder of receipts hidden behind the bath panel.

This time, he paid closer attention to the dates.

CHAPTER 7

De Freitas looked at the printed listing headed "Grey Motive" and wondered if it might be worth placing a small ante-post bet for the 'sheer fun', as Chris had suggested. Apparently, nursing what sufficed as a lottery ticket for a year was an enjoyable pastime. He sighed wearily and added the BHA documents to the betting shop file, returning it to his desk drawer. He looked across at McCulloch.

'You're not by any chance an alcoholic are you, Will? Or wrestling with depression?'

''Fraid not, Les.'

'Unhappily married and kids going off the rails, perhaps?'

'They remain but twinkles in the eye of a woman I've yet to meet, but other than that my free time is a carefree and happy existence.'

'I was afraid of that. It's a wonder we've ever solved a single crime between us.'

'I refute that malicious slur, sir – I closed two cases this week. And assisted Hector in the recovery of a kidnapped cat. Catnapped?'

'But not the betting shop theft.'

McCulloch nodded sagely. 'A TV cop would have had that one sewn up in six episodes. And spent more time away from their desk than at it; have you ever noticed that? But at what price, eh?'

'Point taken. Personal happiness above public safety.'

McCulloch's grin bordered on a chuckle, eventually limited to an amused outtake of breath.

'It is annoying that it's still sitting in the file, no further along, though,' he admitted. 'Two suspects cleared, but the remainder water-tight still. There'd normally be some headway by now.' Money, he'd found, was usually more easily traced than people.

'I'm concerned that Heidi Jones shares a racehorse share with her boyfriend,' de Freitas mused. 'How many others might be hiding one of our suspects behind their name?'

'It takes trust,' McCulloch pointed out reasonably. 'You hand me cash to invest in my name, when you look for it back, I deny all knowledge. Always supposing the theft was opportunist and the money is there to invest. But I could check out the shareholders, see if I run across any connections.'

'Thanks, Will. I shall call it a day and leave you to it; I'm done in.'

'You won't be going on a drunken binge and teetering on the verge of a nervous breakdown, then; just to help the cause?'

'To be honest, a quiet game of crib with Mrs de Freitas and an early night holds more appeal.'

Just for the fun of it, on the off chance that it would be, de Freitas stopped off on his way home at a little independent betting office with a handy parking spot outside.

Explaining his purpose to the cashier, he was redirected to the manager.

'No, it's not an issue,' the manager assured him, 'but I've not entered it on the system. It hardly seemed worth it, for a one-off, but if the whole stable are going to pile in I might have to! What are you, the assistant trainer?' He eyed the detective doubtfully. 'You don't look like stable material?'

'Owner.'

'Ah, well. For today and today only I'll let you have the same odds, seeing as it's a sentiment bet.' He tapped at a screen and twisted it round for de Freitas to see, rather like a bank transaction.

'I thought it would be a single bet?' de Freitas remarked, studying the information overload before him.

'One bet only? The Triple Crown comprises of three races, you know. You could be supremely optimistic and just have a plunge on the Triple Crown itself. I'd advise each-way, we'll call it a quarter the odds, for sentiment.'

'I have no idea what you're talking about, but here's ten pounds for said advice.'

The manager laughed and printed out a detailed receipt. 'Return this to me September next year and I'll have three-thousand one-hundred and thirty-five pounds waiting for you.'

'If you say so. Incidentally, I take it one of the trainers backed him already, then?'

'They're ex-jockeys, aren't they? They've not backed him in here, that's for sure. The young lad from Brookhills Betting Office in the precinct is our only other punter on your horse. It's a safe bet they went in there. I'd watch it if I were you, news of your good thing is leaking out, the odds will plummet to mere double figures at this rate!'

De Freitas returned his amused smile and tucked the betting slip into his wallet. 'You would think another betting office manager would have more sense.'

'We do. The Brookhills' lad is just a trainee. He won't last long if he gives back his wages so gullibly. Good luck!'

Gullible. That was a matter of which side of the counter your viewpoint happened to be, de Freitas reflected as he continued his journey home. If the Sainte Bastien team were correct in their assessment, it was the betting office manager who had just been a mite too gullible. De Freitas was more inclined to trust the equine experts with their years of experience; and the confidence of the horse itself. Yet one of them now had a tenner while the other had only the possibility of three-thousand-and-something to come in eighteen months' time.

Chris had been right, though – the purchased printed confirmation of the fanciful objective had suddenly made it quite real and, dare he think it, possible. The returns were a drop in the ocean compared to the actual racecourse returns Chris and Terry and the unconditional shareholders would receive, but he could understand their need for the little slip of endorsement to provide encouragement over the coming year. He wondered whether he might, come the time, cash it in or frame it as a memento? Of course, Mrs de Freitas would probably prefer a nice little holiday or perhaps a garden summer house...

'And that's how they have you,' he said aloud to himself, 'the race not yet run and I'm already spending it.'

It occurred to him then that the betting office money might not be being spent because it had already been spent in advance...

* * *

Jack sat quietly on the wall outside the classrooms, studying the slip of paper Mandy had given him, along with his money back. There was no mention of two-thousand to one, although if he could manage to do the heap of maths required it probably all accumulated to that. He was having a hard enough job just working out how many different bets there were and how much it would all cost. If he was right, he needed a hundred and twenty pounds, not twenty.

He was aware of someone approaching from behind and tucked the paper back in his pocket, retrieving his phone and switching off the music he'd been listening to.

'You got finished up quick,' Mai remarked, sitting beside him to await the rest of the group. 'What are you listening to?'

He pulled out his earbuds and popped them into his pocket. 'Just random.'

'Random what? Who do you like?'

It was a question he'd often tried to side-step at school, citing some current popular download if he could remember a name quickly enough.

'Just old stuff, from the 1960s,' he told her truthfully.

'What, like The Beatles?'

Normally he found it easier to just nod in agreement, even though he had yet to hear a Beatles song he liked.

'Not really,' he said, stepping outside his comfort zone and feeling strangely comfortable about doing so. 'I like R and B – rhythm and blues. Manfred Mann and The Animals and The Rolling Stones and stuff.'

'I've heard of The Rolling Stones. An old rock band, weren't they?'

'Well, yeah,' he agreed. Normally he didn't continue the conversation. 'They didn't start out that way, though. I don't like anything they did after 1965.' Stop. Now, he warned himself, but she was leaning forward, interested. 'Except Aftermath in '66. There were a couple of good ones on that.' He should have said anything after 1966, really, but he'd never let it go further than The Beatles before. What dumbass said nothing after 1965 except 1966? She was probably laughing at him inwardly at this very minute.

'Can I listen?'

'What?'

'Which is your favourite?'

Shit. It was so not cool to listen to old people's music; and he so wanted to be cool. Just say the battery's dying. 'Of The Rolling Stones? "Off The Hook", I guess.'

Like an idiot, he gave her the earbuds and switched on the phone, scrolling instantly to the well-played selection and watching her in anticipation, so hoping she would love it, or at least wouldn't laugh scornfully at him.

Her expression betrayed nothing, but after a moment he saw her foot tap gently in time to the rhythm. Somewhere past the first chorus she turned to him and smiled her approval.

'They're OK. Different.'

'You might like this better,' he suggested a touch over-eagerly, pushing play on a Manfred Mann song even as his inner common sense screamed at him to quit while he was ahead.

"The One In The Middle" didn't lessen her smile, and her head began to nod in time with her foot.

'And is he?' she asked, handing back the earbuds.

'Is he what?'

'Sweet? Because he's way not modest, is he!'

He laughed with her and showed her the EP cover image linked to the song.

She studied it with faux seriousness. 'OK so he's stood in the middle of four cringey dad types, but, yeah, I pronounce him sweet. I like his style.' She nodded approvingly.

He tried hard not to think about how carefully he mimicked that style.

'Who do you like?' he asked, hoping it was someone he'd at least heard of.

'Old stuff too – not that old, but I can't stand all that boring samey rubbish out at the moment. Ever heard of Valentine Crime?'

'Yeah, my sister was into them a few years back.' The lead singer was a total muppet, he recalled.

'They'd be my favourites; and any in the same genre, really, they're all pretty good. Matt Valentine is such a genius. Your sister's not such an arsehole then! I might actually like her!'

Good luck in that, he thought. Mandy's dodgy taste in music was hardly a redeeming feature; although she'd been pretty approachable recently, almost human. Then he remembered the receipts.

'She's still an arsehole no matter what she's listening to,' he said, with feeling.

'I'll have to set her up with my brother, it'll be a match made in heaven!' She stood up. 'Come on, everyone's going in already.'

The reminder of Mandy and the receipts she had sensibly kept hidden marred his concentration throughout the language class. He had been finding Japanese easier than French, but that afternoon he would have struggled with basic English. It happened; lapses in concentration had dogged his schooldays, although more often than not it had just been lack of interest, mainly on the teacher's part. Preoccupation with staying invisible didn't help, either.

There had been no need to blend in or evade notice here at Sainte Bastien. His new classmates didn't seek to involve him in crimes against his conscience, or force him to choose between becoming Friend or Victim. He had prudently chosen Friend, while skipping school kept his conscience clean. It had also sealed his unearned reputation with the teaching fraternity, who had expected nothing less from Mandy's sibling.

His sister had a lot to answer for.

* * *

'Can't beat a day off on a school day,' Paul said cheerfully, walking across the bedroom en route to the hall and pausing to waggle his naked backside at Joy.

'That thief has a lot to answer for!' Joy joked, but her appreciation of the rare freedom of getting the house to themselves was clear.

Paul returned with two mugs of tea and sat back on the bed beside her.

'The great Cure All.' He winked.

'Pity it can't cure everything.'

Despite the pleasant afternoon, the day hadn't started out so well. Had Paul not been home to provide a much-needed shoulder, she didn't know what she would have done. Sat sobbing in the kitchen 'til the kids came in and teased her, probably. Maud's phone call had been a right kick in the teeth.

'You gonna walk around like that all day, or put some clothes on?' she chided.

'Drink this, shower, dress; promise.'

'You must be mad, it's bloody freezing.'

'It's bloody freedom is what it is!'

They drank their tea in silence for a while.

'As they cross each of us off the list, the noose tightens on the one left,' Joy observed grimly.

'And you'll be the next crossed off, don't worry, love,' Paul assured her, leaning over to give her a kiss.

'Maud was obvious, though, weren't she? She's got like a quarter of a million in the bank and she only sent the family over what their holiday usually costs them for Christmas. She hasn't been spending anything either. We're all too bloody scared to.'

'A quarter of a million!'

'Well she has; near enough, prob'ly. She said she had a hundred grand, between poor old Jim's insurance and Cardi's house he sold. And she's not spent a penny of it, so what would she be wanting with forty grand? They already go on holiday to Barbados every year. And Madam's ticking off all the Greek islands twice a bloody year! Christ, it's only enough to buy a bleedin' caravan in poxy Tenby, and the cops know that.'

'Because you told them!'

'Because they asked! Even if we miraculously had forty grand, we could hardly buy it now, could we? I'd be thrown in prison quicker than you could sign the cheque! This is going to hang over us for the rest of our lives, you know that, don't you?'

'Look, they've let Maud and that Saturday girl go; you'll be next. And then it'll all be over.'

Joy forced a smile enough to reassure him, but he was hopelessly optimistic, she knew. There was no reason for Maud to be a suspect. And Anita would be next off the list, too. And Rhys probably wasn't short of a few bob. Lee had been in flippin' Portugal, for Christ sake, which only left Gareth. The bugger had probably slipped it in his pocket before announcing it was missing; but he wasn't on a cashier's salary, either. It didn't take Sherlock Holmes to work out who'd be the last suspect standing.

'Have you thought about taking Maud's place at the food bank?' Paul suggested, as he got up and got dressed.

'And who'd run this food bank?!' she laughed. 'I like being home. If it wasn't for the money I'd be happy to never go back.'

'Yeah, but there's being home and then there's never going out.' It had been playing on his mind long before Maud had rung them with her good news and shattered the fragile calm.

'How can I go out, with them following me?' Joy demanded.

'They're not following you!' Paul argued, but it was always futile.

'Just because we can't see them! We're under surveillance, they told me so. I'm followed everywhere and the neighbours'd soon start to notice and wonder why. It wouldn't be long before the fingers started pointing and the gossip started.'

'You didn't do it, love, and they can't prove you did.'

She looked up at him. 'And they can't prove I didn't, can they?'

* * *

'Have the DCs ask around a few of the loan sharks, would you, Will. There's a possibility we're coming in at the wrong end.'

De Freitas sat at his desk, staring once more at the Brookhills file, hoping something might suddenly leap out at him. Three months and still no evidence. Lack of enough proof to allow two of the suspects to return to work and escape his file, but it was proof, and not lack of it, that would close the file completely.

McCulloch frowned. 'Spent before stolen? Nothing in their lifestyle suggests that.'

'I paid a visit to a bookmaker the other day and understood nothing, but nevertheless came away a tenner lighter. It's very easy to leave with less than you went in with.'

McCulloch arched a brow. 'Even when it's your profession?'

'True. But we're grasping at straws at this stage. No harm in seeing if any unlicensed debt collectors have been calling.'

McCulloch nodded thoughtfully. 'The Reid girl has a hobby beyond her means. Nothing she couldn't have saved up for, but isn't today's generation the now not later brigade?'

De Freitas slipped the folder back into his desk.

'It's puzzling me where these type of people could come into contact with the wrong type of people,' he pondered aloud, 'but the school is a great starting point. You may be on to something.'

'I've never seen it crop up on our files. Nothing much other than truancy. Racking up debt with dealers who have managed to stay off our radar?' McCulloch shook his head.

Nevertheless, he double-checked his notebook, which only confirmed his memory. The Reid girl had spent four hundred pounds shortly before the theft and, given the timing, it was hard to see her racking up enough interest to already owe forty-thousand. That type of loan shark would definitely be on their radar.

De Freitas was lost in his own thoughts. Joy Reid was intrinsically honest. You got to know the types. If she were to be driven to steal four-thousand pounds to protect her daughter, de Freitas suspected there would be thirty-six thousand still sitting in the floor safe.

'We're drawing too many blanks,' he admitted, 'it's time to go back in again.'

* * *

'I think my sister wants to rob a bank or something.'

Jack and Mai were sitting on the bus together, Mai tapping busily on her phone sharing the day's latest events while Jack watched the outside world pass, preoccupied with the weight of his own small world.

'You what now?'

Mai's fingers were momentarily stilled. He wished he'd not let his thoughts escape onto his tongue. But it wasn't as if he could talk to Mandy about it; or Mum.

Like his music, it was out there now.

'She's got college forms that cost thousands and my mum and dad are never going to pay all that and now she's buying guns,' he told her. 'They come in millimetres, don't they? You hear it on telly, sixteen mill shotguns and all that?'

'Your sister?! How do you know? Did she tell you? Have you seen them?'

'I found the receipts.'

'You found the receipts? The receipts. For guns. So, what, like, criminals write receipts now?'

It did sound kind of stupid, now that he actually thought about it.

'Pipes and stuff come in millimetres, you sure it's not just some science project?'

Jack shook his head. 'She's spent loads, and she goes out target practising in the park, really early. Dawn, like.'

'So maybe they're legal,' Mai suggested. 'She's joined a gun club. You know, for sport instead of bank robbing?' Her tone was teasing, as was her grin. 'You don't need a gun to go to the bank for college fees, you know!'

Jack kicked himself; for voicing his suspicions, not misplacing them. Gun clubs were country club territory, not Whitley Wood pastimes. Guns were purely for gentry, gangs and criminals. Even the price tag and acquisition was decidedly suspect. He'd Googled sixteen-millimetre shotguns, and only a gangster would sell one for the prices Mandy had paid. Even then, at a tenth of the cost, they were beyond her budget and she would have had to rob someone in the first place just to buy them.

'She's not really a shooting club type,' he tried to explain, picturing Labradors with pheasants dangling from their stupidly grinning mouths. 'She'd definitely be more of an armed criminal type.'

'Cool!'

'What's cool about it?'

'Well, nothing, I suppose. But at least she's gone out and done something different. It's a bit different to just going out clubbing or shopping.' She smiled at him reassuringly. 'It's an Olympic sport, you know. Shooting. She's probably aiming her sights a bit higher than armed robbery. Get it? Aiming her sights!'

'You think?' He definitely didn't; but it was probably best not to confess to having an armed robber as a sister, after all.

'Have you tried asking her?' Mai suggested.

'No way. I wouldn't dare.'

'Safer to ask her now, before she gets to be a better shot!'

'What if you found out Arsehole had a gun?'

'Him?' Mai snorted in disgust. 'No question – pheasant and deer murderer! There's no money in Olympics and he wouldn't get his hands dirty robbing banks!'

Jack was grateful the conversation had become a joke, although it had done little to ease his concern. In Mai's world guns were only on TV; in his, too, until he'd seen and heard otherwise. It was so much easier not to believe.

Mai returned to her social media posts, while he watched the world beyond the window grow ever more claustrophobic, the quiet green Downs of Lambourn soon replaced by the busy grey suburbs of Reading.

'See you tomorrow,' Mai said, disturbing his reverie as she stood up. 'And you know something?' She added, dangling her backpack off one shoulder. 'Only criminals know criminals. D'you really think the likes of us could actually meet a villain and be trusted enough to buy something off them? A receipt is legit. And traceable.'

'Are you getting off or do you want me to fix up a camp bed for you?' called the driver.

Mai grinned and saluted a farewell.

Jack found her parting words reassuring, making a lot more sense than any of the other chaos in his home life. If Mum could be a suspect in a shop theft then Mandy could certainly be a member of a gun club. Snobbery went in both directions; he didn't blame her for keeping it secret, the kids at school would have a field day if they found out. It wasn't hard to do; they'd all managed to keep Mum's suspension secret.

At least Mum's penny-pinching backed up her story of becoming a stay-at-home mum to help him and Mandy through their exam years. Just a pain in the arse she had to take alibis so literally. The frugality he could live with, now she'd become a pretty decent chef and turned out cakes and stuff daily. But taking an interest in his classes and homework sucked. His stuff was his stuff and he hated any snooping, 'specially when it came to his games and records. No wonder kids on TV always had those big "Keep Out!" signs on their doors.

Mandy may have been a total arsehole, but she also had her head screwed on. There was a lot to be said for keeping stuff covered up and hidden.

'You getting off or setting up bed for the night?' the driver demanded impatiently, glad to be making her final drop. Her tone quickly changed as she opened the door and surveyed the scene outside. 'Would you like me to walk you to the door?'

Jack shook his head and stepped slowly off the bus, into the suddenly very visible chaos of his home life, now anything but covered up and hidden.

CHAPTER 8

Grant had been right about the fleet of matching squad cars, three of which were parked uniformly outside Jack's house. They still didn't look like police cars, but the swarm of plain clothes officers sort of gave the game away. A uniformed officer, taking Jack's rucksack from him at the door, had ushered him straight to the living room where the rest of the family were gathered, sitting anxiously together on the sofa.

Mum and Dad were in their dressing gowns, Jack couldn't help but notice. He tried hard not to think about strip searches as he took his place beside them; perched on the arm of the three-seater directly alongside Dad.

'It's just a routine search,' one of the detectives assured him gently. 'Much as before; we'll put everything back as we found it, unless we find items of interest.'

'Your Dad and me were just out the bath,' Joy told Jack, trying to sound relaxed and cheerful, and knowing her voice was anything but.

It was the same lie she'd instantly told Mandy on her arrival home, as though being caught by the kids having an illicit afternoon's love-in was worse than the search warrant presented to her earlier that afternoon by DS McCulloch and his team. That in itself had been somehow less traumatic than opening the door to them in a state of undress in the middle of the afternoon. Conspicuously dry, Joy had babbled to them about a bath and had barely been aware of the official warrant handed to her to read.

Now, she sat anxiously, clinging tightly to Paul, thinking only of the scene outside the house rather than the ordered search being conducted inside. Three detectives were systematically taking apart one room at a time, under the direction of McCulloch; but outside, their cars were causing raised eyebrows and the traditional policeman in full uniform was clearly no Stripagram. God knows what the neighbours must be thinking.

'Can I go to the bathroom?' Jack asked, after an awkward silence.

'Are they done in there yet?' McCulloch checked with the uniformed constable, who was then assigned to accompany Jack.

'Only to the door?' Jack checked.

'Sorry, no one's allowed out of our sight until the search is complete.'

That information was enough to suppress Jack's bladder. He pulled a face at Mandy, who seemed to find his discomfort amusing.

'Pack it in, you two,' Joy said, from force of habit, as though their current situation were perfectly normal.

From time to time a sixth member of the team, who mostly sat with them looking mildly uncomfortable, was called away to look at something, only to return slightly buoyed by the activity, but with a shake of the head that did less than buoy McCulloch.

'Are you forensics?' Jack asked, having observed his apparent advisory capacity. He wondered if the expert might let him try out fingerprinting dust, which had always intrigued him. Surely dust would just fill up all the little lines the fingerprints made? Still, it must be dead boring just wandering round a crime scene trying to find a single hair. The guy looked bored, anyway.

'No, I'm not actually with the police,' the man responded, 'I'm a valuator with an auction house. Just helping.'

'No wonder you keep coming back disappointed!' Joy observed.

'Grandad's records are valuable,' Jack pointed out, aggrieved they were always referred to as old rubbish.

'To the right collector, certainly,' the man agreed; prompting what Jack hoped was an "I told you so" look.

'A deaf one, he means,' Mandy teased.

'What were you checking?' Paul asked, intrigued by the idea that there was anything remotely valuable in their home.

'Comics, magazines, books,' the valuator informed him. 'You'd be surprised how many rarities people have without knowing.'

'Yeah? And how many have we got?'

The valuator smiled ruefully and slowly shook his head.

'Yep, thought not. What about those pop annuals from the sixties, you've got three of them, haven't you, Jack, off Grandad?'

Jack pulled a face. 'Someone drew moustaches and glasses on Cliff Richard and Brian Jones. And blacked out Sandie Shaw's teeth.'

Paul grinned. 'God, yeah, I remember getting a proper bollocking off your Grandad for that! Don't tell your Mum what I did to Lulu!'

'Silly beggar,' Joy chided. 'That could've been his inheritance.'

'Three-hundred at the most,' the valuator reassured her; his view of three-hundred pounds vastly different to her own.

'Three-hundred!' Jack protested. 'You wait 'til I tell Grandad!'

Another awkward silence was broken by one of the detective constables seeking further help and McCulloch's place was taken by the uniformed officer. Joy watched the disappearance of the senior detective with some apprehension, wondering what could be raising suspicion.

She felt Paul squeeze her hand tighter.

'It's alright, love,' he whispered softly; but that was an easy reassurance to make if you weren't the one about to be carted off to prison at any moment. Joy wished the other detective were here, the older one. He'd seemed less trigger happy.

Her stomach churned as McCulloch came back in. What could he have found?

'Mandy, I'd like a quick word if I may; it's nothing serious, just some clarification,' he said. 'You'll need a parent with you.'

'Dad, then,' Mandy chose, without hesitation.

It was Paul's turn to look anxious, but everything about the detective's tone and demeanour seemed relaxed and non-threatening.

They were gone for some time, suggesting a little more than just simple clarification, but it did at least herald the end of the house search, which had extended to the garden. Everything had been put back with such care and diligence it was hard to know there had even been such detailed intrusion.

McCulloch waited on messages from his colleagues elsewhere before finally giving the Reids the freedom to move once more, unaccompanied. Jack made the most of it, pushing past Mandy to get to the bathroom before her.

'Thank you for your time and patience,' McCulloch acknowledged as he departed, the last of his team to leave. He'd had a final check round to ensure no unnecessary damage had been done. The usual raids, which invariably found more than enough incriminating evidence, were not so diligently tidy. His team were under no obligation to repair breakages or restore order where seizures were made. But he'd learned from de Freitas to treat suspects with respect, until they provoked the loss of it.

'So what was that little chat about?' Joy demanded, the moment the front door closed behind the departing visitors.

'Just her college choices,' Paul said lightly, hoping it was old enough ground not to turn up any fresh dirt. 'They wanted to ask about a stack of college stuff she had that's way out of our league.'

He wasn't in the habit of keeping things from Joy, nor was he any good at it, but he felt her stress levels were bad enough as it was. It wasn't as if it was anything she needed to know. He just hoped she'd accept that part-truth and not press him into a lie.

'Christ almighty, we went through all that when she started sending off for it all, what's the matter with her!' Joy fumed. 'Now they think I've robbed the shop to put her through bloody media studies!'

Paul reached out and pulled her to him, giving her a hug.

'They don't think that. Mandy still thinks she's gonna get a scholarship and she was being as honest as she was stupid, poor kid. They're not gonna arrest you just cos Mandy's living in cloud cuckoo land.'

'And that's why she asked for you, not me? I bet you encouraged her, didn't you?'

'I didn't shoot her down in flames. Let her have a dream for a bit.'

'You're a bloody softy! They get away with murder!'

She didn't know the half of it, but he just gave a guilty grin.

* * *

'Not getting soft in your old age?'

De Freitas smiled as he continued to read through the report McCulloch had given him.

'Not necessarily a bad thing, Will. But, no; just relieved my hunches are still to be trusted.'

'Pity you haven't a hunch as to who's guilty.'

'None of them, according to this.' He closed the file and reached for the coffee McCulloch had thoughtfully provided. 'This one is hanging around like a wasp at a picnic, it's beginning to annoy me.'

'Have you had many cases go cold?'

'A good few. It happens.' De Freitas sipped his coffee. 'People go missing, Will, but money? It never fails to leave a trail. You don't steal money just to hide it away.'

He sat back and finished his coffee, considering. It was an opportunist crime. His department had twenty or thirty cases open at any one time, half of them already concluded, as far as he was concerned, and pending Crown Prosecution; a few had gone as far as they could, without success, and would get filed. Cold, as McCulloch put it. Never closed, just forgotten.

Opportunists rarely got passed on as far as his office; uniformed usually had them nabbed or filed pretty smartly. In this instance, they weren't dealing with a criminal mind, but an ordinary person seizing a chance. A chance that had been under his or her nose for much of their working life at the Brookhills betting office. Why had it only now been noticed and seized? Why risk a career, a lifetime's reputation, for less than two years' salary? What could be so important, so worth the risk, and yet so invisible?

'I'm not ready to file this yet,' he admitted, setting his cup down. 'There has to be a trail. We're just not finding it. And if we file it, those innocent employees lose their job and quite likely any chance of a future decent job. As much as I like to collar the guilty, the most important part of our job is protecting the innocent.'

'No trails, but a bit of trodden down grass blade,' McCulloch pointed out. 'Mandy Reid's spending spree was pre-theft, but her objective is still a year ahead. Future college fees are our only motive so far.'

De Freitas had severe doubts, but he wasn't one to shoot down the only lead McCulloch or any of the team had come up with.

'And another thing,' McCulloch added, 'the Reids' regular outgoings have decreased quite noticeably over the period. There may not be any evidence of luxury items or spending, but maybe the lack of visible spending is evidence of another supply of cash?'

'They're being too careful,' de Freitas agreed. 'Have surveillance stepped up. We need to catch someone dipping in. Desperately.'

* * *

'So they caught you. Dad knows about the guns, then? ' Jack stood hesitantly at the foot of Mandy's bed, not sure if they were now comrades in the face of a common enemy, or still the same old enemies as always.

'The what now?' Mandy looked at him scornfully. His loopy friend Amad had the whole street believing the cops had been looking for some ancient stash of guns. Mum didn't know whether to laugh or cry, but at least guns were easier to laugh off than the truth.

'I know what you and Dad and that detective were talking about,' Jack insisted, 'but I can get us out of this. I can get everything you want and get Mum her caravan money and pay back her work. You don't need to do anything but put that bet on.'

Mandy laughed, but not unsympathetically. 'It's not Hollywood, dumbass! We can't just magically win a happy ever after!'

'Not if we don't even try!' He sat down on the bed. 'What were you planning?'

'Trust me, a safer gamble.' She sighed. 'Still a gamble, though. At least it rests on me and Tisha's skill, and not just a horse.'

'What did Dad say?'

'Like it's any of your business! But he thinks we'll just fail and get hurt.' He'd meant well, of course, but, god, a little bit of faith wouldn't have gone amiss, as she'd pointed out cuttingly at the time. What made him so sure she'd fail? And now here was Jack, just as bad.

'The bet might lose as well, but at least no one gets hurt,' Jack reasoned.

Mandy smiled. 'Go on, then, give me the bet and the money. Have you worked it all out yet? The guy in the bookies said it was a multiple or something.'

Jack had painstakingly worked it out. The Triple Crown turned out to be three races, not one. And all three limited to three-year-old horses, so a horse only got one shot at it.

Grey Motive would have to prove himself the best of his generation in three different races over three different distances. At Sainte Bastien they had been learning about pedigrees and physique and specialist horses, but the Triple Crown needed a versatile horse with speed and stamina.

'Well, first there's the Two Thousand Guineas, run over a mile in May,' Jack explained. 'Then The Derby, a mile and a half in June. Then the St Leger, a mile and three-quarters in September.

'In two hundred years only fifteen horses have managed it, and none for over seventy years. No one's even tried in forty years. Chris says it's prob'ly not even possible any more, but Mo has got loads of speed and Chris and Terry think he'll have loads of stamina from his parents. It's massive. Like really massive. Like Reading Town winning the League, the League Cup and the Cup Final!'

'As good as free money, then,' Mandy teased.

'If anyone can do it, Mo can.'

'Just give me the slip written out and the money.'

Jack hesitated. ‘See, the thing is, like, there are six bets and I’ve only got sixty pounds. That’s ten pound on each bet and we’ll only win fifteen-thousand.’

‘Is that all? Shame,’ Mandy said with heavy sarcasm.

‘You could double it?’ he suggested hopefully.

‘Great idea, between us we can lose twice as much!’

‘He’ll win!’ Jack protested. ‘Even if he only wins one of the races, at the very least we’ll get fifteen-hundred. If you chipped in, too, that would be three-grand!’

Mandy reached for her handbag and pulled out her purse.

‘I’ve got twenty quid, that’s it, no more.’

‘OK.’ Jack did the maths. ‘You chip in eighteen pounds. That’s thirteen pounds per bet and an extra four and a half grand in winnings!’

‘For Mum?’

‘For Mum.’

Mandy shook her head, adding her note to Jack’s betting slip and carefully folded notes. ‘Thanks a lot, creep, now we’re both friggin’ dumbasses!’

He grinned. ‘You can see how it’s addictive!’

‘Yeah, right, a girl could get used to being twenty quid down every week.’

Jack hesitated before making his escape. ‘You won’t do anything stupid, will you; you and Tisha? Mum’d go spare.’

‘Oh for god’s sake, one total moron in the family is enough! We’re not making a Muppet movie; you’ll be able to show your face and brag to Amad when it’s done, trust me,’ she said bitterly.

He retreated to his own room and the sanctuary of his records, trying not to think further about the risk he and Mandy were determined to take. There was no point in balancing one bad act against a worse one; he knew Mum’s low opinion of gambling and she’d be just as hurt by his own well-intentioned crime as Mandy's. Their only hope was a successful outcome. Hopefully before getting caught.

* * *

'Another successful outcome,' McCulloch remarked, slipping a file into his out-tray. 'Down to twenty-four open cases for the moment.'

'Successful up until the point a judge says not guilty,' de Freitas muttered, glancing disapprovingly at a letter recently popped into his in-tray, one of the less satisfactory aspects of his work.

'Have we overlooked blackmail?'

De Freitas looked up at McCulloch. Several facetious responses crossed his mind, but the sergeant didn't give him long enough to voice one.

'I've just put the Freeman case to bed, it's gone over to the CP now, but it just made me think – blackmail is by its very nature an invisible crime. When we were investigating blackmail, it was pretty easy. Someone trying to keep a secret, only so-and-so could possibly know and the whole process leaves a pretty obvious trail. But with the Brookhills Betting Office case, we've only been looking at theft.'

'An instant need for money that never appears to get spent,' de Freitas agreed. 'You could be seriously onto something here, Will. Have you still got your notes of first impressions when we initially spoke to the Brookhills suspects?'

'I have indeed.' McCulloch sorted out the relevant file and handed it to de Freitas.

After a considered perusal de Freitas handed it back. 'Your thoughts?'

'Joy Reid jumps out,' McCulloch concluded, after a careful read through.

'Very much so. In as much as, from this new angle, none of the others do.'

'The million dollar question being, why?'

'A mere affair isn't enough. An illegitimate child somewhere, already been done by the husband. A previous theft?'

'If Brookhills were made aware of it, she'd lose her job.'

'Is the theft of forty-thousand comparable to job loss?'

McCulloch perched himself on the edge of de Freitas' desk. 'They're a supportive family; I watched them the other day, during the search. The husband seems pretty easy-going and forgiving, and I think she knows that. It would need to be extreme to drive her beyond owning up and into committing theft.'

'Not her directly, then, but protecting one of the kids? What's our most common blackmail?'

'Company fraud, sexual deviancy. Or, in the Freeman case, both.' McCulloch thought back to the house search. 'The husband is keeping some of Mandy Reid's aspirations from Joy Reid. In fact, it was news to him, as well. So, what else is Mandy Reid hiding, and her mother in turn hiding from her father? The Los Angeles connection?'

'You said it all looked innocent?'

'On social media, certainly. But beyond the innocent contact? Provocative photos exchanged?'

'Surely the recipient would make the better target, unless it is the recipient blackmailing her?'

McCulloch smiled. 'I think the girl's canny enough to be the blackmailer, not the victim. I'm thinking more of the recipient targeting Joy Reid.'

'That makes sense; well, to the degree we imagine the whole notion makes sense. We are probably barking up the wrong tree, but blackmailers don't stop. Joy Reid will be under pressure for more.'

'Cutting back on their usual household spending,' McCulloch agreed. 'She'll be desperate.'

'We'll pull her in for informal questioning.'

CHAPTER 9

Joy had talked about the noose tightening, but she hadn't quite expected to physically feel it. She felt the roughness of it now, burning at her throat, restricting her breathing, crushing her chest, making her head spin as the sweat pricked her skin.

The noose may not have been real, but the effects of its tightening very much were. The rising panic of being asked questions she had no answer to had seen her kindly detective send out for tea and biscuits, as if they would have helped! More likely choked her! Instead she'd flustered her way into ever-deepening guilt, about as real as the noose. Like the noose, the reality of it made bugger all difference to the outcome. Without proof of her innocence she was guilty as charged.

They'd fetched her back home about an hour ago. Paul at work, the kids at school, no one to see her come or go. She'd stopped sweating about her impending incarceration in prison and wrestled now with the dilemma of whether to confess to Paul or just stay schtum. They didn't need this grief; she could worry for all four of them.

Of course, staying schtum meant not being able to give vent to her fumes at Mandy; she could murder that little cow! What the devil was she up to that the police thought her mother would rob a bookies for?

Disguising her fear as anger and redirecting it at Mandy went some way toward loosening the imaginary noose and its genuine affects. As the nausea and dizziness subsided, she decided that now was probably the time for that cup of tea and biscuit.

Of course, none of this should have come as any surprise to her. She'd been steeling herself for the inevitable from the moment Gareth had first announced a problem with the cash, all those weeks ago. The memory of it was still vivid and chilled her now just as it had chilled her then. She'd known at once the money was missing; and had known at once who would be blamed.

No; no need to say anything to Paul about being questioned today. It wasn't as if she'd been arrested. They'd just wanted her to answer a few questions, ever more bewildering. The more she'd answered "no!" the more perplexing the questions had become, until she could no longer make sense of any of it. Her emphatic "no" had become increasingly uncertain and suddenly it had become all about Mandy and those stupid bloody prank calls and god knows what else.

'We paid the bill off ages ago and she's got her own pay-as-you-go mobile and I unplug the house phone and take it to work with me!' Joy had protested in confusion, the implication being that she'd stolen the money to pay off Mandy's debts. 'I can't bail her out if I don't know what she's s'posed to have done! We haven't got anything we'd want to spend it on!'

And that was the crux. They did have something they wanted, had dreamed of, and it fell neatly into the forty-thousand pounds price range, too. Even if she weren't arrested and imprisoned, even if they did somehow save up enough money or win the lottery, the caravan could never be bought now, the police would always be waiting. It would never be anything more than a pipe-dream.

She didn't know why she was now crying, it had always been a bloody pipe-dream.

'Silly cow,' she scolded herself out loud, as she dabbed her eyes with the tissue up her sleeve and gave her nose a damn good blow.

She dropped it in the bin and the lack of any replacement was enough to curb her emotion.

She thought of Maud, happily back at work, not a care in the bleedin' world. Joy wondered if Anita and Rhys had been hauled back in for questioning and which of them would be the first back at work? She barely knew Gareth, maybe he really had pocketed the cash before calling the police? And yet the police still thought it was her, so he'd left no evidence and had all the alibis and would get away scot free while she went down for his crime. Huh. Bloody typical. She and Paul could never catch a break.

The tea and biscuit did help a lot in the return of normality to her life. She washed up her cup and the other bits left on the side from breakfast and tried to forget about that dreaded knock on the door and trip to the police station. Done and dusted and not worth a mention.

Yet still she jumped when the door banged again, an hour or so later.

Jack appeared at the kitchen window a few seconds later, tapping impatiently on the glass until she let him in the back door.

'I thought you was never letting me in, I'm froze!' he complained.

'I never heard you,' Joy lied. 'If you've lost your key again you can pay for a new one!'

'It's upstairs on the side, I forgot it this morning, and my Japanese essay, but it was OK, they didn't mind, I can hand it in tomorrow.'

Jack still couldn't get over how enjoyable the whole learning experience was when tutors treated you like a human instead of an annoyance in their mind-numbing day. The Racing Futures Programme was the best thing to ever happen to him and Mo was brilliant and his policeman friend who owned him even better. He knew having a policeman to talk to would help Mum.

'You need to pull your socks up,' Mum complained now, 'they'll turf you out if you make a habit of dodging your homework.'

'It's fine, Mum. When's dinner?'

'Yer Dad'll be in at six.'

'Great!' Jack grabbed a couple of the homemade biscuits from the tin and raced off upstairs, eager to get his homework for that day finished.

Joy shook her head, marvelling at both his enthusiasm and the fact that he was doing Japanese. Japanese! A pity there hadn't been that scholarship available for Mandy when she was going off the rails.

Unless, of course...

The new train of thought put a new fear of god into her. Jack had already won a scholarship and was really blossoming as a result. Mandy's dream of university was totally unrealistic, but what if Jack actually got offered a place?

They couldn't pay for it.

Lack of money had once been her only worry. But now it was the spending of what little they had that petrified her.

* * *

'Kind of scary, isn't it?' Chris admitted, as he looked at the budget Anne had been busy working on.

They'd never really let lack of finances worry them before, with a perpetual circle of borrowing and repayments so far yielding profit, at least enough to live on and carry through to the next cycle. But that old loop had closed. This year's projections had no definitive end. Unless, Chris noted, you followed the fifteen pounds a week losses through to an inevitable conclusion.

'Well done, love, you've kept the annual loss to under a grand.'

Anne smiled ruefully. 'And our wages to fifty pounds a week. The BHA training grant just about covers it, but we need to get some prize money percentages or sales commissions to actually pay our own bills. At least we've got the rent from our place; Su and Terry can't get by on a hundred pounds a week between them.'

'They could let the cottage and move in here as well. It's not like it's not big enough.'

'Seriously? Could you ever see them giving up the cottage!'

Chris studied the spreadsheet, even though figures were not his forte.

'You've got twelve sets of training fees, but our own two horses aren't actually being paid for.'

'Their price included the training fees,' Anne reminded him. 'The income from sales and syndication is forty-thousand short because I put that over here into training fees. We got eighty-thousand for the forty percent in each colt and an advance on the training. All we need to do now is pray to god the other pinhooks turn a profit!'

Chris grimaced. He felt more like he'd sold his soul to the devil, having kept the only two horses likely to cover any losses. But while the pinhooks still provided a lifeline, he knew it would all come down to judgement and the success of the only two colts in the yard who now mattered.

'Send Jack into me tomorrow,' Anne said as she packed away for the evening and shut down the computer, 'we'll go through the entries process and I'll get him used to the calendar.'

'When do our big two-year-old races close?'

'Oh, god, slow down there, not 'til June onwards! We won't actually be making any entries, but we'll make a plan, maybe. I think he'll enjoy that.'

'How's things at home for him, do you think?'

'Ask Mo, Jack tells him everything! But I think he's got something weighing on him, I've never known a kid so miserable about breaking up for the Christmas holidays!'

'Not serious?'

'No, thankfully; I did report it to the counsellor, but all's well, apparently.'

Chris moved to behind Anne's chair and leaned over her, embracing her tightly.

'It might all be a headache, but I do really love what we're doing here,' he admitted, 'we're really making a difference to these kids.'

Anne put her hands over his and squeezed them.

'It does make you feel proud,' she agreed. 'Who would've thought it, all those years ago out in that same yard?'

'Less of the "all those years ago", it still only feels like a few!'

Anne smiled and reluctantly pulled free of the hug. 'I'd never have thought it of the old guv'nor, though, curmudgeonly old devil that he was, letting a load of inexperienced kids loose in his yard! Who'd have ever guessed he had a soft spot?'

'Not me! He used to find mine easy enough with his boot or that bloody tin mug he'd hurl at us!' He grinned. 'Happy days!'

And they had been, genuinely, Chris reflected. He and Terry had eventually moved on, but a tragedy had, in an odd way, brought them all back to the yard that had shaped their transition from youth to adult. Chris forever regretted his own part in that tragedy, but there was now consolation to be found in helping to shape a new generation and give something back.

It was a funny old world, much smaller than it seemed; the old guv'nor's legacy bringing them all back round again. Less a circle of life than a circle of living, students growing into teachers and a fresh cycle of students to fill their shoes. And DI de Freitas, too; an unexpected link to where it had all started.

'It's funny how Fate works,' Chris said, as Anne closed up the office for the evening. 'You can't help thinking Les might find his missing money after all.'

'What, the detective? I should've thought they'd given up by now, it's been months, hasn't it?'

'They never give up, apparently. Still, we might all end up on one of those unsolved mystery channels on the telly in a few years' time!'

Anne followed him out and locked the door.

* * *

Jack knocked at Mandy's door, simultaneously pushing it open and entering her bedroom in a single deft movement, circumnavigating the "piss off" option while still able to retain his holier-than-thou insistence that he had knocked first. Their life together was one long war, with minor battles won and lost on a daily basis.

Mum had long ago given up her own battle of trying to end the war, but what Jack wanted now, more than anything, was a ceasefire and an ally, other than Amad who thrived on drama and Mai who condoned it.

Mum was in trouble, but more than that there seemed to be something else very wrong and Jack sensed she needed help. He knew that the only help they could manage was likely to go disastrously wrong and only add to her woes. He could keep his betting slip hidden and eventually buy his way out of trouble with the production of thousands of pounds. But Mandy? Even if it all went to plan, how could she explain away her windfall without Mum and Dad both having a heart attack and probably disowning her and throwing her out? That was way worse than prison and would break Mum's heart. People could die of a broken heart, he'd heard of it loads of times. Dad always said Nanny Walker died of a broken heart, after Grandad Walker moved to Scarborough with his girlfriend.

He thought the fate of Nanny Walker would be a strong enough argument to sway Mandy and a good starting point, but instead he found her room unoccupied. He momentarily considered going out and waiting for her before coming back in again, knowing she'd eat him alive for "snooping behind her back", but he wasn't there to snoop, he was there to talk and had a perfectly valid reason to sit on the bed and wait.

Listening out for the bathroom door, he sifted through the mess on her chest of drawers, school stuff and notes mixed in with make-up and jewellery. And her phone, plugged in to charge.

It was no use without her password, but as he peered into it, hoping the face recognition would be fooled by sibling likeness, it momentarily lit up with an incoming message. From Tisha. It flashed up for just long enough for him to read, "well? news agent or offie? both?!!!!" and not to hear the door.

'Shit!'

'Shit what, you little freak! I'm telling Mum! MUM!!!'

'No! Wait! Please!' he pleaded, 'I wasn't snooping, I only wanted to talk and I just saw it light up is all, I swear!'

'MUM!!! Come throw him out of my room!'

'Mandy, please!' he sat down on the bed heavily, crestfallen. 'It's about Mum. I wanted to talk to you – I don't want her having a massive row or dying of a broken heart.'

He could hear Mum calling back from down the stairs, threatening to come up and sort them both out.

Mandy went to the door and yelled back with a little less venom this time, 'It's OK, he was just giving me back my game. AND perving while he waited!'

She closed the door and smiled at him as though he needed special help. 'So, what now, you think Mum's dying?'

'No, but she might, if you and Tisha don't call it all off.'

'Jeez, you really are a bigger dumbass than I've ever given you credit for! You really think it will kill her? What, having to eat her words when we actually succeed and get a place in the Met? Or dying of embarrassment when we don't?' She shook her head, more in disappointment than disgust.

'Look, I did see a bit of the message, alright,' Jack admitted, 'I'm sorry. But you can't do both, you shouldn't even be doing one. Have you thought about the people involved, how they'll feel?'

Mandy sat on the bed beside him.

'Is that what this is all about?' She smiled at him with something like genuine respect. 'Not such a dumbass after all, are you? I never had you down as the thoughtful type, I s'pose it's all that looking after horses stuff. But I'm not such a complete bitch either. Wha'd'ya think we were gonna do, just march straight in without asking? Of course we've spoken to them. We've set it all up so's they're completely happy. We've even had rehearsals and everything, like proper professionals.'

'Really?' Jack was stunned. It had never once occurred to him it might be a set-up, like an insurance scam or something. 'And they don't mind?'

'Don't mind?' Mandy grinned. 'They love it! All the publicity and everything. Stardom! It might bring in more customers.' She ruffled his hair. 'You've been watching too many of them sensationalist fly-on-the-wall documentaries and stuff. You know they're totally scripted, right? Tisha and me are doing it right. Professionally. The prize is the Met and a BA and sod all the teachers who say I can't get in and Mum and Dad having no faith and thinking I'll just fail and get hurt. Because I won't. Trust me.'

'I'm worried for Mum. She can't handle any more drama.'

'There won't be any; promise. This is my thing. Mine and Tisha's. It doesn't involve Mum and Dad or you.'

Jack wasn't reassured, but knew he couldn't stop the plan already in motion.

'How did you pay for it?' he asked instead. 'I saw the receipts.'

'Nothing's sacred in this house! That's why it's all at Tisha's, thank fuck. As if it's any if your business anyway, but we've gone half each on everything. I had a bit saved up and then I used,' she paused, almost imperceptibly, 'some money Nan gave me.'

Jack had picked up on the hesitation and rounded on her instantly.

'Nan gave you money?!'

'So? Grandad gave you his records!'

'Only cos no one else wanted them.'

'Yeah, well, Nan was clearing out her stuff too and no one wanted the cats, Mum said they creeped her out.'

'What cats?'

'All those ornaments she used to collect, Cats In Costumes, done up in fashions through the ages. I always liked that Mary Quant one, I used to play with it when I was little. It got all chipped and she threw it out. But anyway, when Grandad gave you the records, she gave me the box of ornaments. They're not worth anything, they'd've only gone to the charity shop.'

'And the money?'

'You'd better not breathe a word of this, you hear me? I will literally kill you if Mum finds out.' Mandy looked him in the eye, leaving him in no doubt. 'One of the cats had this Limited Edition sticker under it, so I looked it up online. It was the Suffragette one and they're selling on eBay for like a hundred quid, so I sold it.'

'But Nan gave it to you!'

'Yeah, I know, I felt a bit bad and I know I should've really given the money to Nan. That's what Dad said, when he found out, the other day when the police came. But he was pretty OK with it. Mum would've gone spare! But me and Dad agreed Nan was only gonna hand them in to the charity shop anyway and even if I gave her the money, she'd give it back so's I can use it for college. And if you tell Mum, you're dead!'

'It's OK, I won't.'

Jack considered the revelations, marvelling at the hidden world even within his own family.

'How d'you even learn about all this stuff and how to shoot and everything?' he asked. 'I always thought some of your boyfriends were a bit dodgy.'

The tacit truce evaporated.

'My what?! Some of?!'

'Well it's not like the whole school didn't know,' he said defensively.

'Are you really that thick? Haven't you twigged yet that those who do, do; and those who don't, talk about it? You need a reality check, Jack, before you become just another one of them.'

It was rare for her to use any other endearment for him than Freak or Creep or Dumbass. He paid attention.

'Have you ever actually seen any of the "cool boys"', she drew the inverted commas in the air with her fingers, 'with anyone? They big themselves up so much until their cronies'd rather lie than admit to being the only one who hasn't been laid yet. Seriously, what would you say the morning after to all your mates? Oh, I got slapped round the face and sent packing before we were even out the school gates! Or, I got laid and then I dumped the bitch?'

As Jack considered her words, it slowly and unpleasantly dawned on him why he didn't so much mind her current boyfriend.

'I'm sorry, Mands; it's just a bit crap thinking the school slag's your sister. And you're always sneaking in gone midnight.'

'I'm sorry movies don't end in time for me to get in early,' she retorted sarcastically, 'and I'm sorry you think I'm a slag, and apparently the whole school does, which doesn't bother me one incey bit, like!'

Jack remained silent, but spontaneously threw his arms around her and hugged her tightly. He felt her inhale to let out a predictable curse, then relax a little and instead reciprocate the affection.

'Twat!' she said kindly.

'If you need help with any of it,' he volunteered.

'No family or outside help,' she insisted, 'it's gotta be our own work.'

He was privately relieved. And kind of happy to have a Big Sister instead of an Arsehole.

'What happened to all your Matt Valentine posters?' he asked, as she stood up and checked her phone. 'If you've still got any, can I have one?'

'Took you long enough to come out!'

'Ha ha, very funny; it's for a friend at the stables. She's big into them.'

'Yeah, OK, I'll sort you out one.'

She was lost in her phone messages for a moment and Jack thought he'd got safely away with it, as he stood up and made his way to the door.

'Mind you don't get a reputation, Jack The Lad!' Mandy said, without looking up.

'Do NOT mention her to Mum!'

'I'll keep yours if you keep mine,' she promised.

A little later, Mandy tapped at Jack's door, waiting patiently for a response. With none forthcoming, she went in anyway, unsurprised to find him totally enveloped in headphones and a handheld game controller.

He was aware of someone's presence and looked up, lowering the headphones to his neck.

'Here,' she said simply, handing him a large poster rolled up and fastened with an elastic band.

'Oh, wow, thanks, Mands!'

'And if you want to help Tisha and me, we're having a practise shoot Saturday morning outside Haydary's, seven o'clock, before the sun comes up. No involvement, but you can help us carry the gear and get set up, if you like.'

Jack hoped his face wasn't mirroring the reaction he was biting his lip to silence. He so didn't want to help or be involved in any way; but he so didn't want his sister to be in this alone.

Oh, god, they were both so dead.

'Yeah, OK, if you want,' he agreed.

CHAPTER 10

Most fourteen-year-olds hated alarm clocks, but Jack had grown to love his, lying wide awake ahead of it in anticipation of the music that would begin his day; the days spent at the stables, with the people he liked, the horses he loved and the subjects he enjoyed.

Saturday was not one of those days and he had lain awake for much of the night, dreading the sound that would ring in the morning. He rose wearily and sorted out every item of black clothing he possessed, wishing now he had a polo neck sweater that he could pull up over his face when the need arose. At least it was cold enough for him to wear his big ski gloves and avoid leaving fingerprints.

Careful not to wake Mum and Dad, he crept downstairs to wait for Mandy in the kitchen, but she was already sitting calmly eating breakfast with Tisha. He marvelled at their composure. Even if it was only a practise run and just a pre-arranged insurance scam, it still seemed to him way bigger than real life, more like a movie plot. His heart was pounding before they'd even started.

Too anxious to stomach breakfast, he eyed up the long black sports bag by the door. He and Amad had googled guns, but he had no idea what to expect. Sixteen millimetres were shotguns, twenty-five millimetres the most common and thirty-five millimetres cannons, apparently.

'What's in the bag?' he asked. Maybe helping with equipment didn't mean carrying weapons.

'All the gear and it's fragile, right, so be super careful.'

'How big is the thirty-five mill one?'

Mandy gave him a withering look. 'The clue is in the name! Like, der, thirty-five mills!'

'Just over an inch,' Tisha offered, unhelpfully.

That didn't seem much like a cannon. Jack figured the sixteen-millimetre shotgun must be tiny. They all looked so much bigger on TV and in the movies. Surely just a toy one would've been enough?

'And it's just practise shooting, right?' he checked.

'To get the lighting right and set up angles,' Mandy agreed.

Tisha sniggered. 'Shooting! He makes it sound like a drive-by!'

'Leave him alone, the whole idea scares the pants off him for some reason. He thinks, right, we're gonna end up all over the telly, embarrassing him!'

'Well, like, der, I hope so! That's the dream!' Tisha pointed out.

'Seriously?' Jack snapped. 'All this just to get on telly and you don't even care why or how?'

'Calm down, Freak! All this to give us the opportunity to learn to get on telly and films. What else can we do?' Mandy protested. 'We know we won't get enough points to get into the Met, Mum and Dad can't pay for the BA course, and it might be scummy in your eyes, trying to win a place, but at least it's an option. Our only friggin' option. So stop putting us down and either give us a bit of credit and support or fuck off back to bed!'

'OK, OK, I'm sorry! I'm just scared is all. This is a really big deal.'

'For us as well.' Mandy stood up and took her coat from the back of the chair. 'So are you coming or what?'

Without hesitation, Jack walked across and picked up the bag. It was lighter than he would have thought, but then guns, it seemed, were smaller than he ever thought. He couldn't wait to tell Amad, he found himself thinking. Would he tell Mai? It was so easy to get swept up in his friends' versions of "cool".

It was just a short walk to the local set of shops. The little supermarket was closed, as were the off-licence and laundromat, but Mr Haydary was already unlocking the newsagents as they arrived and he waved to them cheerily.

Jack couldn't help noticing he was dressed much smarter than usual, and he could see Mrs Haydary just inside. She hardly ever worked behind the counter, unless it was busy. She was also dressed for a fancier occasion than work, her hijab a striking purple silk and her make-up glamorous, like when Mum was going to a party.

Mandy was already pacing out a line from the shop entrance and marking the pavement with chalk, while Tisha held some gadget in the air and studied it.

'Get the tripod out and set it up on this spot,' Mandy instructed Jack. 'Don't touch anything else! It's like sooo expensive.'

'The Switar,' announced Tisha decisively.

'The Flektogon's better, 'specially for full and direct sun,' Mandy explained to Jack, as she fished an object from the bag and removed it from its packaging, 'you don't get any flare whatsoever. But this,' she brandished what looked like a camera lens, but was obviously some sort of gun sight, 'is the Kern Paillard Switar, what every professional has used since the Fifties.'

'How do you even know all this stuff?'

'By asking. We read all the professional magazines and stuff, but we also spoke to experts. They don't mind helping if they know you're serious and keen to learn.'

Jack had been told the exact same by Chris and Terry. Keep your ears open and your mouth closed, was their mantra, as well as never stop asking questions, which was contradictory in a way, but he got it totally. They said they were still learning new things, even with their years of experience. A bit like him and Grandad and music, and Dad and the football. Mandy and Tisha had a proper passion and Jack understood it. It didn't really matter anymore that it was wrong.

'And this,' Mandy declared with obvious pride, 'is a Bolex!'

She showed him something more akin to an old-fashioned cine camera than a weapon, but most likely what the rounds were kept in, like what attached to machine guns in war movies.

'The Dogs Bolex!' Tisha joked, taking it from Mandy and mounting it on the tripod.

'A second-hand Bolex Paillard would set you back a couple of grand, easy,' Mandy informed Jack, 'but Tisha's mum picked this up at the church jumble sale and it just all started from there.'

Jack stared at the mounted Bolex in wonder. He'd never seen Mandy like this before, so confident and knowledgeable and animated, sharing her passion with him. He could've been anyone and she would've still been this excited and talkative.

'It's a movie camera!' he exclaimed in amazement.

'See! I told you to trust us, we weren't wasting our time! Everyone else will be shooting their samples on video cameras or iPhones, but we're using proper vintage equipment. We're demonstrating every skill they set out on the admissions form. And we've been practising loads of tips from the best cinematographers in L.A.'

'L.A? Like Hollywood, you mean?'

Mandy nodded. 'Mum went demented when she saw the phone bill! How was I to know it was like a tenner a minute or whatever? But if our samples get selected, we get a free scholarship to the Met – the MetFilm College in London!'

'You're gonna make a film?'

'Wha'd'ya think we were gonna do, pretend?!'

'Told you!' Tisha declared triumphantly. 'He thought we were making a porno!'

Mandy grinned. She'd had fun stringing him along.

'It's about the camera work more than the subject,' she explained, 'we're not filmmakers, we're cinematographers, but we're taking no chances, Zohib Haydary and Solomon Kamara, in the offie, have such good stories to tell. There's only three places up for grabs through the open competition route. Either both our entries win or neither does.

'Now piss off out of it and keep quiet,' she ordered, as Tisha held up a whiteboard for the first take.

* * *

The crisp white cloak of heavy frost and icy mist blanketed the downs, creating a comforting stillness in the quiet of dawn. De Freitas had come to love these mornings, shrouded from the outside world, awaiting the eerie rhythmic breathing of the horses emerging from the mist. For a heavy animal they were surprisingly quiet of foot, the rapid gulps of breath breaking through the dense air long before the hoof beats, muffled as they were within the all-weather surface of the purpose-built gallop.

It reminded de Freitas of a helter-skelter, prolonged anticipation for a flash of excitement, over in an instant. The horses broke through the silence, appeared briefly, their snorts rising to a rapid crescendo that faded just as instantly, then gone, into the distance. To his untrained eye it was impossible to gauge anything other than the horses were all in one piece and able to keep up with one another.

Alongside him, Chris had clearly ascertained a little more. His satisfied smile bordered on delight. Apparently the snorts, that de Freitas could never quite put a satisfactory name to, told the experts many different things, all of them good right now.

'We won't start getting serious with them 'til next month, but he just does everything we ask of him without fuss and with so much ease,' Chris explained. 'That mental attitude is as important as ability. The one is pretty redundant without the other.'

De Freitas nodded his understanding and hopped up into the jeep beside Chris. They tracked the horses back along the downs, Chris winding down the window and conversing with each rider as they cruised slowly alongside. It was a similar conversation in each case, most of which went over de Freitas' head. Instead, he read Chris's expression and body language, which told him all he needed.

They arrived back in the yard and rather than avail of the offer of a warming coffee in the house, de Freitas lingered in the yard, watching the activities. He knew that Chris was always privately relieved at the regular refusal of hospitality, his place out here in the hive of activity, not sweet-talking patrons.

He nodded to Jack as the boy and the horse they all now called Mo passed by, heading to the wash bay and the walker. He followed them, at a safe distance, and watched the cooling off process; falling into step with Jack as he returned to the yard.

'I'm told that was an impressive piece of exercise,' de Freitas remarked conversationally.

'Well it was just routine, nothing special like, but he never does a thing wrong,' Jack agreed. 'The breezers are the ones looking good at the moment. We're getting them ready for the sales in April and May.'

'No good to keep?'

'They probably are, but they're pinhooks. Terry and Chris bought them last year 'specially to sell. Grant says they're the opposite of cars – the older they get, the dearer they get!'

De Freitas smiled. He remembered now, Chris' initial explanation of the cycle of racehorse ownership quashing any hopes he and McCulloch had harboured of tracing the missing betting shop money. The broodmare's assignation with the stallion being the first major cash haemorrhage, the resulting foal a year later representing profit or loss based on nothing more than its physical attractiveness.

Some bought foals to sell a year later, in the hope of profiting; apparently sixty percent made a loss. Others waited and bought the yearlings, in the hope of profiting the following spring when selling them as unraced two-year-olds. And those that bought the two-year-old horses at the breeze-up sales hoped to profit by racing the horse, maybe winning a race, then selling it; apparently only forty-five percent of foals born each year ever went on to win a race.

And some, like Chris and Terry and their syndicate members, bought a horse to race and keep, in the hope of turning a profit from the prize money it would win and the resulting stud career that would then beckon, so that the whole moneymaking and money-haemorrhaging circus could begin again.

Still, de Freitas reasoned, it at least kept the get-rich-quick schemers away from easier pickings, such as crime. The draw with racehorses, of course, was not so much making money as the chance to pay one's way while experiencing the joy of working with these addictive animals.

And some, of course, simply bet money on them. A fiver each-way in the hope of reaping thousands. Addictive animals indeed.

'I had a little bet on Mo, to win the Triple Crown,' de Freitas confessed. 'Everyone always seems very confident and happy when they're around him.'

'He has an aura,' Jack agreed, 'Chris says it's "Class". It's how you tell the good ones.'

De Freitas nodded. He'd seen similar in people – upper management effortlessly commanding respect, the criminal hierarchy oozing menace. Some just had a presence about them.

'Do you come in early just to look after him?' he asked the boy, aware that the students' day didn't start this early, and yet several of them were conspicuously present.

'Breakfast Club,' Jack informed him. 'You're allowed to come in early if your parents work or something and you need breakfast.'

'Oh. Is your mother working now, Jack? I seem to remember you saying she was at home?'

Jack shook his head. 'No; she's still at home, so's to help us with our exams and stuff, but I signed up anyway, just to be able to come in longer. They don't check. You won't say anything, though, will you?'

'No, of course not. If you promise not to say anything about me being here when my colleagues think I'm held up in traffic on my way into the office!' He gave a wink.

'You can't really solve crimes from an office,' Jack said doubtfully. 'Can't you just say you was out investigating something?'

'Funnily enough, we solve most crimes from our office,' de Freitas corrected him. 'Most of my work is reading through evidence. There's only so much you can collect; after that, it's just a matter of evaluating it.'

'Are you sure you can't work as a private investigator at the weekends? The muppets looking for evidence where my Mum works can't find any and my Mum's still not allowed back at work and she's going mental at home.'

'Not good, then?'

'My Dad's really worried. My Mum's OK and everything; but she won't go out.'

'I'm sorry to hear that, Jack.' De Freitas paused. 'You know, if I were investigating your mother's workplace, I would be watching for anything unusual. Perhaps her colleagues visiting places they wouldn't normally go; having new things. People behaving oddly.'

From an office, Jack thought disparagingly? But he said nothing, instead considering the policeman's words.

'Does she speak with any of them?' de Freitas asked.

'I think so,' Jack acknowledged. He'd heard Mum and Dad talking about them alright, but hadn't really paid any attention. He'd pay attention now, though.

De Freitas unzipped his thick padded jacket and reached into the breast pocket of the suit within. He handed Jack his card.

'If you ever need to talk to me or ask for any help, I'll always listen.'

Jack relayed what he regarded to be this good news to Mandy later, that evening. She was less enthused.

'They're called business cards for a reason – to get business,' she pointed out. 'Mum said the police who interviewed her gave her a card as well. They just want you to do their work for you, an extra pair of ears and eyes.'

'He's not the same as them,' Jack argued. 'He's a proper high up boss, he's on a huge wage, enough to own a racehorse, he doesn't walk the beat or anything, and we can just get his help.'

'With what? What do you even know that the police don't? You know Brookhills have called in a team of forensic accountants now? Mum's freaking out. Dad said they can only look at Brookhills' accounts and bank and like, they're not actual real police, but Mum's having a meltdown. I'd like to see your Mister Big solve that one.'

'Well maybe he won't have to – these forensic accountants will solve it and Mum can go back to normal.'

He took that reassuring hope with him back to his own room and bed, but he couldn't sleep. All he needed to do was spot someone acting unusual; and all he had to do for that was stay at home. What if Mum was freaking out because she really had taken the money? She wasn't a thief, but if she thought Mandy needed it for college and it was just sitting there in the floor safe, never even looked at or used? Just borrowed it...?

* * *

De Freitas sat quietly at his desk, pondering a conversation he'd had with the Reid boy. As much as he'd liked Joy Reid and his first instincts had screamed innocent, everyone involved in the Brookhills case had been innocent up until the point of opportunely stealing forty-thousand pounds.

Watch for anyone behaving out of character...

So far, that was only Joy Reid. And what Surveillance were reporting back seemed to be the mere tip of the iceberg, if young Jack were to be believed.

He glanced across at McCulloch, busy clicking through files on the computer screen as he showed young DC Pritchard whatever it was he required.

'Imagine this,' de Freitas said, interrupting their work. 'It's your job to take all the old property out of the Evidence Room to the Property Warehouse, where chances are it will never see the light of day again. Half the items down there have long gone cold. Every so often, when the room here gets a bit cramped, you take a few bits off to the warehouse. And every time you're in the warehouse you look longingly at that old set of golf clubs you've been eyeing up for ages. If you were to take them, no one would ever be any the wiser.'

'The perfect opportunist crime,' McCulloch agreed.

'Do either of you play golf?' Pritchard ventured.

'Only figuratively,' said de Freitas.

'Then it would destroy your game.'

'They're good clubs,' McCulloch tempted him.

'But useless,' Pritchard argued. 'The guilt would put you off your swing, who do you play a round with, chances are it's colleagues, and the first thing they'll do is remark over your new clubs and where they came from. From never seeing the light of day in Properties to never seeing the light of day in your garage. Useless.'

'Pritchard, you've a bright future ahead of you,' de Freitas said in praise. 'Now let that be a lesson to you in life should ever Hector and his gang have you moving property to the Evidence Room or Warehouse.'

The young recruit looked a little bemused.

'Don't mind him,' McCulloch advised him, 'he's just irked that you've solved his cold case where I have failed. Which means you owe me a coffee. With a plain chocolate digestive.'

'Custard cream for me,' added de Freitas.

'You're thinking of the Brookhills money again, aren't you, Les?' McCulloch guessed, as the young constable departed on his errand. 'I've noticed your mind always turns to that one whenever you arrive in with wood shavings stuck to the sole of your shoes.'

'Really? You'll make someone a very good detective one day,' de Freitas observed. 'He has a good point, though, doesn't he?'

'They're not stealing because they need to, simply because they can. And now it's nothing but a curse to them and they don't dare spend it,' McCulloch mused. 'I think they might have seen that coming, though. They would have been deliberating about it long and hard.'

'True; but you have the benefit of knowing this will haunt them forever.' De Freitas leaned back comfortably in his chair. A myriad of thoughts ran through his mind, but it always helped when someone else voiced one of them. 'Tell me what you've learned from our television colleagues?'

'They solve these types of cases in a single episode.'

'And?'

'Getting punched doesn't hurt?'

'I think you had it with the first one. People expect us to work methodically on one case at a time and then put a line through it. Our TV friends go away. So you take the money and you sit on it. Yes, it's a curse, but eventually we give up. In a few years' time you have a useful nest egg and no longer have to look over your shoulder.'

'I guess that does make sense. They're playing the long game.'

'Which just leaves who?'

McCulloch called up the file on his screen to refresh his memory.

'Maud Simmons, the merry widow, already eliminated. Clearly no need for such a risk, for less than she already can't spend. Joy Reid, a retirement caravan. Anita Wallis, just a retirement fund to keep up the lifestyle. The highly ambitious Rhys Fordham, too young to be playing a long game? You noted that when you last spoke to Wallis, she accused him of setting her up to take her shop. The long game seems too immediately risky for one who values his career above all else.

'Then we have Lee Baxter, blank canvas. No ambition, no obvious need. Gareth Rogers. Now he's a bit of a blank canvas. No obvious need, but no lack of ambition either. Hard to imagine how he could have got the money out of the shop before calling us. The cameras were on him the whole time. We've put a line through him.'

'But with a "but",' de Freitas reflected.

'Hmmm. Not actually eliminated yet. And Tracey Pattinson, unaware of a floor safe or contents. It's possible she may have found out from other sources, but not possible for her to have access to the keys. So eliminated.'

'Back to Wallis, Reid and Baxter, then. Any gut feelings, Will?'

'Joy Reid. Very edgy, erratic spending patterns, typical behaviour of someone racked by guilt. Not obvious initially, but increasing rapidly with time.'

'She thought the long game would be easier, but hadn't bargained on being intrinsically honest.' De Freitas welcomed the coffee and biscuits set before him as the DC returned. 'If villains had a conscience, our job would be so much easier.'

'If we didn't have a conscience our job would be easier,' McCulloch observed.

'By the way, your hypothetical golf clubs,' DC Pritchard interjected, 'if it were me and I played golf, I'd just take the one club. No questions likely to be asked, relatively guilt-free and my game duly improved.'

'You're wasted on tea trolley duty,' McCulloch noted.

De Freitas silently considered the possibilities as he finished his biscuits.

Clearly, McCulloch had done the same. After Pritchard had departed he perched himself on de Freitas' desk and voiced his thoughts.

'Our golf club theory. I take one club at a time, as and when I need it. Replace it, take another. Not an opportunistic whim at all, but a calculated risk. Dip in whenever I need to, with growing confidence I'll have it put back before it's checked. Classic Wallis behaviour. Successfully juggling bills and credit from one month to the next, in the full knowledge she's the only one who actually confirms what's there and what isn't.'

'So why is it all missing instead of a few hundred?' de Freitas asked. He had asked himself the same question when attempting to make a case for Joy Reid stealing college fees.

McCulloch shook his head. 'Your guess is as good as mine. But as this could have been going on for years and we can't track cash transactions, we can't track bar tabs or restaurant bills, but we can match a lifestyle profile. Reid takes half the year to pay off her Christmas debts. And anyone other than Wallis knows they can be caught on any given day.'

'Wallis knew she would be caught on that precise given day.'

Again, McCulloch shook his head. 'No. She didn't. Lee Baxter should have been in there.'

CHAPTER 11

May

It was the letter Joy had been dreading.

She picked it up off the mat and held it out in front of her, divining no clue to its contents. It made no difference either way, whatever was in it was bad news for her and the family. Bugger it. Stupid bloody Mandy and her stupid bloody dreams.

She tapped it against her hand as she took it into the kitchen and reluctantly relinquished it, laying it centrally on the table. She continued to eye it accusingly, before tearing herself away and switching on the kettle.

She only just had time for a quick cuppa before heading off. She hated the late shift, but seemed to draw the short straw more times than not. As a part-timer, there weren't many good shifts to draw. Unlike the precinct shop, the Broad Street shop stayed open for late nights and Sundays. Seven days of eight a.m. starts and nine p.m. finishes were a far cry from the cushy number in the precinct. Her twenty-five hours a week were all over the place, not to mention fifteen hours a week short of her previous pay packet.

There were Maud and Gareth and Tracey back permanently in the precinct, their lives safely back to normal, while her and Lee and Rhys were farmed out on reduced hours to the crappiest shops in the chain, their managers pointedly restricting their access to all but their own till. No one was supposed to know about the precinct theft, but rumours had been rife and the staffing shuffle only fuelled them further. The lack of in-store trust was just an added kick in the teeth.

Talk about innocent 'til proven guilty! She'd been better off on full pay and suspension! Lee was fighting it like crazy, she knew, with Citizens Advice and lawyers on his case, but she had lacked both the finance and energy to join him. Meanwhile, Madam was still sat on her arse all day doing bugger all for a bigger pay packet, while supposedly guilty. And screaming blue murder about it!

And there was the dread letter, ticking away like a bomb ready to maim her when she got home way too late that night.

She never could catch a break.

* * *

'It would've been nice to catch a break.'

Terry's expression, as usual, mirrored his glass-half-empty tone, as All Things Pass cruised by. Watching the smart two-year-old, one would never have suspected the horse had been in an equine hospital recovering from a broken leg only seven months' earlier.

It was a textbook perfect recovery, but for coming just one month too late.

A gallop like that would have seen him top the last of the breeze-up sales a fortnight earlier, providing financial security for the foreseeable future, not to mention the recognition and status of being high-end consignors to be respected and trusted. But as Terry morosely observed, preparing him for that date with destiny would have pushed him too far too soon.

Patience had saved his day and cost them theirs.

'We'll find him a nice little maiden next month,' Chris said cheerfully, their glass happily overflowing in his own opinion. 'It would be great if we could have him ready for the July Stakes.'

'It would be a shame to waste the entry fee,' Terry agreed bitterly.

'Don't panic, we've not made any entries yet. But speaking of which, we'll need to put Mo in the Chesham Stakes and find him a prep race.'

'Seriously? He's an autumn horse and you know it!'

'Yeah, I know, but he's working so well. Even backward, he has to have a bit of a squeak. Imagine taking the syndicate to Royal Ascot!'

'He's our shop window display, Chris, we have to get it right. If he does win a Classic next year, we can't be the ones to have screwed it up and blemished his record just so the owners can have a day out at Royal Ascot.'

'Goodwood, then. He's a proper Vintage Stakes horse.'

Terry shot him a patronising look. 'You'll be writing your letter to Santa next! I mean, it is May already.'

Chris smiled, point taken. He recalled the arguments to keep the little grey colt in the first place, one of which had been to prevent a lesser trainer taking advantage of the horse and over-racing him at two instead of gently nurturing him for his three-year-old career. It was easily done. The colt made everything look so attainable. There was an excitement about the yard pretty much like Christmas Eve, every day.

The fact that Mo's full-brother had only a month ago won the well-regarded Wood Ditton Stakes on his first start, having recovered from the health issues that had kept him from the racecourse last year, only increased the fervent expectation. The colt had since added the Newmarket Stakes to his unbeaten record, bringing the long-awaited "black type" to

Grey Motive's "page". Perhaps that catalogue page would never be needed.

'The Champagne Stakes, then,' he conceded, wondering how they'd contain themselves until September. But Terry was right; they owed it to the horse to campaign him with the utmost care. Patience and restraint, patience and restraint, he reminded himself. But the mantra couldn't quell the excitement.

* * *

'Have you heard, Brookhills have run out of patience and let Anita Wallis back to work!' McCulloch announced with some incredulity as he read the incoming email. 'Apparently she's a relief manager, until further notice. They're not trusting her in the one shop.'

'The Super won't be too happy,' de Freitas observed. 'I believe the Brookhills' CEO has been bending his ear about getting a result before the six-month suspensions expired.'

'You never know, this might help. Wallis might drop her guard, now life seems to be back to normal.'

'The others didn't.'

De Freitas brought up on screen the collection of graphs reflecting the weekly spending of the Brookhills Case suspects. Where most were pretty much level, Joy Reid's had been on a constant nosedive, suggesting either unsustainable frugality or a hidden cash source. Pointing to the latter, her family could barely be subsisting on the monitored expenditure.

And pointing to the former were Jack Reid's grim accounts of his disintegrating home life. If Joy Reid's guilty conscience wasn't destroying her, then she was finding her questioned innocence just as hard to live with. Damn it! He wished they could just find something and put that case to bed, for the sake of the innocent kept hanging.

* * *

'Well? What's your news? Are you going to keep me hanging all night?'

Joy looked at the unusually quiet household, patently waiting for her as she dropped her coat on the stair ready to take up and put away later.

They weren't good at stony faces and bluffs, she'd never had a surprise birthday or Christmas present from any of them.

'ACCEPTED!!!' Screamed Mandy in delight and Paul and Jack immediately competed for volume as they declared their pride and the fact that, now the doubt was gone, they'd always known she would do it.

Joy's head spun.

All afternoon at work she'd gone over the various scenarios and how to play it. But all she could do now was simply give Mandy a hug and a kiss on the forehead.

'Well done, love, that's some achievement.'

'You could sound a bit happier about it!' Mandy complained.

'I am happy! Just tired is all. We'll talk about it in the morning, eh?'

Joy's lack of enthusiasm was contagious and flattened the mood.

'I'll warm your dinner up, love,' Paul said, 'and fetch in your tea, go and put your feet up. There's a film just starting on plus-one.'

'That could be Mandy soon!' Jack declared, his own excitement uncurbed. 'Coming up in the credits. Way down at the bottom, though!'

'Cretin!' Mandy retorted, without malice.

'Seriously, though, Mum, it was so cool,' Jack related, as he followed her through to the living room and flopped onto the sofa beside her. 'Mands let me go and watch, I carried the equipment and everything. Zohib Haydary just sort of narrated his day and whenever it was quiet he just talked about stuff, like how him and Mrs Haydary escaped from Afghanistan, cos he did music at college and it was banned and he might've got shot or beheaded even, and they had to learn English and everything, but all the time Mandy was just doing like really clever stuff that you wouldn't even notice, like stuff I can't even remember, but it'll look totally amazing if you watch it and it said in the letter the judges were totally amazed!'

'Blown away by our use of resources,' Mandy corrected him. 'Yes, Tisha did get accepted too, thanks for asking.'

'Sorry, love, I was worrying about it all day, honest, it's just that I'm bushed. Show us the letter, then!'

She feigned the necessary excitement as she read the glowing praise of her daughter, which had become genuine pride by the end. She handed it back to Mandy.

'Bloody hell, eh?!'

Mandy grinned. 'Isn't it, right! And I like they could see our individual touches, even though we shared equipment, and they loved that we did that! Tisha did a shoot of Solomon Kamara in the offie, he fled Sierra Leone with his family, they chose here cos English is the language over there, we didn't even know that, so it was really cool and totally different to Mr Haydary's story, but we thought the subjects were really good and might help as well, even though all you really had to do was send examples of camera work, so I shot in daylight and used indoor for my dark shots and Tisha shot at night and used the indoor lighting and we really covered absolutely everything the L.A. guys told us, it took us like months of practise and we couldn't even really shoot it all cos the film's like sooo expensive, we only got one real go at it each, I can't believe it!'

'A genius in the family, who'd've thunk it, eh?' Paul said, fetching in a tray laden with Joy's dinner and a mug of tea. 'One Steven Spielberg and one fluent Japanese speaker, we must be doing something right!'

'I'm only learning,' Jack protested.

'And it's more Roger Deakins than Spielberg!' Mandy complained. 'I film, someone else writes and directs.'

'Who the hell's Roger Deakins when he's at home?'

'A wannabe Mandy Reid!' Paul quipped. He raised his mug. 'To Mandy and Hollywood!'

'To Mandy!' Joy gently raised her mug to his. Tomorrow could wait, let them have their moment for now.

'How are we going to pay for all this?'

The kids had gone to bed and they finally had the sofa to themselves, cuddled up together in front of a movie that had been just as bad the first time they'd seen it. Bed beckoned, but they couldn't be bothered to move.

'The college is paying all the fees, it's a free place,' Paul assured her.

'Huh! The place is free. But what about all the stuff she'll need? Is she going to commute or stay there – a Travel-card's as dear as bloody rent! We can't afford this, Paul. She can't go.'

'Christ, love, lighten up! Other kids pay their way through college, so can Mandy! The college'll help us, they won't just give her a free place then abandon her! Jack's not costing us anything.'

'Yeah, but that's just a school, isn't it? College's different, isn't it! What kind've job will she get, fresh out've school, no decent grades, London rent to pay, god knows what, more than the hundred-and-fifty a week train fare, that's for sure. Food. Film! She said that was bloody expensive!'

'We'll cross that bridge when we come to it, stop worrying. It's a film school, they must supply the film! Sleep on it, eh?'

Joy grunted agreement; but she wasn't going to sleep that night, that was for sure.

And Mandy wasn't going to film school, she was sure of that, too.

* * *

'Sorry, Jack, you're not going to Windsor.'

Chris didn't look or sound too concerned about it; but he wasn't the one who'd marked the date on his calendar and counted off the days all the past week.

'Are you withdrawing him, then?' Jack asked, looking across at Diverse Reality, one of the older geldings in the yard, due to run in an apprentice handicap on Monday evening.

The pupils' names had been put in a hat and Jack's had been miraculously pulled out, to accompany and lead up the horse in the eight-thirty race at Windsor. It was a big deal and Chris and Terry had given him a suit to wear for the occasion and told him to invite his family. They'd arranged their shifts to be there.

Grant had been the first of them to get to go racing, accompanying Dundalk Gakk to Lingfield Park in April, with Danno there to assist as they led up 'Gakk in tandem. It was the first time Jack had ever known Grant to be quiet and nervous, but his confidence had returned with gusto the next day, when he told them all about it. Even the bit about feeling self-conscious walking around the parade ring with all eyes on him.

They'll only be looking at the horse, Jack had told himself all week. No point being nervous, that would only make his horse feel nervous. He would simply keep his eyes ahead, or turn and talk to his horse, if he felt the eyes of the race crowd burning into him.

Which was irrelevant now Diverse Reality wasn't going to run. He tried to mask his disappointment. After all, that was racing. More lows than highs, Chris always said, but the highs made it all worthwhile.

'He's running, but we drew Yvonne's name out instead,' Chris explained, his eyes twinkling.

Chris had this way of smiling with his eyes, they kind of creased up like the edges of his mouth, Jack and Mai had noticed. It was infectious and always made them smile, too. But not now.

'Why?' Jack demanded, a little more crossly than he'd intended. Now he knew how Mandy felt, to have a dream snatched away at the very last moment. Not that he was about to throw a tantrum and scream about how unfair it was. He'd just put in his earbuds and retreat into his music, like he always did.

'Because we've just finished the entries and we want you to take All Things Pass to Salisbury on Tuesday instead.'

Jack slowly absorbed this new information. All Things Pass. His first ever race. With him leading up!

'His first race? Really?'

Chris smiled reassuringly. 'We think you're both ready. We didn't want to send any of you with a horse making its debut, no point both of you being nervous and inexperienced, but you have this knack of keeping him calm. You're just the man he needs with him; and Danno will be there to help. No different to Windsor, but maybe you'll be leading up a winner!'

'Wow, thanks! Thanks, Chris!'

* * *

'Thanks, Chris, I'll see what I can do.' De Freitas put down the phone. 'Curses!' he said aloud, unintentionally.

McCulloch stopped what he was doing and glanced across.

'Sorry, just talking to myself,' de Freitas admitted. 'You remember the Brookhills case and the racehorse shares?'

'How could I forget. What's up, has the bill arrived?'

'A dividend, if anything. Only I can't avail of it. One of the horses is due to run at Salisbury on Tuesday.'

'That's a pain, you're in court all day. I could go along, if you think it might be useful?'

De Freitas considered it. 'I don't know; do you? It's highly unlikely our man's invested in a racehorse. I'd written that one off as a bit of a tilt at windmills the minute we followed it up.'

'On the other hand, Les, we've had nothing else to go on and it would make a nice change from court rooms and crime scenes. I could just mill about a bit and keep an eye out for faces.'

'Other than Anita Wallis, our faces will be at work. Was Wallis a racegoer?'

'Not that we were aware of. So catching her at Salisbury would be more than useful. And if the others use their day off for a day out, more than coincidence, wouldn't you say?'

'Sounds like useful surveillance work to me, Will.'

'Great! And this horse of yours, Les – will it win?'

'You'll just have to ask it that on the day.'

They returned to their duties, McCulloch preparing paperwork for his own day in court on the coming Monday. He was soon joined by Pritchard, being passed around for tuition by those who had bored of the task. Like the others, McCulloch conveniently set him up with his own chores, assigning the more mundane of the material needed for court.

For a while the room fell into a busy silence, broken only by McCulloch's sudden conscientiousness as he took pity on Pritchard.

'I'll just stop you there,' he interrupted, 'that is how we all do it, but technically the correct way would be to log-in here and gain access yourself. You can sort by date or alphabetically or use the search. It's a pain in the neck and the tech' boys don't mind, they're only twiddling their thumbs half the time, but you should at least know how to, if anyone does ever ask you.'

He watched as Pritchard carried out the task himself, rather than simply emailing a request to the technical department. The latter was quicker and easier, of course, which was why no one ever bothered to follow protocol.

'We all cheat a bit and no one minds, but technically this way there's a direct path to everyone who's had access, rather than just someone in tech' trying to remember who they last sent attachments to,' McCulloch pointed out. 'Not that it really matters.'

De Freitas sat back in his chair and watched the more experienced sergeant showing the new constable the ropes. Had the Brookhills case not been fresh in his mind he wouldn't have paid any attention to the trivialities. As it was, they triggered a light bulb moment that he chose for the time being not to share. Hopefully he wouldn't need to, if McCulloch was on the same wavelength.

McCulloch, it transpired, needed prompting.

'You've a good way with the newer DCs,' de Freitas observed, as they finished up for the day and reached for their coats.

'It's all just give and take, isn't it? We give them valuable experience in paperwork; they do our work for us.'

De Freitas grinned. 'The Anita Wallis method, minus the teaching! You have to wonder how the new kids like Fordham learn under her care.'

McCulloch paused, with one arm in his coat sleeve, and did wonder.

'They'd learn to leave it all to the cashiers,' he said slowly. 'Until someone, like Lee Baxter, for example, showed them how it should be done in other shops.' He finished putting on his coat. 'And how it could be done in this shop?'

'It took us a while to think of it,' de Freitas agreed, 'but you could imagine at least one of them might spot the invitation, the very moment the words were out of Baxter's mouth.'

McCulloch considered the words.

'"They never count the cash here".'

CHAPTER 12

June

It was a pity his family couldn't be here, Jack reflected, as he brushed a gleam into the coat of All Things Pass that Danno felt sure would win him the Best Turned Out prize, a small sum of cash awarded to the groom responsible for the best turned out horse. The standard hundred pounds was usually reinvested straight back into the horse, grooms tending to have a natural bias toward their own charge down in the betting ring.

It was a prize Chris and Terry liked to win, their grooms always nailed-on certainties had there ever been a similar award for the staff. Jack felt comfortable in his smart grey three-piece suit, a good fit despite being one of a few spare kept in the Colours Room. His shirt and tie had been purchased specifically for the day, carefully chosen to match the owner's colours worn by the jockey. The balance of "smart" and "loyalty" was often tilted a little by "gaudy", depending on the owner's chosen colours, but fortunately for Jack and the identically-dressed Danno, the Sainte Bastien Racing colours were a tasteful blue and black.

Danno had given him a tour of Salisbury racecourse on arrival, showing him where everything was and when and where he was to fetch "Thingy-Bob", although with Danno with him the whole time he didn't need to worry.

He was secretly glad his family had stuck with their intended trip to Windsor the night before. Mum had taken a lot of convincing, virtually kidnapped by them, still under duress at the racecourse entrance and dubious that the under-eighteen Jack and Mandy really would be let in for free. 'If we have to fork out for them as well, we're going home,' she had warned, tugging uncomfortably at the hem of her smart dress that she'd not worn in a while.

She and Dad had booked the evening off and Dad had convinced her they could afford it and that the police wouldn't arrest her for spending money. She hadn't quite believed him on either count and had been visibly anxious all day.

They couldn't have swapped their pre-booked day off to Tuesday in any case, but Windsor had turned out to be a much prettier, quieter racecourse than Salisbury, Jack felt, and a far nicer introduction to his new world. Especially when they all invested on Diverse Reality on the Tote and Mum's insistence of 'a place bet only' paid off with a small dividend when he finished third. Yvonne had been over the moon, jumping and screaming from their position on the rail near the finish as though her charge had actually won. They'd all hugged and for a moment Mum had been happy, sharing the Sainte Bastien team's delight, her own troubles briefly forgotten.

Salisbury was nice, too, Jack observed, the parade ring more open, with fewer trees, as he walked All Things Pass round several laps. Rather than nerves, he felt pride, especially when he was aware of the pay-for-view TV camera focused on him, for what seemed longer than on all the other runners. "Thingy-Bob" did look a lot more impressive than his competitors, smaller and more muscular, if a little tubbier than some. The favourite looked very lean and fit.

Chris and Terry had taught him about physique and conformation, but he was too involved with his own horse to be able to cast a look at any of the others. Fit was good, but tall and lean not so good for a five-furlong sprint, the minimum racing distance. Tubby was bad, but the powerful round quarters and short back of All Things Pass were very good traits in a sprinter; and so it proved in the race.

The fit-as-a-fiddle favourite finished a distant third, while the two leaders fought out the finish, All Things Pass losing out to a fitter rival by just half a length at the line. Again, the team celebrated as though they had won and even Terry mentioned the magic words 'Coventry Stakes' at some point in the aftermath. Thingy-Bob soaked up the praise and attention, his ego visibly swelling.

For Jack, leading up a horse at Royal Ascot seemed the ultimate dream, even the Triple Crown forgotten in the heat of the excitement.

* * *

'A pity you weren't there,' McCulloch reported the next day, 'it was quite exciting. Your horse was up at the front for most of the race and only just got beaten at the post. A nice-looking horse, a bit of a swagger to it. The Reid boy was all done up in a suit and tie, a few others leading round horses were just in jeans and t-shirts. Good quality suit, too, not cheap.'

'Any sign yet of Reid having paid for it?'

'Not with a debit or credit card.'

'Something always tempts them into spending it. A simple little thing we wouldn't even notice such as ensuring your son looks smart for the races.' De Freitas glanced across at McCulloch. 'Did you lose much?'

'As a matter of fact, I did. Five pounds was the minimum bet, so I rather recklessly put it all on "the nose", as the bookie advised.'

'Living dangerously, eh? Ah, what it is to be young. I suppose the coffees had better be on me, next time we're out.'

'Or we could bring Pritchard along for some experience...'

* * *

Joy knew she may not have had the best parenting skills in the world, but she did have sixteen years of the finest battlefield experience, which entitled her to a Victoria Cross in her book. And she knew a double agent when she saw one.

Mandy had gone predictably ballistic when she had categorically refused to sign the college forms. Tears, anger, pleading, more anger and bitter silence. They definitely weren't on talking terms for the foreseeable future.

It had been OK for Joy to forget herself and bestow an ecstatic hug at Windsor, when they had each won four pounds fifteen pence. But it was way out of character for a cold-shouldering Mandy to be just as forgetful and reciprocate. In fact, since the initial fight, Mandy had been way too normal by far. Not a child whose future had just been cruelly denied.

Not so much denied as deferred.

'It says quite clearly you can defer the place 'til next year!' Joy had argued reasonably, but for which she might have ripped the forms up there and then. 'It's not a lot to ask, just to stay on at school another year. MetFilm isn't going anywhere, you'll still go next year when all this bloody mess is cleared up.'

'IF it's cleared up! You'll prob'ly be in prison by then and they won't take me cos of your criminal record!'

That had been the final straw for Joy. 'They won't take you this year, not without a parent's signature! So live with it! You think I want you hanging round the house an extra year? But we've no money – Read. My. Lips. No. Money. You're not going!'

And that had been an end to it; the battle, not the war. She'd barely noticed the war petering out as well. An early truce had been revealed at Windsor and, when she'd finally got over the fear of immediate arrest, it had triggered her suspicion.

She pulled open the sideboard drawer and rummaged through the various documents. Passports, TV licence, a list of passwords, credit card bills; she must remember to sort through and throw out some old stuff. No college forms or acceptance letter.

In their house, a parent's signature meant her signature. It wasn't that Paul couldn't read forms or write his own name, it was just that he never bothered to. Paperwork was her department.

That bloody underhanded treacherous scheming little cow!

She was waiting for him when he came in that evening, dropping his car keys and sandwich tub on the kitchen table and his coat over a chair. He gave her a kiss and asked after her day, opening a newspaper he'd picked up off the bus and folding it open on the puzzles page.

She followed him through to the living room.

'So how was your day, love? Any excitement?'

'Just the usual. They've still got the road up round by the park, we were sat there for twenty minutes on the last run, it was a right bottleneck and no bugger'll let a bus out. May as well rip the timetable up!'

'Yeah, I was nearly late in this morning. Gwen's sister has the dreaded Big C, so she wants to go part-time, so it looks like I'll be back to full-time next month.'

'Only if you want to? We're managing alright, aren't we?'

'Hmph! Hardly! Anyway, you'll need me back full-time if you want to sneak Mandy up to London without me noticing come September. You signed her form, didn't you?'

'You weren't really gonna make her wait 'til next year, was you?'

'You never gave me the chance, did you! She has you wrapped round her bloody finger!'

'She deserves a break, she's worked bloody hard for it. You can't seriously make her wait,' Paul argued. 'The college'll help, she can get a job, we can help her out a bit – we'll manage, trust me. Trust her. She's a good kid.'

'And you, Paul Malcolm Reid, are a good man. Too bloody good! You'll be the death of us.'

She gave him a hug and a long, loving kiss.

'She said I'd be the first to crack!' Paul revealed, with no small satisfaction, as their embrace ended.

'Mandy didn't crack, she just went off the boil way too easy for my liking. The three of you are as useless at secrets as whatever it is that's useless at secrets! You were behind Jack's suit an' all, wasn't you?'

'He said the stables supplied it.'

'Same as he told me. You didn't give him the money for it, then?'

'Definitely not guilty.'

Joy thought about it. 'Oh. OK.'

Later, as they ate their re-heated dinner, the kids off doing their own thing, she continued to think about it.

'Schools supply all that kind of stuff, then? Even vocational places like Jack's stables?'

'I know as much about it as you do, love, but so it would seem. That's why I say don't worry about Mandy, she'll get by. They can't give free places then expect you to pay for everything. There's probably some grant in place.'

'Mandy gave us all those grant booklets, but they only paid for the course. Seriously, Paul, they can't rent her a room or buy her a Travel-card.'

'Well, they'll have to, it's as simple as that. You saw the letter. They're giving someone with talent an opportunity and that has to be all-inclusive, otherwise what's the point? She can live on beans on toast if she has to.'

'I might speak to Tisha's mum.'

'Good idea.'

Her mind continued to tick over.

'That form?' she said. 'You sure you filled it in right?'

Paul grinned. 'Not a clue! All I did was sign it where she told me to! Her and Jack sat together and did it. It'll be fine, they're bright kids.'

'Must be your side they get it from!' they both said in unison, and laughed.

Paul couldn't remember the last time he'd seen her laugh. He reached across the table and put his hand on hers, squeezing it reassuringly.

'Everything'll be alright, you'll see.'

She smiled back with more sorrow than joy, the brief moment of laughter quickly gone.

'You'd tell me, wouldn't you, if you was in any sort of trouble?' he asked her, hesitantly; instantly regretting his mistake.

'Wha'd'ya mean?! You think I took it, don't you?!'

'I nev–'

'You do! You think I did it! I took the money!'

'I didn–'

'It's all over your face! And the kids! You all think I took it! That I'm a common dirty thief! Same as all the rest of them, checking my till every time I go for a pee, the neighbours looking through the curtains at me, pointing their fingers at me!'

'Joy! I don't think you did it, seriously I don't, but you're getting all upset and paranoid!'

She ran out of breath and emotion, and simply sat, drained.

Paul took both her hands in his once more and squeezed them so tight, as though he could transfer all his positive energy and refuel her.

'You need to stop all this worrying; never mind any pointing fingers, who cares what anyone thinks? If you're innocent they can't prove you did it.'

'If?'

She pulled her hands away.

'Oh, come on!' Paul protested, exasperated. 'You know what I mean! They've torn the house apart, had you in for questioning and still they can't pin it on you.

'In all the years when we were really struggling, saving up to get married, trying to raise the kids when they were small, scraping together bits of furniture, trying to keep crappy cars on the road and get them through the M O T, a quarter of my wages going to bloody child support – never once did you complain or dip into the till. So why now? Why now, eh, when things are just picking up for us?'

She raised a half-smile. It was a reasonable argument; but the police didn't know all those things. They only knew she was dreaming of a forty-grand caravan and the kids were about to leave school and need college fees or cars, and Christmas just got more expensive the older they got, pound shop toys replaced by games consoles and the games that were nearly as dear...

But he was right. He usually was.

'I'm sorry,' she said. 'I know I've been a bloody idiot; but I'm so scared...'

Paul gave her the biggest hug.

'Christ, of course you are, love. We're all scared. But it'll be alright; everything'll be alright, you'll see.'

* * *

Jack lay on his bed, enveloped in headphones and loud music. *The Magnificent Moodies* spun at a relaxed thirty-three-and-a-third revolutions per minute, shutting out the world. It had been rare for Grandad to have only one album by a band, but later listening to subsequent long players from The Moody Blues had revealed why. Like everything else in a world not to be trusted, the band who had already been hit-and-miss at best, in his mind, plummeted to rock bottom thereafter. Prog-rock bottom. Leading the Manfreds over the edge with them. Even his idols The Animals had caught the dreaded psychedelia after just three LPs.

Life sucked.

At least with music he was on solid ground, with no surprises. Yeah, Grandad's bands had given him a nasty surprise when he'd tracked down their later work online; but he'd already known by then that there was no more to come. He wasn't like Mandy and Mai, waiting fervently for the next Valentine Crime or whoever release, only to be bitterly disappointed. He'd been given a limited number of songs and no amount of online searches were going to add to them.

Imagine how Grandad must have felt, rushing in to buy *Winds of Change* and hearing Eric Burdon in hideous technicolour? Hurricane of change, more like. Why did people have to let you down? Gaining your trust and adulation, only to just go off and do something stupid, as though you didn't matter.

Dad's words played over and over in his mind, as it wandered through "It Ain't Necessarily So". He normally skipped that track, but he couldn't be bothered to move off the bed.

So why now? Why now, eh, when things are just picking up for us?

He'd come back from Amad's just in time to hear a row in the kitchen and had scooted past, only catching Dad's litany of stuff they'd survived without Mum dipping her hand in the till.

Until now.

So why now?

Those words had stopped him dead in his tracks, waiting breathlessly for the denial that never came.

Instead, an apology. She'd been stupid. And now they were all scared.

As much as he longed for Mandy to get home, he fretted now over whether to tell her. A problem shared was supposed to be a problem halved, but that was a load of crap and why inflict this misery on her? What good would it do?

It wasn't that long ago that he couldn't have talked stuff over with her anyway, and wouldn't have wanted to. But he could still talk to Mum and Dad, back then. Now he was on his own.

Except that he wasn't. As he reluctantly roused himself to put on another LP, the awful realisation flooded through him. In the belief Mum was innocent, he'd asked a policeman for help! Now he knew Mum was guilty, that didn't seem quite so clever. Somehow he'd have to call Les de Freitas off, without arousing any suspicion.

Crap. He really did need to talk to Mandy.

* * *

'We really need to have an Open Day,' Chris suggested, as they all sat together in the office, contemplating the Royal Ascot entries. An outlay of fifteen-hundred pounds had just seen All Things Pass secure his place in the opening day's Coventry Stakes in ten days' time. And in case they were concerned about the extra furlong in elevated company in the Group Two six-furlong event, they would also enter him for the five-furlong Norfolk Stakes on the third day of the Royal meeting. It was still a Group Two event, but tended to be less littered with future Classic winners, as Terry had pointed out.

Whether the elite "Formula One" level of the Group One races or the "mere" free-for-all of the handicaps, Royal Ascot's glittering five-day programme of races was the Olympics of Flat racing, attracting the best horses from around the world.

And All Things Pass had every right to take his place alongside the other swans who had managed a good place in their only racecourse outing, before the future could cruelly reveal them as ducks.

'They always let you down,' Terry had warned, as Anne made the online entry and clicked the button that sealed their fate.

'Except the good ones. The good ones never let you down,' Chris corrected him.

Terry shot him a glance. 'We don't know which he is yet.'

'Well, he was good enough to get himself injured at the worst possible time,' Su pointed out breezily, 'and rubbish horses can play buckaroo on a motorway without ever coming to harm! Sod's Law has that in his favour!'

'Well if it does all go safely to plan, he'll be at Ascot in a fortnight,' Chris said, 'together with a mish-mash of syndicate owners who don't yet know each other. We should have everyone down for the day, a pre-Ascot party. A bit of a consolation for the owners whose horses won't be going.'

'So you're not thinking of a post-Ascot celebration, then?' Terry observed, wryly.

Su slipped her arms around his waist and gave him a squeeze. 'We'll have that, too. Can we get a flag made, to run up the pole when we have a Group winner?'

'The old guv'nor only flew the flag for Group One winners!' Terry reminded her.

'We're not the old guv'nor, though, are we? He was tripping over Group One winners every time he stepped out in the yard! I'm happy to settle for a Group Three if we have to! A flag for black type race winners, until we get a Group One!'

'Why not?' Anne agreed, 'I bet the original flag's knocking about somewhere, out in the Colours Room, probably. If I can fish it out, we'll fly it!'

'IF we have a black type winner,' Chris reminded her. 'Neither of our superstars have won anything yet. We don't know what conversation we'll be having in a fortnight, but right now, Open Day?'

'I'm all for it,' Anne said, 'the kids can invite their friends and family, it will give them a proper sense of pride and achievement. And I bet the BHA will help, they have funds for this type of thing. Party time!'

Even Terry smiled.

Chris couldn't help reflecting on the apparent bad fortune that had saddled them with two horses they hadn't really wanted and couldn't really afford. And now it had changed to apparent good fortune. The two colts had brought a definite positive vibe to the place. The job hadn't changed, their lives hadn't changed, and yet here they were talking about open days and parties.

For the first time since his retirement as a jockey, he felt life was pretty good.

CHAPTER 13

Jack hid within the wall-to-wall, or rather ear-to-ear, mono of "Kinks", the world that he had not so long ago considered sweet now soured and blocked out. He had wrestled with his conscience and struggled with the need to discuss his problems, coupled with the knowledge that he expressly shouldn't, but no ready solution had presented itself.

Life for Mandy was decidedly sweet, which was why he had delayed for so long in souring it for her, too. Now, it seemed, he had no option. The Open Day at Sainte Bastien was forcing his hand.

The classic R and B collection drew to its final crackling silence. The Kinks' subsequent LPs had been another of life's let-downs, but had at least had a modicum of tolerable pop. Grandad had them all and even liked them. He wasn't such an 'R and B snob', as he often teased Jack.

Sliding the vinyl back into its paper case and cover sleeve with the usual care, Jack noted the time and knew he could put off the dread visit to Mandy's room no longer. He had practised and practised his speech over and over in his head, but knew he wouldn't know what to say when the moment actually came.

'Piss off!' came the usual response as he tapped tentatively at her door, but her tone never backed up the words these days.

He had come to like his new, college-bound sister. But he turned the door handle down on that peaceful era and joined her on the bed.

'What's up?' she asked, without looking up from her phone.

He took a deep breath.

'OK, so we're having this Open Day at the stables next Sunday and you're all invited and I really want you to come and everything, but there's this policeman who'll be there cos he owns Mo, and I don't know he'll be there but he's invited and everything, so he prob'ly will be, but I don't want him to meet Mum.'

Mandy looked up from her phone. 'Why not?'

'I told you about him. He's like a top detective or something and I kind've asked him to help, to see if he could prove Mum didn't do it and catch the real thief. To be honest, he doesn't seem to have done anything, he's as bad as the muppets who are actually doing all the detecting, but he's more of a desk job detective really and–'

'Your point being?' Mandy interrupted impatiently.

'What if he can prove Mum did actually do it?!'

She returned her attention to her phone.

'Cretin! A, she didn't do it and B, not even the cops hounding us can prove she did.'

'They can't prove she didn't.'

'Innocent 'til proven guilty, remember?' Mandy looked up at him reassuringly. 'They don't have to.'

'Yeah, but just s'posing Mum did actually take the money and now Mo's owner will recognise her and put her face to all the evidence and arrest her.'

'Again – cretin. Mum didn't do it and they have no evidence. End of. Go back to bed.'

'We don't know that she didn't.'

'Oh for god's sake, Jack, who cares if she did or not – they've no evidence! They've torn the house apart three times now, AND Nan and Grandad's! Good luck to her if she has it stashed away somewhere, cos it's so well hidden even she can't friggin' use it! Go to bloody bed, Jack, you're even more paranoid than Mum!'

'Why is she so paranoid?'

'I don't know, why are you?!'

She told Dad she took it. He was itching to blurt it out. He stopped himself.

'How do I stop Mum going to the Open Day?' he asked instead.

'Tell her it's a tenner to get in! What's up, are you ashamed of us or something in front of your little horsey friends? It's that girl, isn't it?!'

'No! I want you there. But...'

'Yeah, go on?'

'What if I've dropped her in it?'

'What exactly did you tell your detective buddy, then?'

'That she didn't take it. And she won't go out and won't buy anything and they make her check her till all day at work.'

Mandy smiled gently and gave him a hug.

'No one ever got hurt from telling the truth, Jack. Stop panicking. He isn't going to know Mum from Adam anyway, big bosses leave it all to the plebs who keep ransacking our house. And you know they know nothing! It will be a lovely Open Day and you can go to bed and sleep soundly. So do it, go, now!'

* * *

'Lovely, an Open Day. That'll be nice,' McCulloch commented, looking at the invitation de Freitas had left on his desk. 'Can I come?'

'That is the nature of an "open day",' de Freitas pointed out, 'bring a friend, why not.'

'Will Mrs de Freitas be going?'

'Yes, indeed.'

'Debuting The Hat, by any chance?'

De Freitas winced. 'Like the family silver, it will not be taken out of its box for anything less than a Royal Garden Party.'

'Or a wedding.'

'We don't get any of those at our age, it's all funerals.'

Mrs de Freitas' hat had been an office topic since its purchase the previous weekend, the majority of colleagues unaware that mere hats came with three-figure price tags. Kindly members of Uniform had even offered to lend her theirs.

The painful discovery had been additional salt to an already open wound. Royal Ascot Owner badges had been limited to the syndicate members, leaving any plus-ones to pay their own way in. Where a usual race day was twenty pounds, the Royal ticket had been nearer a hundred. And, of course, his good lady wife just had to bring her sister, for whom he had felt obliged to pay. He had, however, insisted she buy her own hat.

'As a matter of fact, Will, I'm rather hoping you will be there. An extra pair of ears and eyes won't go amiss.'

'I thought we were tilting at windmills in that direction?'

'The Reid family will be out in force, grandparents included. Guards may be down.'

'Mrs Reid may even wear her good hat by accident...'

'You are skating on thin ice, Will,' de Freitas warned with a chuckle.

* * *

'Any more ice?' Chris checked, as he set out another cooler with two champagne bottles.

The champagne or Prosecco argument had gone in favour of the "public face" of Sainte Bastien rather than the behind-scenes finances. If they looked like a home for Derby winners they might be sent Derby winners was the adage constantly instilled in their students, now coming back to bite them in the wallet. The yard certainly looked fit for the entertainment of Derby-winning owners, even if most of the expected visitors were just the family and friends of their students.

'They won't go hungry, that's for sure,' Su observed, looking round the pristine yard.

The same thought occurred to Jack, as he ushered his family in through the gates a short while later. He had insisted on arriving early, to ensure Mo and his box were in sparkling condition, allowing him time to rectify if not. But Danno and Greta had done a great job and the students had nothing to do that day but eat and drink.

The centre of the courtyard was awash with heavily-laden tables, mainly finger foods but with interesting urns of what could be soup or stew dotted around. It seemed the other students had had the same fears as Jack, and already Mai and Grant could be spotted returning from their recce', to a group of adults standing awkwardly beside a hot water urn.

Jack steered his family toward them, running into Anne en route.

'Welcome to Sainte Bastien!' she greeted them cheerfully. 'Feel free to explore before the tour starts. None of the horses bite, unless you give them good cause to, and we'll be doing a full presentation later on, so I'll just leave you in Jack's capable hands for the moment. Grab something to eat and drink, help yourselves!' And she was gone, to impart the same wisdom to the other nervous families.

'Is that your little girlfriend?' Mandy nudged Jack.

He ignored her.

'D'you want to see the horses, before everyone else arrives?' he suggested instead, and his family readily agreed.

They strolled from box to box, standing cautiously back from enquiring equine muzzles, or peering into boxes at disinterested occupants, as Jack told them who was who. He showed them where the classrooms were and introduced them to the assortment of dogs, who followed along.

'Why Cheddar?' Paul asked, having been introduced to a small ball of white fluff.

Peanut, the brown miniature Jack Russell, never seemed to arouse the same bemusement, Jack had noticed.

'He's a Bichon Frise,' Jack explained, 'so Terry said if they were going to have a dog that sounded like a cheese it may as well be one they could spell!'

They returned to the main yard and Jack was thankful to see a good deal more people had arrived, relieving him of the embarrassment of having to introduce them to his friends. He abandoned them, as they made a start on the food and chatted with other similarly deserted parents.

'Is that your mum and dad?' Jack asked Mai, joining her and Grant over by the tack room. 'Didn't Arsehole come?'

Mai grinned. 'He is coming, but with some of his old college friends. I think he's got some new girlfriend; we've not seen much of him in a while. Bliss!'

'When do the owners come?' Jack asked, as though double-checking would put their arrival back further. He so wished his family would be gone before then.

'One, I think,' Grant confirmed. 'After the school tour. That'll be when the horses get fetched out.'

They chatted together until Su and Terry led half the families off on a tour beginning with the classrooms, while the remaining visitors followed Anne and Chris out to the paddocks first. It was too much to hope for that none of Jack's family would want to stay for the parade of the horses.

'Come on, we may as well go with them,' Grant suggested, and they tagged along behind their respective family groups.

By the time the two groups converged once more in the main yard a handful of new visitors were among them, drinks and nibbles in hand. The main owners were regular visitors throughout the year and well-known to the staff and students, but several less-familiar faces now swelled their numbers.

Stable Open Days were common enough in Lambourn and those in the know were happy to pass a Sunday afternoon with free food and drink, while horses were led before them like Time Share opportunities. A mix of syndicate members and mildly-interested locals now hovered by the buffet tables.

Jack's heart sank as he saw that de Freitas was among them. To his horror, even worse, the policeman who had led the search on their house was with him. Jack shot a glance at his Mum and Dad, but they were still walking on air at the elevated status of their youngest child and busy in conversation with Anne.

Their obvious pride hadn't escaped the attention of Mai, whose own parents had adopted a visible air of disdain throughout the tour. Classrooms and the latest in equine technology, it seemed, did nothing to disguise the fact their daughter was still "just" working in a stable. Even Grant's parents had looked impressed.

'I am soooo going to get it in the ear when my brother turns up,' Mai complained. 'They'll probably gang up and send me to business school!'

'You wait 'til they see you ride,' Grant assured her. 'They'll be falling over themselves to brag about you!'

Jack was barely listening, consumed by his own problems. It occurred to him that if he disappeared off early to get Mo ready for the parade, there was no reason for de Freitas to speak to him and meet his family. But what if the other cop pointed them out? And Mum was surely going to spot the cop at some point and freak out.

He opted for an ostrich-like head-in-the-sand approach.

'I'm going to hang out with Mo,' he told his friends, 'coming?'

'Where the devil does he keep disappearing to?' Joy complained to Paul, as they looked around for Jack for the umpteenth time that day.

'He doesn't want us to meet his girlfriend!' Mandy informed them, happy to rat him out. 'That's her mum and dad over there, the snobby pair who were asking all the questions about the school curriculum.'

'Doesn't want them to meet you, more like!' Grandad pointed out unhelpfully.

Nan poked him in the ribs.

'I thought that bloody horse was his only love interest,' Joy joked.

Both she and Paul were now keeping a surreptitious eye on Mai's parents, Mandy noted with relief.

Mandy had recognised the young Detective Sergeant the minute he'd walked into the yard, presumably with his parents. She'd been conscious of Jack's anxiety at police presence, but had hardly expected the entire force to be out. It made sense, though, all the big-shot's workmates coming to look at his wonder horse.

She knew the effect the detective's presence would have on Mum's nerves, so took care in redirecting her attention. If Dad noticed, she hoped he'd have the sense to stay schtum. Given the good turnout of people, it was easy to keep plenty of bodies between the police and themselves.

'I'm very much looking forward to seeing these horses of Lesley's, has he been showing you the photos?' Mrs de Freitas asked McCulloch conversationally.

'They're more popular in the office than baby photos!' McCulloch acknowledged. He glanced around at what was, by now, a large gathering; and not all with children in tow.

'An awful lot of people appear to have a spare forty-thousand pounds to invest in racehorses,' he remarked.

'I do hope you two are not simply going to talk shop, I thought we were here for a nice day out,' Mrs de Freitas chided lightly.

'I sincerely hope not, too,' McCulloch assured her, 'I'm off duty!'

'If you want to get away with murder, do it on a Sunday,' de Freitas observed wryly.

The parade of horses was announced as imminent and the groups of people began to form more of a line. De Freitas dropped back behind his wife and nodded to McCulloch to follow suit.

'We may keep our heads down,' he advised. 'From what the young boy has been saying we don't want to give Joy Reid a heart attack. It's a family day, after all; and as you and my good lady wife so correctly point out, we're not exactly on duty.'

'We might be yet,' McCulloch corrected him, 'I think we may be about to go on the clock.' He nodded toward the newcomers gathered at the hot food table.

An ornate bell in the centre of the quadrangle chose that moment to peal, as Terry gained attention to introduce the first of the horses. He and Chris took turns in introducing each of the horses, led out by Su and Anne. Price tag, pedigree, race results and entries were listed for each, with personal comments such as a preference for carrots or a tendency to pick pockets in search of Polo mints. When Grey Motive was introduced as the stable's Derby hope, with dreams of the Triple Crown, he brought forth oohs and aahs, but it was the pet goat who accompanied Six Minute War who ultimately stole the show.

'Activity?' de Freitas asked quietly of his sergeant, looking toward their Person of Interest.

'The iPad came out specifically for that horse of yours who runs at Ascot. Several selfies with the horse in the background.'

'And not for the other horses, or the goat? I'd call that interesting, wouldn't you?'

'I'd call it the only positive movement we've seen on this case – and all he's done is eat a sausage roll and take a selfie!'

'We're grasping at cheese straws?'

McCulloch laughed. 'It might be prudent to disappear. I've seen enough to keep me occupied tomorrow and we don't want any crumb trails cleaned away in the meantime.'

'Mrs de Freitas will eat me alive, but of course you're right. Enjoy what's left of your weekend, Will.'

De Freitas glanced across at the buffet tables and knew he needed to melt away just as expediently, but not at the cost of domestic bliss.

'Damn! I meant to give Will my desk key for the morning!' he told his wife, patting an offending pocket, 'I'll just catch him up at his car. Why don't you go and say hello to Anne and Su?'

She looked at him suspiciously. 'While you two talk shop after all?'

He smiled ruefully.

'Oh, but there's a riding demonstration on that mechanical horse gizmo, you'll miss it, Lesley!'

'Miss it? I've been on it!'

Jack was relieved to see the young detective depart and even happier when de Freitas left soon after. For the first time that day he relaxed a little.

'The police have gone,' he whispered to Mandy.

'I noticed.' She smiled at him, like a cat eyeing a mouse. 'And here comes your little girlfriend. Aren't you going to introduce us?'

He glared at her, and she winked.

'Aren't you giving a demonstration on the Equicizer?' he asked Mai, as she joined them.

Her star rider status had seen her chosen to demonstrate the mechanical racehorse simulator, which would entertain any visitor who wished to give it a try themselves.

'Yes; but not for a few minutes yet. Arsehole has turned up, so I'm hiding. They'll start shooting me down at any minute!' She lowered her voice. 'Speaking of which, your sister seems cool. I'm beginning to think it's just a brother thing; are you sure you're not the arsehole?'

He grinned. 'She's not so bad; now she's shooting films instead of bank staff!'

'Hey! I heard that!' Mandy smiled at Mai. 'Brothers are the pits. Was that yours, talking to your dad?'

'Hatching a plan to rescue me, before I make the mistake of becoming a champion jockey instead of just some company C E O.'

'Come on, you lot, I want front row seats for this exerciser thing,' Joy interrupted, ushering the family to the semi-circle of people already gathered around the Equicizer, pulled out from the pair of boxes that had been converted to a gym.

They widened the semi-circle and a second and third row of onlookers quickly gathered behind them. The electronic mechanical horse, with speeds from slow canter to full forty-five-miles per hour gallop, looked just like the real thing, with the exception of a base instead of legs, making it easier to mount and more appealing to the non-horsey volunteer riders. Even the lifelike head and neck simulated the movement of a galloping horse.

Terry showed them all how it should be done, building up to a fake finish, tightening reins and pulling his whip through, driving out with hands and heels, and between breaths explaining every move. He made it look easy, as did Mai, who repeated the sixty-second exercise. Most races were run in well under two minutes and the powerful driving finish wasn't something sustainable for either horse or jockey.

The onlookers were clearly unimpressed by the brief workouts, until they each had a go themselves. Thirty seconds at the gentle half-speed was enough to turn all legs to jelly. Reins and whips were dropped, and the advised positioning of legs and backs and rear-ends was instantly forgotten with the increase of speed. The fun continued afterwards, with the participants allowed to use the Pro-Cush whips with unlimited force on whomever they chose.

Even Joy had reluctantly joined in, at the insistence of her family members, and after Grandad had given the Equicizer a go she could hardly refuse.

'I'm glad they teach you on something safe like that and not on the real thing,' she told Jack approvingly.

He thought it best not to correct her.

They moved away and enabled those waiting to get nearer to the action. Many of the younger children were queuing already for second and third turns. Jack couldn't help thinking he was part of a minority pursuit when, in the presence of racehorses and even a Derby contender, goats and mechanical horses were the stars of the day. At football academy there would be nothing but footballs.

Still, it gave him space, much like his minority-appeal music, and allowed him to remain invisible.

Invisibility had stopped being a preoccupation since arriving at Sainte Bastien, where he had felt at once that he fitted in and belonged. Today, with a crowd of at least one hundred milling about, he still felt strangely comfortable, happy to talk to complete strangers about the vocation he loved. The successful invisibility – or at least early departure – of the police had been an added bonus.

That last thought apparently tempted Fate and he was disturbed to be greeted by the wife of his friend, the detective. Was she Mrs Chief Inspector or could the introductions slip by unnoticed, he wondered, in a brief moment of panic? Oh god! Where was Les? Maybe he hadn't left after all...

'I've heard so much about you and the horses,' Mrs de Freitas gushed, mercifully turning at once to Mai to praise her on her Equicizer skills. 'Will you be riding at Ascot?'

'Not until next year, when I'm sixteen,' Mai informed her, 'but I want to ride on every track in Britain and be Champion Jockey!'

'Then I very much hope you do.'

Mrs de Freitas turned, as though looking for someone, and Jack's heart sank. He glanced anxiously at his parents and saw Mum's gaze focus beyond him, her expression of puzzlement turning to surprised recognition.

To his utter consternation Mum raised a hand in a slight wave, acknowledging a presence now directly behind him. He couldn't tell if she was pleased or not as she declared,

'Fancy seeing you here!'

CHAPTER 14

'How did we miss that?' de Freitas wondered, as he stood over McCulloch's desk, staring at the social media page on the sergeant's computer screen.

'Someone on the team should have picked it up,' McCulloch agreed, 'but then again we didn't know what we were looking for. Not so much hidden, as simply not acknowledged.'

Rhys Fordham, for a reason best known to his parents, had been given his mother's maiden surname, despite the fact his parents married a few years after his birth and subsequently christened their next child with their marital surname. His connection to one of the Racing Futures students at Sainte Bastien had been a helpful coincidence that had therefore eluded them.

His presence at the Open Day could have been purely due to sibling support. Or, more relevantly, due to his close companionship with Heidi Jones and her circle of friends. It was no secret that Heidi's hitherto disregarded boyfriend had chipped in unofficially with her share in All Things Pass.

The uploads from the previous day's Open Day betrayed nothing, other than an anecdotal connection with that particular horse. That the connection had come via an unknown and still to be detected financial source was now central to the case.

To an extent they were still tilting at windmills, but no longer on a whim. A relief manager showing a trainee manager how to count cash and, in so doing, inadvertently stumbling on how to steal cash, was suddenly looking a lot more plausible.

'Do we bring him in?' McCulloch asked.

'No, not yet. What we have is still purely conjecture. But if it's correct, he's beginning to dip into the money. And if we let his confidence grow, so too will our evidence.'

'You didn't arouse any curiosity yesterday, nothing that will feed back to him?'

De Freitas shook his head. 'Mrs de Freitas is very much more than just a pretty face. She chatted away with Su Jones, was introduced to the two children and their friends and found out more than we ever would. Certainly a lot more than had I not discreetly left her to it and waited in the car.'

'Discretion on our part being the operative word here?'

'Exactly.'

'It's going to cost you in strawberries and champagne, though,' McCulloch observed. 'That's Ascot, isn't it? Or am I thinking of Wimbledon?'

'Both, I shouldn't wonder. But I think Mrs de Freitas rather enjoyed playing Miss Marple and knowing more than us! I'm afraid you've gone down rather a lot in her estimation, now she knows how easy this detecting lark is.'

'It was only a matter of time,' McCulloch agreed. 'A life of coffee and custard creams, we were bound to get found out at some point. Although in fairness, you'd had Fordham and Baxter earmarked for a couple of weeks now.'

'I didn't tell her that, though. Have you seen the price of strawberries?'

* * *

'Have you seen these prices?' Joy complained, scrolling through her phone. 'Even the second week of September is more than we paid last May.'

'Should've booked before Christmas,' Paul pointed out, 'you always say the Early Bird saving is massive.'

'So's a prison sentence for theft.'

'A deposit on a week in Tenby?'

'They watch everything, Paul – everything.'

Jack, trying to read The Racing Post news on his phone, had come to loathe their discussions about money; or apparent lack of it.

'What's the point of having forty-thousand pounds and not even having a week in a caravan in Wales?' he complained, most of his words a parting shot as he retreated upstairs to his room. 'You should be looking up cruises in the Caribbean.'

'Exactly!' Paul declared. 'He gets it! And the police get it! You're the only one who doesn't!'

Jack didn't linger, having no interest in the outcome of the debate. He liked their week in Tenby, but since Mum had battened down the hatches on anything more luxurious than bread and water, he'd ruled out the possibility of any sort of holiday that year or any other. Life had been a lot richer when they hadn't had a fortune stashed under the floorboards.

He put on his headphones and The Rolling Stones' eponymous debut LP. It was a long word for such a lazy action, Grandad had told him when he'd asked why so many of the albums didn't have titles.

He wondered what Nan and Grandad would say, if they knew?

Mum had always instilled in him and Mandy a strong sense of right and wrong. He'd hated Mandy all the more when he'd felt she'd been letting Mum down. He'd been wrong about his sister; and wrong about his mum.

He knew something extreme must have pushed her to stealing money and it wasn't really the fact that she was a thief that hurt him. What hurt was that it had taken her months and months to tell Dad and even now she still wouldn't tell him and Mandy, as if they were little kids or something.

He didn't care about the money, although if she'd just taken it to make life better then life really might have been better and kind of cool in a way. But not his mum, not the mum he respected and admired and was kind of proud of. She wouldn't steal just to make life better. She had stolen money to get herself out of big, big trouble. Something very big. Maybe not her, even? Maybe to get Dad out of trouble?

It didn't make sense, they never did anything that would get them in trouble. He'd seen programmes on TV where you owed a small amount of money or a parking fine or something and the next thing you owed a massive amount and bailiffs came and took your car and stuff. But there was nothing they'd ever had that could have got them so in debt.

"Little By Little" drew to a close and he knew he'd have to get up and turn the record over. Sometimes he preferred just a playlist on his phone that he could listen to for hours without being disturbed, but he always missed the crackle of the vinyl and the familiar occasional jumps that not even a coin on the record player arm could prevent, the trick Grandad had taught him.

He roused himself from his bed and thought of Nan and Grandad, and their grand clear-out. Nan had said it was so they could clear the rooms out for a fresh coat of paint and half of it was rubbish anyway, especially Grandad's records. But how could it be rubbish when they'd had it all for so long? What if it was stuff they didn't want to lose and it was them about to have the bailiffs round?

Mum was honest.

And honest enough not to break someone else's trust.

* * *

'I'm trusting you to keep these somewhere safe,' de Freitas had instructed his wife, upon picking up the expensive package that landed through their letterbox; but instead the contents had rarely left their sight since.

The Royal Ascot tickets were not only suitably impressive, a cut above the average theatre ticket or cinema stub, but enclosed within a veritable encyclopaedia of information. Maps, history, dress code, fashion guide, terminology, betting guides, menus and horse welfare were among the de Freitas household reading list in the evenings leading up to the big day.

Mrs de Freitas needlessly measured the length of her hemline below the knee, reassured that several inches of fabric protected the sensibility of the Monarch, and questioned the legality of Fascinators, which surely didn't comply with the rule that the crown of the head must be covered. Her own Gainsborough-style headgear not only complied but would cover the crown of anyone within a three-foot radius, her husband pointed out.

De Freitas himself was more focused on the technical aspects, not out of any technical interest but more because of the various departments listed. He had been given a stack of relatively unhelpful information by the British Horseracing Authority when first the betting office investigation had begun, but had binned it all in favour of the simpler details supplied by Chris Marsh.

Now he looked up the BHA Ownership Department and BHA Director of Integrity and Regulations, the latter a former senior within the police force, he discovered. This time, he took a great deal more interest in the reams of Rules and documentation and wondered whether he might be able to put any of it to use with the Brookhills case. He decided to set McCulloch on the task when he was back in the office on Friday.

For now, however, he dutifully donned the hired morning suit, complete with top hat, and posed with his wife outside in front of the rose bushes, while his sister-in-law took photos and the couple next door came out to compliment them all on their attire. The photos were just as dutifully dispatched via his phone to McCulloch, to be shown around the office.

'Bride's side or groom's?' came back the reply.

* * *

'They look like they're going to a royal wedding!' Mai observed, as Terry, Su, Chris and Anne said their goodbyes and issued final orders to those left behind in charge for the afternoon.

Danno and Greta had looked almost as smart, loading Thingy-Bob into the horse box and driving him away to his date with destiny. There had been no usual draw to pick the accompanying grooms. The day was far too important for the inexperienced students; the trip to the Royal meeting reward for the two senior members of the team.

The students were left to their afternoon classes, interrupted by the television coverage of the racing, which they had been following all week. The opening day's Coventry Stakes had engendered mixed feelings and no little debate. The impressive winner, bred in the purple and now favourite for the following year's Two Thousand Guineas, had been astutely dodged according to some, while others felt the accolades steeped upon him should have been going to Thingy-Bob, had he run. Both camps, however, were now unusually quiet, torn between confidence and doubt.

'Is your brother there?' Jack asked Mai, watching the paddock scenes on the TV.

'I doubt it, he has to work, it's one of their busiest weeks. Besides, he's not a proper owner, whatever he likes to pretend.'

It had been a bit of a turn-up, discovering Mai's arsehole brother was one of Mum's workmates, which meant he was also a suspect for the theft. It also meant that he knew Mum was, too. Mai hadn't mentioned it, but Jack had felt increasingly uncomfortable all week.

If Mai's silence on the matter meant she was embarrassed and ashamed, then she would be just as embarrassed and ashamed of his own family. He knew he might well have been looking at Arsehole bitterly as the culprit threatening Mum's innocence, had he not now known better. Was Mai harbouring a similar grudge against Mum?

'OMG, Greta looks amaaazing!' Mai now gushed, as the television camera focused on All Things Pass in the parade ring.

Both Danno and Greta had coordinated their smart suits with the owner's colours and Greta also sported a fetching fascinator.

'So does Thingy-Bob!' Jack agreed, the colt at the peak of condition, his coat shining in the June sunshine.

The TV camera focused on him long enough for the pundit to big-up his chances, but there were at least eight of the fourteen Norfolk Stakes runners equally praised. The classroom fell into an eerie silence as each student stifled the heart-pounding mix of excitement and trepidation.

The preliminaries took only five minutes, with glimpses of Thingy-Bob cantering to post met by excited cries of 'there he is!' and an audible holding of breath as he backed away from the stalls and took a couple of attempts to be loaded. Sharp intakes of breath accompanied the dramatics of another of the runners, playing up in the stall alongside.

Just when Jack felt he could take the suspense no longer, the stall doors sprang open and the commentator began his sixty-second race call. Jack wasn't sure if it felt like longer than a minute, or whether it was all over in a lot shorter flash.

For a while, the clock did seem to stop ticking and the winning post was never going to come. All Things Pass was up at the head of the race throughout, making it look easy as others around him came under pressure, until he too was asked for a bigger effort and rivals dropped away, while others came into contention.

The commentary was lost amid the classroom screams, urging their horse on. Everyone was standing now, the scraping of chairs adding to the crescendo. As the horses swept past the winning post, Jack was aware he had been holding his breath.

The room erupted; hugs and kisses reminiscent of a drunken New Year's Eve party. The thrill of finishing second in a Royal Ascot Group Two race far outweighed any disappointment at not winning. All Things Pass was now an elite racehorse, their trust in him vindicated.

They talked over all the replays of the finish, out-punditing the pundits. 'Nearly' was the word of the day, Thingy-Bob finishing strongly rather than weakening at the line, regardless of what any of the experts might have been saying in the post-race analysis.

Jack's tongue was joining in as vociferously as everyone else, but it was on autopilot as he sat back in silence in his own mind, absorbing the euphoria. He knew it would last with him always. There might be better moments; there would definitely be worse. But this was a life-defining moment.

The euphoria died as quickly as it had come.

'It would have been good if he'd won,' someone said; and the talk turned instantly to the July Stakes in three weeks' time, seemingly already in the bag.

'There'll be offers,' Mai said, beside him.

'What?'

'Offers. Huge money. The top end of six figures, Su reckons, even for finishing in the first three.'

'Do you think they'll take them?'

'It's their job, isn't it? By all rights he should have made six figures already at the breeze-up sale.'

Jack thought of Mo; and his life-defining moment took on a new perspective.

* * *

'We had to queue for ten minutes for that,' de Freitas told McCulloch, as he showed the sergeant the photo on his phone. The floral backdrop bearing the Royal Ascot insignia hardly looked worth the wait, although the three beaming faces reflected none of the inconvenience.

'Your rose backdrop was nicer,' McCulloch observed.

'Mmm. Especially five minutes in.' He returned the phone to his pocket. 'It was a crying shame the horse didn't win, but we've been told he'll win his next race.'

'Did you back him?'

'Mrs de Freitas and her sister had a place bet, but won very little. I lost a great deal on a jug of Pimms. Several, in fact.'

'Painless, then. Any sign of our P O I?'

'None at all. Not a glimmer of evidence, either. I dug out some names at the BHA, though. I wonder if it might be worthwhile contacting them and letting them do some donkey work for us?'

McCulloch looked at the short biography details of the BHA hierarchy, published on the website. The Director of Integrity and Regulations appeared to have been offloaded from their own department, which begged the question of why? And the Head of Ownership and Accounts sounded more clerical than investigative.

'Carmel Currid seems to be all anti-doping and anti-cheating,' McCulloch noted, 'and Guillaume Desprez more like our man, with access to accounts. But is he capable of tracing our P O I?'

'The problem is, Fordham isn't a registered owner. Heidi Jones is the officially registered name, Fordham isn't included in our group chat when Chris Marsh sends out videos and updates of the horses. I always keep an eye on the group members, just in case.

'But maybe Desprez can trace her payments? Has Fordham given her cash or PayPal gifts, or a bank transfer? We can't find it from this end and his accounts; and we haven't access to Heidi Jones' accounts. But perhaps Desprez does have access. How exactly do they police this system they're so proud of?'

'Discreetly?'

'Good point, Will. I'd like this to remain very much a covert investigation. But we're not asking them to do our work for us; merely share their own information. It can't hurt to ask.'

'I'll give him a call and arrange a meeting. They're based in the City, High Holborn. Do you fancy tagging along?'

'I'm never one to turn down a day Travel-card trip, Will. Your turn to drive.'

* * *

Ascot had been kind to the Sainte Bastien team, in more ways than one. Grey Motive's full-brother had continued his belated winning ways by landing the Group Two King Edward VII Stakes the day after the Norfolk Stakes. The weak catalogue page had, too late, been transformed to a superb one.

And Su had been correct about the offers that might flood in for All Things Pass following a good Ascot run. Flood wasn't quite the right word, only three serious offers had been made, but they had been serious enough to warrant discussion.

As usual, it came down to a gamble. Take a good offer and run; or sit tight and wait for the horse's value to rise after the July Stakes. The gamble being that his value could as easily plummet if he ran badly next time out. Like every punter, they were simply placing a bet on their horse, which could go either way.

Naturally, Terry was in the no-risk camp, happy to now reap the profit denied them when injury had cost All Things

Pass his place in the sales ring. Coupled with not knowing the result of the July Stakes, three weeks before it was run, was the fact the race was run over an additional furlong. An eighth of a mile was a considerable addition for a sprinter. It was, he argued ineffectively, a no-brainer.

When not a stalemate, a four-person Democratic State often turned out to be a Dictatorship. Even the usually cautious Anne was adamant the additional furlong would suit their colt and see him valued as a Group Two winner, rather than just a Group Two runner-up.

'A Group Two runner-up with potential,' Terry reminded her. 'All you're planning to do is take away the potential.'

'Or add the potential of becoming a Group One winner and stallion!' Su fought back, with what turned out to be the winning consensus, their bet placed.

Still, it was nowhere near the enormity of the decision made eight months earlier to retain Grey Motive as a long-term investment; and that was beginning to look a very smart move. Terry relaxed somewhat, no more than a minor battle lost.

'And now for the really big news,' Chris announced, as the discussion closed. This one, he knew, would need no debate. 'We've had an offer of a horse from a new owner, he rang me there in the office about half an hour ago. And with the promise of an order for maybe three more at the sales, if he's happy with us. Bona fide big league trainers!'

'Imagine the offers of horses we'll get after the July Stakes!' Anne said, only half-jokingly, the dream well and truly alive.

* * *

'Oh my god, it's just a proper fairytale!' Mandy said excitedly, holding her letter out in front of her, re-reading it still, even as she tried to show it to the others.

As Joy and Paul craned their necks to see, Mandy pulled it to her chest again.

'They're giving us a studio apartment as part of the bursary, Tisha's got one too! It's three minutes' walk from the college! And it's Ealing Studios, can you believe that?!'

'What, like Ealing Studios who made all the old classic black and white movies?' Joy asked, imagining her daughter roughing it on site; filming by day and putting up a camp bed each night.

'Like studio apartments in Ealing, more like!' Paul said. 'Here, give it here, let's have a look.'

Mandy handed over her letter as though it might crumble to dust at any minute.

'Bloody hell, it's nicer than this place!'

He showed it to Joy, who echoed his approval. It was no more than a tiny bedsit, but the answer to her prayers. No rent, no Travel-card, no anxiety.

'And you were gonna stop me going!' Mandy reminded Joy bitterly.

'I didn't, though, did I, so stop your griping.'

'Maybe things are looking up at last,' Paul remarked; and both he and Joy rapidly tapped the wooden doorframe, just in case.

* * *

DI de Freitas was used to gathering information from various official sources, none of whom had ever so far offered to actively take over the case. Despite the fact that he and McCulloch had solicited the offer, he couldn't help but feel a sense of foreboding as the BHA's Carmel Currid and Guillaume Desprez now attempted to arrest more involvement than he considered necessary.

For a particularly petite woman, Currid was overbearingly officious. Desprez's silence, for that matter, was just as annoying. Between them they brought up files and data on their laptops, which they seemed unwilling to share with their visitors, while firing intrusive questions at the two detectives in what McCulloch noted down as being a very accusatory manner.

"Has forgotten she's not still a Metropolitan Police Assistant Commissioner" McCulloch tapped into his notes, showing de Freitas under the guise of calling up case notes.

De Freitas stifled a smile.

'We don't, of course, actually know that and have no evidence to even suggest it,' he reminded Currid, who was bristling with hostility in the face of a suspected criminal sneaking past her into quasi ownership. 'But we're hoping to draw a definite line under that possibility, with the evidence of your Accounts Department.'

'Inspector, having an unregistered owner in a yard is a highly prohibited flaunting of our very exact Rules,' she retorted, unable to over-emphasise her position enough, but trying all the same. 'Nor are we obliged to share any of our data with you, unless on production of a warrant. This is highly confidential information and not for the domain of general public such as yourselves.'

De Freitas felt certain the four-letter word McCulloch was currently tapping was "ouch". He wondered why she hadn't gone so far as to ask them to call her "Ma'am" and was tempted to do so anyway.

'There is no evidence to back-up your theory,' Desprez announced sharply, closing his laptop purposefully. 'We run a tightly-policed ship here and would have picked up on any such irregularity long before you did.'

'We'll be sure to keep you updated on any findings,' Currid said pleasantly, rising from her chair to bring their meeting to an unproductive close. There was nothing pleasant about her manner or expression.

The two detectives stood up, de Freitas merely nodding a farewell.

'Thank you, Ma'am,' McCulloch said pointedly as he pulled the door closed behind them.

'Well, I've half a mind to go back with a bloody warrant just to look at his damned data and turn my nose up at it!' de Freitas vented as they headed back out to the car. 'Mrs de Freitas would have my guts for garters for saying it, but that woman is a thorough–'

'MPS?' McCulloch ventured, interrupting him; not that there was any real rivalry between the Thames Valley and Metropolitan Police Service.

'This must be what it's like to gate-crash a Masons' meeting, talk about closed shop! Either they solve it on their own, or block us from doing so. Would it have killed them just to show us the bank account? The lodgement references and sources?'

'We only needed the account number, to trace it on Fordham's transactions,' McCulloch complained, 'which she knows full well. Could we do them for withholding evidence?'

'When Desprez insists there is no evidence?'

'He didn't actually show us, though.'

'They're avoiding stains, Will. It's not easy maintaining a whiter than white outfit.'

'So possibly Desprez spotted a stain?'

'It's a difficult one to read. Would you want her to find out if you had?'

McCulloch shook his head, smiling ruefully. 'At least they don't have the POI's name and account number. We didn't actually give them Fordham's account number, did we?'

'And have that pair trampling over any evidence? No, I did not. Just the IBAC, which actually tells us one thing – Heidi Jones isn't with the same bank as Fordham, or Desprez would have had to ask for the IBAN as well.'

'And that helps us how?' McCulloch unlocked the car and got himself comfortable in the driver's seat.

'Time only may tell. In the meantime, we've had a totally wasted trip.' De Freitas clicked in his seatbelt. 'Still, it got us out of the office and no harm done.'

'Famous last words, those.'

CHAPTER 15

August

Having their first Royal Ascot runner had, as a result, seen June pass in a blur of preparation and excitement for the entire Sainte Bastien team. With the July Stakes falling in the first week of July, at the more relaxed and informal Newmarket July meeting, Chris and Terry had hoped to take a much-needed breath and get back to normal, but the flag still proudly flying above the stable-yard entrance heralded a different story.

All Things Pass running out a narrow winner of the Group Two July Stakes had brought delirious joy and far more very serious offers than they could have predicted. And with them, headaches. They had expected to lose the horse, but gained a number of options and new horses instead.

His next intended target, under new ownership, had been the Group Two Gimcrack Stakes a month later, but a very minor bruise to his foot had ruled him out; a reminder of the fragility of horses, hopes and plans. A test, too, of trust, for both new owner and trainers.

And now, with the all-important St Leger meeting at Doncaster just a week away, the chance to catch breath was still at least a fortnight away.

The easy victory of Grey Motive on his debut appearance in a Maiden race, specifically for two-year-old horses that had not yet won a race, at their local Newbury track had done little to ease Jack's heart-rate. He had led the colt up, all by himself, with his family looking proudly on and his policeman friend safely on holiday in Devon; and he had been there alongside his beloved Mo for all the post-race photographs, one of which now adorned his bedroom wall.

Although Chris and Terry had emphasised beforehand how immature Mo was and the race was more of an education than an opportunity to win, Jack had never once doubted his colt. The only brief anxiety to cross his mind at Newbury the previous week had been the possibility that Mandy might in her excitement blab about their bets on the following year's Classics, but as Mum hadn't given him a lecture on the stupidity of gambling, all seemed well.

With one Group race already to the stable's credit, it was now up to Thingy-Bob and Mo to triple the tally at Doncaster next week – and he, Jack, would be leading up both.

All of which he now discussed with Mo as he gave him a brush and cleaned his hooves in readiness for the morning's exercise, tacking him up with the usual care and attention to detail.

'We're not expecting you to win, now,' he assured Mo, 'not stepping up to Group Two level on only your second run, but there's plenty others in your race who've only won a Maiden; and that Group winner from Goodwood, Chris says he's a sprinter really and your class will find him out, so don't let him worry you.'

He stepped back from Mo to check his appearance and looked him in the eye.

'If you're as good as we think you are, Chris says you'll win doing cartwheels, just like at Newbury. And you don't have to be scared of them selling you like Thingy-Bob because Chris says they won't let you go at any price and Thingy-Bob paid for you ten times over and he's still here.'

He was suddenly aware of a presence and turned to see Chris looking in over the stable door. Not there long enough, surely, to have heard him, but he felt embarrassed nonetheless.

'You've done a great job on him, Jack, it's not easy getting a sheen on a grey coat.' Chris smiled. As if reading his mind, he said, 'They're easy to talk to, especially the good ones. The good ones listen. It's a confidence thing. If you treat them as though they're special, they think they are special. Put someone down or pay them no regard and they won't have the confidence to try.'

'Do you think he'll win next week?'

'I can't see anything beating him, to be honest. He's a bit weak still and backward, but he put away some good horses in that Maiden. I'll be surprised and upset if he doesn't, but bloody nervous until he does! No one makes a fool of you as easily as a horse can!'

Jack shook his head. 'Not Mo, it's not in his nature to be unkind.'

He led Mo out as Chris swung the door open for him and walked toward the group of work-riders, Mai stepping forward to meet them. She rubbed the colt's nose in greeting before being deftly legged up into the saddle by Terry.

Her riding that summer had just got better and better, the bad habits picked up at pony camps ironed out and forgotten. It took strength to ride a racehorse and Mai never missed a day in the stable gym, improving her upper body strength and performing physics-defying miracles on the exercise ball to perfect her balance.

Her dedication showed. Jack rarely missed any televised racing and could recognise the better jockeys simply from how they sat while led round the parade ring. Mai sat like that, even with her stirrups slightly longer for riding exercise.

He couldn't explain it; just an ease, a fluidity, a oneness with any horse she sat on. He could see the difference in Mo and the other horses compared to when he or one of the other students rode them.

It was like Chris had said – she gave the horses added confidence. He knew he lacked that quality and would never be anything more than an adequate work-rider. He wasn't a natural rider, but he loved the very different relationship he had with the horses he rode, as opposed to simply being with them on the ground. As soon as he sat up on a horse he felt himself merge with the horse. He could feel the language of the muscles beneath the skin, could feel every notion before it became action.

Down here, on the ground, his conversations with Mo were very much one-sided; but up there Mo's words flowed silently in a steady outpour. A rider didn't just see the twitch of an ear but felt it, before ever the ear had moved.

He and Mai absorbed like sponges the stories with which Chris and Terry would regale them, of their experiences race-riding, good and bad. For Jack they would never be more than stories to cherish, but for Mai they were an education; he could see the intent in her eyes, every word stored away for future reference.

He knew that Grant was a little envious, Grant's own aspirations of becoming a jockey not looking so good; but Jack was content with his own skills. The jockey could take care of a horse for ten minutes at the races and those crucial seconds of the race itself, while Jack would be taking care of the horse for every other moment of their working day, all year round. He already knew he wouldn't swap that for the world.

'Penny for them?' Anne asked, as he stood quietly watching Mo walking away.

'Sorry, just watching Mo,' he apologised.

'No apology needed, not many get to look upon a horse like that, we should make the most of it while we can.'

Jack considered her words. It wasn't only the races themselves that were fleeting.

'Has your sister moved to London yet?' Anne asked amiably. She liked to chat with him about his family, worried that things might not be entirely happy for him at home. And yet she had met his family more than once and her fears couldn't have seemed more ungrounded.

'Next week,' Jack said comfortably.

'Well, if she needs a project, she can always come and make a film about Mo!'

Jack didn't like to question her wisdom, but he was only just ridding himself of his sister, albeit a more tolerable sibling in recent months. Nevertheless, he didn't want to be sharing his workplace with her as well. It had become what Su called "a legal high" and Mandy could just go and find her own highs somewhere else.

He was just about to reply with a grudging, yeah, I'll ask her, when Anne's attention wandered. He followed her gaze to a pair of Range Rovers pulling up in the yard.

'Not another stable inspection,' Anne muttered.

Her guess looked accurate to Jack, who had been there for the BHA inspection in the spring. The random inspections primarily checked for documentation compliance and welfare, the horses also blood-tested for possible contaminates. It wasn't anything to worry about in a well-run yard, merely an inconvenience disturbing the routine of the stable and the horses.

The Sainte Bastien team was more accepting than most, given that the stable and student programme fell under BHA ownership, but receiving a second visit in the space of four months was unusual enough to raise some concern. Particularly when the usual veterinary team had been joined by the head honcho herself.

Carmel Currid, wearing highly unsuitable shoes for a yard visit, stepped down cautiously from her gleaming Land Rover. Fortunately the yard was always kept immaculate and no passing horse had yet sullied the freshly-swept surface. But it was the multitude of passing horses in close proximity that presented a greater problem to Currid, who did not appear to be at all comfortable in their presence.

'She shouldn't have parked her Chelsea tractor in the middle of a working yard if she was worried about the paint-work,' Anne hissed under her breath to an amused Jack.

It crossed Jack's mind that it wasn't the car the visitor was chiefly concerned about. Mum had been equally nervous of the horses, but then again Mum hadn't taken a job in the horseracing industry. Maybe the short lady in the tall heels thought she'd taken a desk job.

'Let Chris know they're here, but I'll see to them,' Anne told him, 'no point disrupting work, it's the last Lot anyway.'

She headed off toward the visitors, greeting them cheerfully.

With four of them running the place, it was easy to maintain a well-ordered office and the surprise BHA inspection shouldn't have concerned Chris. Now the officers were actually here for a second time, in relatively short succession, he felt illogically flustered and guilty of some improbable oversight.

He jumped down from his last ride of the morning and hurried across to the office, keen to offer some sort of belated support to his wife, if only moral, leaving Su and Terry to sort out any horses selected for samples.

Anne was bustling about the office, locating and furnishing each individual equine passport for every horse in their care, the Health and Safety Statement, Staff Hours Book, Accident Book, Medicines Register Book and every other document demanded of her.

Currid's presence surprised Chris, who had expected the usual minions, not the head of Integrity herself. She appeared to be there only for the day out, giving the items no more than a cursory glance before handing them back to Anne. Her people had seen everything in April, after all, and very little had changed since.

Or maybe a seismic change, if you happened to be where he was sitting. But a couple of new horses and first Group winner weren't really of any interest to the powers that be. He wondered exactly what was?

'How do you communicate with owners?' Currid asked of the air in general, without looking up.

'Mobile chat groups, daily videos and updates, all via the Equisoft system, and individual emails and phone calls.' Chris felt confident they followed data protection laws to the letter, but Currid was beginning to make him anxious.

'May I see the Equisoft group listing for All Things Pass?' Currid asked, looking up at last from paperwork in her own file.

Anne opened the horse's details on her phone and handed it to Currid, who stared at it, nonplussed.

'No group? You've only one name here?'

'Alfawz Farms is the new owner, but we only send updates to the racing manager, Pete Allen,' Chris clarified. 'Everything goes through him.'

'Alfawz? But what about the syndicate?'

Chris and Anne exchanged glances. The purchase of their July Stakes winner by racing's latest super-power had been all over the media for days. The public loved a rags-to-riches story and their little stable selling to Alfawz and retaining the horse to train for the high-profile owner had been a media meal ticket. Didn't the BHA management ever read the racing press or watch TV coverage?

Chris peered over her shoulder at the Ownership Form Currid was holding.

'That's the old form you have there,' he pointed out.

Currid tutted disapprovingly, looking blankly at the paperwork Anne now handed her. It was annoyingly in order and showing just the sole ownership.

'Have you the previous owners on your system that I may see, then?'

'No; Equisoft updates automatically,' Anne assured her, taking back the phone.

So that was it; just a data protection fishing trip that might, without Anne's diligence, have earned them a hefty fine of a few thousand. Chris took a deep breath and tried to mask his exasperation.

The smartly dressed Currid turned on her designer heels and re-joined the BHA vet outside, who had been checking the yard and taking samples.

'A waste of time,' she muttered to the vet, declaring more audibly, 'Everything's in perfect order, thank you for your time.'

'What does she expect?' Chris remarked, watching the BHA hierarchy departing in a spotless Range Rover. 'This whole place belongs to them! If it wasn't in perfect order we'd be out on our ear!'

'Well, it's out of the way now, we can relax again.' Anne exhaled deeply, only now aware of how tense she'd been. It was true, one error and this could all be taken from them, just when things were going so perfectly.

'You won't believe it,' Chris complained to Terry as he wandered over, 'that woman's in charge of our sport and didn't have a clue Thingy-Bob had been bought by Alfawz!'

'Huh! It figures, though. Sitting in a London office, totally disconnected.'

'Not sat in an office today, though,' Anne pointed out. 'I'm guessing they're short staffed!'

'Guillaume in Accounts was too busy to tell her about All Things Pass, anyway!'

They laughed, and Su gave Anne a grateful hug, reflecting what they all felt. None of them had any particular skill or inclination for office work, but it had been Anne from day one who had been willing to give it a go; and successfully so. Keeping the horses fit and happy was the easy bit and second nature to them all; they'd done it all their lives. The office was very much a necessary evil.

And yet their livelihood depended as much on paperwork as horses.

* * *

'Anything exciting in my absence?'

'More so than toffees?' McCulloch remarked, as De Freitas handed round the obligatory boxes of clotted cream fudge. 'Not unless you count paperwork and court. Mind you, Surveillance just dropped a file on you, our luck could change.'

De Freitas picked it up and read the top sheet.

'Bingo; enough for Crown Prosecution on your body in the woods.'

McCulloch took it from him. 'We've still got her detained; we can get the arrest warrant now and keep her. That was a quickie.'

'I can't say I like domestic murders and missing children, but they do tend to be easy overnight jobs,' de Freitas observed. 'Any advances on anything I left pending?'

'I think you've only the jewellers robbery left open; Surveillance are still on that, our POIs have gone to ground. A nice new bundle in your in-tray instead!'

'So I see.'

'Hang on, one more – there are two files here,' noted McCulloch, handing back a second slim manila file that had slipped unnoticed beneath the more interesting of those sent up by Surveillance.

De Freitas sat back in his chair. 'Well, would you believe it? It's the Brookhills case! I wouldn't have given it a thought but for the horse winning the other week. Shame we were away for that.'

He opened the file and read through the contents.

'Movement on Fordham or Reid?' McCulloch enquired.

'Movement on Baxter, as it happens. Another late deal to the Algarve.'

'And?'

'And he's put a deposit down on an apartment there.'

* * *

With Mandy settled into her apartment, the two families having travelled to Ealing en masse to move her and Tisha safely in and allay their own fears; and now Jack temporarily in Doncaster for two overnight stays at the racecourse, Joy and Paul should have been enjoying their empty nest. They had had every intention of doing so, love and romance the only things that didn't show up on bank statements and trigger alarm bells.

But instead of an empty nest, they had an unwelcome cuckoo. Two, to be exact.

De Freitas had opted to bring in Baxter and Fordham for interviews, without charge. For Joy Reid, however, both he and McCulloch were in agreement that a simple house visit would be more efficacious.

In the station, she had been flustered, confused, but consistent. Slightly more relaxed at home, though that was an overstatement, they hoped her consistency might falter. They were nearly a year into the case and no nearer having a firm suspect.

Ordinarily the file would by now have been gathering dust, but the Brookhills CEO was unhappy at retaining tainted staff without grounds for dismissal, while several of the accused staff were equally unhappy at groundless demotion and unsubstantiated accusation. With people's lives and future affected, the case had ceased to be simply about theft.

'Tea?' Joy offered, less flustered than in the past.

She had become resigned to her guilt and inevitable incarceration; the passing of each week crushing further any hope she may have clung onto. She even got the impression, from the odd snide remark he'd make, that even Jack suspected she'd stolen the money. Hanging out with Rhys' sister probably just emphasised to him how unlikely it was that any of her colleagues would have taken it; and certainly not Rhys.

'No, thank you,' de Freitas declined, sitting comfortably beside McCulloch on the sofa.

Joy sat less comfortably in the armchair, with Paul perched on its arm, his own arm reassuringly around his wife. He was relaxed and confident in Joy's innocence and in the ability of the police to prove it. Her fear, only its iceberg tip showing on her frayed surface, was not his.

De Freitas and McCulloch had considered it to be good fortune in finding Paul Reid home as well. Whatever lies she had told him to cover her tracks most probably didn't quite match those she had so far told them. Trying to convince them now, in his presence, of her innocence could lead to a slip.

'It could be all three,' McCulloch had earlier suggested, as they'd highlighted their case notes for a final time before getting out of the car and knocking at the Reid house. 'Reid taking just enough for the college fees she was expecting to get hit with; and Baxter and Fordham expecting to divvy up forty-grand between them, only to find it a few thousand short. Who are they going to complain to? So you get eighteen-thou' instead of twenty – it's still a nice deposit on that holiday home and the racehorse your girlfriend tells you will be a quick turnover.'

'It was, too,' de Freitas had agreed. 'The shareholders each made seventy-thousand out of the sale of All Things Pass. And time enough to get the money back in the floor safe before it's even missed.'

McCulloch had checked the dates, but the money had been taken before the potential of such a lucrative investment had been made known. Nicely laundered, maybe, but not stolen for the purpose.

And so they had knocked at Joy's door, in search of a purpose.

'Tell me about the American phone calls,' de Freitas began, the lack of need for refreshments established. 'We understand emails were also exchanged?'

'You'll have to ask Mandy, she didn't tell us a thing. We thought she was just making crank calls to Hollywood in the hope of getting through to some random film star!'

'Jack knows more about it,' Paul spoke up, 'he helped her with the project and she was telling him about the help she got from directors.' He corrected himself. 'Not directors, cinema…'

'Cinematographers,' Joy came to his aid. 'They're the ones who film it all.'

'And you're happy it was all above board? It could be easy to take advantage of a star-struck young girl desperate for a career in the industry.'

'Well they can't really take advantage of her down a phone line or by email!' Joy pointed out. 'And if they asked her for money, good luck in that!'

She realised at once what she'd said, for the first time making sense of the irrelevant questions.

'If she owes them money then it's nothing to do with us. She hasn't told us anything,' she protested.

'Look, officers,' Paul stepped in, 'they helped her and Tisha enough for them both to win a scholarship. We're not talking about famous actors or film directors or what-have-you – they're just cameramen who got asked about their work by a kid who's passionate about it. We saw it when we went to Jack's stables – people want to help youngsters if they're passionate about something. They must know she's just a school-kid with no money.'

De Freitas put a mental line through blackmail, online abuse clearly never even occurring to either parent, much less dealing with it.

'So tell me about your budget,' he asked instead. 'We're not seeing any sign of your wages being spent on shopping. In fact, you're adding to your savings, on a lower salary than you've been used to.'

'You think I'm shoplifting!' Joy said with horror, rising up out of the chair. 'I'll go get you the receipts! I've got them all, every one of them!'

'Please, Mrs Reid, that's not necessary, that's not at all what I'm suggesting. And we already have the receipts, in as much as the totals debited from your bank. My concern is with the decrease in spending.'

'They think you're topping up with cash,' Paul said, catching her hand and easing her back into the chair. 'The cash.'

Joy sank back into the armchair, deflated. 'Damned if you do, damned if you don't,' she said quietly, almost to herself.

'We've been going without, everything's been homemade, even biscuits,' Paul told the two detectives. 'Christmas was straight out of Dickens! Joy's been breaking her heart not to spend anything and have you lot banging on our door! It doesn't even look like we'll get a holiday. And now you tell us she's dropped herself in it by not spending money! Jesus Christ.'

'My apologies, but I have to ask; it's my job.' De Freitas smiled gently. 'Maybe we will have that tea after all. Sit back and I'll have DS McCulloch put the kettle on. Four teas?'

'I'll do them, milk and sugar?' Paul volunteered, standing up.

'No, let me,' McCulloch insisted firmly.

'Why not? You know where everything is,' Joy remarked ruefully, holding Paul's hand tightly, unwilling to let go.

'We desperately need to wrap this one up,' de Freitas said, as they climbed back into the car and McCulloch settled into the passenger seat.

'Her kitchen cupboards back up what she and the husband were saying,' McCulloch assured him. 'Everything about the Reids screams innocence.'

'Mmm…And yet the boy seemed alarmed by something. A complete turnaround in attitude toward me; as though he'd found the money under her bed.'

'Don't worry, we've looked under there more than once!' McCulloch reflected on his last visit to the Reids. 'You forget he's just a kid. To him, a couple of hundred is a lot of money. Maybe he saw something that he took to be expensive. The longer this drags out, the more the doubts creep in.'

'Mine certainly are. Instinct tells me they're all innocent; what little we have to go on tells me they're all guilty. But I do like your idea that Baxter and Fordham stole a depleted bundle of cash. The long-term dipping into a ready source of interest-free credit does rather fit the Wallis profile.' De Freitas frowned, considering. 'That would make her a damned good actress, mind you.'

'We'll just have to see what the afternoon brings.'

'Unless it brings a confession, we'll bring Wallis back in, too.'

CHAPTER 16

October

Derby favouritism was a fickle thing. It had, momentarily, rested with Grey Motive immediately after his Group Two Champagne Stakes win at Doncaster. As in his debut at Newbury, he had won without effort; not by any flashy wide margin, but with plenty in hand, a fact known only to his jockey.

Cozee Aribo had jumped down in the Doncaster winner's enclosure and quietly unsaddled the unflustered grey colt, her post-race debrief to Chris and Terry no more than three words.

'He's very special.'

It meant a lot. She had ridden some very good horses indeed.

She'd said almost as much at Newbury, but that had been against unknown opposition in a maiden race for inexperienced young horses. That afternoon at Doncaster Grey Motive's Derby-winning potential had been recognised by enough punters to see him top the ante-post betting market at fourteen to one.

Four weeks later his ante-post odds had remained unchanged, but were already twice that of the new Derby favourite, an impressive winner of the Group One Dewhurst Stakes. Ante-post betting on the Two Thousand Guineas saw both horses in single figures with, bizarrely as far as the stable was concerned, twelve to one offered on All Things Pass.

The latter's target was The Breeders' Cup Juvenile in America the following month and a sprinting career the following year. His narrow-margin win in the five furlong Group Two Flying Childers Stakes, the day before Grey Motive provided the stable double, had endorsed his precocity and speed, neither of which were credentials for the 'Guineas.

Jack thought of his Equine Anatomy and Physiology classes. It was easy to spot a precocious horse who was already fully grown at two and would not improve as a three-year-old, losing its earlier advantage over its peers. All Things Pass had just a small amount of room to grow. Grey Motive looked as though he wouldn't be fully grown until he was four, with a big frame still to fill. All Things Pass was small and stocky, built for speed, not stamina. Grey Motive was slender and gangly, built to comfortably gallop twice the distance that the muscular sprinters could manage.

He wondered how punters couldn't see that? What was the point of studying form and sectional race times if they then just ignored physique? If he was going to invest money with a bookmaker, he'd want to do his homework first.

He found the ever-changing ante-post betting incomprehensible, with Thingy-Bob rated on a par with Mo. It made no more sense than betting on races seven and eight months in the future, at odds no higher than fourteen to one. Of course, he'd been just as reckless himself, but the hundreds to one had made the risk a little more worthwhile.

And now his precious betting slip had become a real bargain, worth ten-times more than anyone else could currently get. If it wasn't for Mandy keeping it somewhere safe he would have taken it out daily just to look at it and work out all the maths involved in changing Mum's life. Maybe it was just as well Mandy hadn't let him have it; it might have faded or got so crumpled with the over-handling that it couldn't be read come May, the first of the big pay days.

Not that Mum needed the money anymore...

He hoped it still would change her life though, even if she probably had just as much money already, hidden somewhere or given to Nan and Grandad to keep the bailiffs away. At least, come May, she could start spending it all without worrying about the police, once she could prove to them it had come from a winning bet and not her shop.

He'd almost forgiven her for stealing the money; it was kind of an OK thing to do if it was to help Nan and Grandad. They were her mum and dad, after all, and maybe he'd do the same to help her, if he had to. But he wasn't so ready to forgive her the lies and deceit. Even if Nan and Grandad had sworn her to utter secrecy, it wasn't fair that she could tell Dad but not him and Mandy.

What lies had she told Nan and Grandad to explain away the money? They would rather have bailiffs taking everything than have a thief for a daughter, he felt sure. A thief and a liar...

* * *

'The Super wants a word with you,' McCulloch said as de Freitas settled down at his desk.

'That sounds ominous.'

'He did sound pretty ominous,' McCulloch agreed. 'I don't think it's for being five minutes late.'

'The jewellers, probably, and how did one of them manage to leave the country.'

'Surveillance's problem, surely?'

'Under my direction, don't forget. He's never really liked me.'

'There's a good reason for that.'

De Freitas looked surprised. 'Really? I've never given him any cause, surely?'

It was McCulloch's turn to look surprised. 'What can I say—do give up the day job?'

'Fill me in, then.'

'You're older and more experienced than he is.'

'Older? That's a trifle indelicate, Will – you mean to tell me no one here likes me?'

'Not so much your age as your position. We all know that at some point you must have turned down the offer of Chief Inspector. He sees that as a kick in the teeth. It's not that you don't respect him; you just don't respect his position. It's still a slur.'

De Freitas smiled. 'Oh, that old chestnut! Good to know you're on the ball, Will, even at a pre-coffee nine-o-five. Still, I'd better grace his office before the first cup of the day, I wouldn't want to rankle him still further.'

De Freitas couldn't help but feel he was on the wrong side of the interview desk as he sat down opposite his Superintendent. The summons had seemed more formal than usual and the carefully positioned paperwork laid out on the otherwise clear desk did indeed appear ominous.

There had been no hint as to what the summons might be about. A discussion on mandatory retirement and the pension situation had been de Freitas' immediate thought, until the heading "Brookhills Betting Office Theft" had caught his eye on one of the uppermost sheets of paper. Even so, there were plenty of other, as yet, unsolved cases on file, some a good deal less trivial than a forty-thousand pound theft.

It was the letter on British Horseracing Authority headed paper that gave de Freitas cause for concern, even though he wasn't able to see its content, obscured by other papers. He couldn't imagine what grounds for complaint he and

McCulloch had given the guardians of integrity and licensing, but suspected he might find out shortly.

'The Brookhills case,' the Superintendent began immediately, skipping niceties. 'One year on, and it would be fair to say that there are no leads or tangible evidence in this case, you would agree?'

'So far, yes, Sir,' de Freitas concurred.

'And yet you continue to invest work hours and documentation in what amounts to a relatively insignificant sum for which compensation has already been received, by way of insurance or accountancy write-off.'

'It was deemed a significant enough sum when we were called in,' de Freitas politely pointed out, 'but I would agree, Sir, that it has become insignificant in comparison to the impact on the suspects.'

'Ah, yes—the POI's.' He paused. 'I'll cut to the chase, de Freitas. I would be a lot happier if the case had been filed long ago and we were not continuing to waste the valuable time of Surveillance. However; the Brookhills CEO does not share my view, nor does he share your softly softly approach, which frankly is being taken to the extreme at this stage. The POIs don't view it as softly softly at all and I'm hearing the words "civil liberties" more than I would care to. I'm not at all happy.'

'Establishing innocence among the POIs is my priority, Sir.'

'The law already establishes innocence—your priority is to establish guilt beyond any reasonable doubt. As it stands, we have three major issues, none of which include the tracing of the money.

'Brookhills are left in the position of unwillingly employing a known thief and risk unfair dismissal suits if they don't.

'Your POIs, despite numerous and recent interviews, are surely not of interest, given the complete lack of evidence. How long into the future can you continue to call them in for spending their salary on impressing girlfriends or on mortgages for holiday homes? The word harassment will surely surface.'

The Superintendent paused once more; reading the face opposite him.

'None of which is of any concern or indeed fault of ourselves,' he acknowledged, continuing. 'We have, until now, been seen to have investigated this matter with due diligence.'

He pulled out the letter spotted earlier by de Freitas, along with the substantial documents accompanying it.

'This, however, states otherwise.'

He passed a single sheet across to de Freitas; although reading the letter, damning or otherwise, was clearly not going to have any effect on the pre-decided outcome of the meeting.

De Freitas read through the listing of owners registered for All Things Pass and Grey Motive.

'Is there a problem?' he asked calmly.

'I should say there is.'

A second sheet was passed across, the original cover letter.

De Freitas smiled at the ridiculousness of it. The BHA Director of Integrity had reported him to the Independent Office for Police Conduct.

'You requested information from the British Horseracing Authority about the possible laundering of money via a racehorse. A racehorse that you yourself happen to own shares in. If that isn't compromising your position then I don't know what is.'

'I was added to the list of owners purely to assist the case, Sir,' de Freitas pointed out. 'I have a very clear contract—no money has changed hands and nor will it. Far from a compromise, it was beneficial. We were able to identify a POI as a direct result.'

'A person no longer of interest,' the Superintendent reminded him.

'Nevertheless,' de Freitas said.

'Nevertheless, it can be seen as a conflict of interest and this Currid woman has involved the IOPC.' He pulled back the pages across the desk. 'I'll be frank with you, de Freitas – I suggest you take a few days holiday while this matter is dealt with further. I really don't want to see a member of my team suspended.'

De Freitas allowed himself a moment to think before he spoke, speaking with firmness when he did so.

'Respectfully, Sir, I would prefer not to. I'm confident the IO will give Ms Currid a slapped wrist for wasting their time and I'm not inclined to receive one unnecessarily in the meantime.'

The Superintendent betrayed nothing in his expression. He nodded acceptingly.

'At some point you may have to, but for now that's all; you may leave. But I would like to see that ownership contract. Email it to me, would you.'

De Freitas exchanged the more usual pleasantries as he rose to leave and returned to his colleagues in the busy office.

'Why won't they just spend the bloody money?!' he complained lightly to McCulloch.

'Not that Brookhills case again? What did he want?'

'One of them to pull up outside in a Porsche and hand themselves in! Preferably before Currid and her sidekick Desprez shut us down. You know she's only gone and reported us to the IOPC? Not us as such, but me in particular because my name is on her list of owners. I'm being investigated for a Conflict of Interest.'

'We discussed that at the time, it seemed pretty harmless then.'

'It still seems pretty harmless, I don't think the IO will be too concerned. You'd have thought she'd know better, given her background.'

'Just marking her territory,' McCulloch surmised.

'On the plus side, the Super credited us with doing everything else right and is inclined to draw a line under it, but for the BHA and the Brookhills CEO. So, yes, a Porsche parked in the Reid driveway would come in handy right now.'

'Not exactly a family car, though.'

'One each, Will, naturally.'

'What about the horse? Time to give up ownership?'

De Freitas shook his head. 'I rather like the involvement, actually. The Super wants a copy of the contract, but unless he instructs me otherwise I shall continue with it. He's running at Doncaster again on Saturday; the horse, that is, not the Super. We half considered going, but it's too long a drive for a daytrip. It's on the telly.'

'It makes you wonder why Currid and Desprez feel threatened? Discrediting us and elbowing you off the case? Our POI might well be involved after all and they know it. The BHA won't want a money laundering scandal.'

'There was a great deal of money made, but no opportunity until after the theft. I checked with Marsh, Grey Motive was just a bit of a long-shot still and they'd planned to turn the other horse around at the sales. And they hadn't made a significant amount on horses they kept to train themselves in the past. Any racehorse investment was an afterthought. What I'd like to know is what the first thought was.'

'Well, you know my thoughts. Murder On The Orient Express. They'd all been dipping in and using it as a payday loan.'

'The Brookhills CEO just wants to sack someone, he won't care whether it's one or all.' De Freitas, however, did care. He would happily arrest all involved in the theft, but his gut instinct told him that none of the suspects were guilty, however irrational that seemed. Certainly, McCulloch's assertion seemed much more plausible.

If only the grey motive surrounding the Brookhills case was as clear-cut as the Grey Motive he might be forced to relinquish his share in...

It was a funny thing, but being around the little grey horse just lifted his spirits, even on days when they were already high. He wondered if he would actually give up his part-ownership, as pseudo as it was, if the Super insisted upon it. It was a stupid thought to have, given that a year ago he'd had no interest in horses or sport. Relinquish Grey Motive or take an early retirement?

He placed a little bet with himself on the outcome of the Futurity Stakes.

* * *

Grey Motive walked around the familiar Doncaster parade ring, watching everyone and everything with quiet interest. He was favourite for the Group One Futurity Stakes, a traditional stepping-stone for prospective Derby colts, and had already earned Jack the one-hundred pound Best Turned Out prize, probably by dint of his remarkably full and beautiful tail. As hard as it was to get a gleam on a grey coat, everyone had a soft spot for 'rocking horse' greys, especially with such luscious silver-haired tails.

There were just seven other runners and none had the presence of Mo, in Jack's opinion. He had allowed himself a glance or two at the nearby opposition as he'd led Mo around the pre-parade ring, prior to being saddled. A couple were much bigger and more imposing in stature, but they lacked that indefinable 'class', as Chris called it. None had Mo's impeccable manners and relaxed disposition, with never a danger of him getting upset and losing the race before it had even been run. His energy was safely reserved for the race alone.

The bell rang to signal it was time for the jockeys to mount. Jack untucked the reins and pulled down the stirrup leathers in readiness for Cozee and continued to walk Mo round the ring. He saw Chris and Cozee waiting ahead for him, but didn't need to slow. They crossed in front of him, Cozee giving Mo's nose a quick rub in greeting, before Chris deftly legged her up into the saddle as they walked.

Some of the other horses began to jig-jog in anticipation, pulling hard to get out onto the track now they were united with their rider, but Mo's calm demeanour remained. He walked quietly beside Jack out onto the track and didn't break into a canter until Cozee asked him.

Chris had remained in the parade ring with the owners, to watch the race on the big screen and welcome back their horse, win or lose. Jack instead joined the other grooms on the viewing steps beside the track, ready to run out onto the track and greet their charges as soon as the race was over, leading them back in to be unsaddled and cooled off before returning to the racecourse stables.

As they stood together in tense silence, each waiting for their horse to arrive at the start and begin the loading process, Jack reflected on just how much was involved for just a minute and a half of competition. They had already walked the pre-parade and parade rings for twenty-five minutes; post-race would see them walking their horse once more to cool off and visit the veterinary sample box if required. Then back to the stables and a return three-hour trip in the horse box home, where all the diligent care and attention would continue. Cozee and the other jockeys were welcome to their minute-and-a-half of fame; although as fellow athletes they had just as much pre-race and post-race prep' as their equine partners.

Jack watched Mo load safely into the starting stalls and reflected on the six-weeks or so of preparation behind every race. Ultimately it all came down to a minute or two of a jockey's skill and the horse's mental and physical ability. Without his own work at home, Cozee's talent counted for nothing. Without her talent, all his hard work could be wasted. There were two athletes out there competing together as one, each fully dependent on the other.

Nevertheless, it would be Cozee alone at whom all fingers publicly pointed if anything went wrong. Not Mo, not Chris and Terry and certainly not him, who no one even knew.

He didn't envy Mai one little bit.

His train of thought was broken by the course commentator declaring "they're off!". He had been anxious after all, for all his positive confidence in Mo. There were so many variables, so many people and roles involved, so much to ensure all went right and so much to go wrong. What had he even been thinking of, convincing Mandy to put that bet on? If Mo wasn't good enough to win today, he was never going to be good enough to win a Classic...

He wished he had binoculars or a better view of the big screen. The commentator was calling Mo in second throughout, but he couldn't see how comfortably Mo was moving or whether Cozee was moving at all. The grooms alongside him were beginning to call for their horses as the runners thundered into full view toward them, easier to see now in the flesh than on the screen.

The shouts and screams and clicking of fingers were almost drowning out the excited commentary. The noise merged into a blur and Jack really didn't know if he was screaming for Mo or not, his lungs aching with the strength of getting the words out, while his ears denied their existence.

'COME ON MO!!' filled the air, somehow disconnected from his own voice, as the ground vibrated with the approaching horses. The hoof beats, slaps of the whips and shouts from the grandstand were now more deafening than the cries around him.

He could see Mo, right there on the far side rail; Cozee as still as a statue, her arms not moving, other than maintaining their position with the rhythm of Mo's stride. And Mo, his head forward, ears pricked, his stride long and easy and comfortable. Neither looked to be trying.

'MO!!! GO ON, MO!!!'

The whole race only took one minute and thirty-seven point nine-seconds to run, as the course commentator declared some moments later, announcing the result. They must have flashed past Jack in less than three-seconds, but it seemed to be in slow motion. Jockeys like Dessaint and the rest of Mai's idols pumping away with arms and legs, whips swinging, trying to get every last ounce from their straining mount. And Cozee motionless, Mo's ears still pricked.

They crossed the line just a length and a half to the good.

But it was how they crossed the line that would stay with Jack forever.

CHAPTER 17

March, Year Three

'I love the Cheltenham Festival,' Terry said, raising the eyebrows of those around him who knew him better. He smiled wryly. 'It means The Flat becomes the headline news, now it's over!'

He dropped The Racing Post onto the desk, folded open on a "Five to Follow" page. Grey Motive featured in four of the six pundits' choices, the two others disparaging about his narrow-margin wins and opting instead for an alternative Classic potential. One of the more favourable pundits even voiced hopes of a Triple Crown challenge for their unbeaten colt.

'We'll be needing to organise a media day,' Anne said, 'best ask Nicky Taylor what he does; doesn't he always have one every year ahead of Cheltenham? I suppose we just give them all tea and biscuits and photo-shoot time.'

'Do we mention the Triple Crown?' Chris pondered.

'Why not? It'll create a bit of buzz and debate,' Anne agreed.

'Or jinx it,' Terry countered. 'Wait 'til we've at least won the Guineas first. Or after The Derby, if the dream's still alive by then.'

'"Too soon to say, but wouldn't it be great for racing if we had a horse we could really dream about?"' Anne said in a mock quote. 'That would work, should one of them ask the question. Without jinxing him.'

'He's jinxed already,' Terry conceded. 'First grey to win since the 1940s, first Triple Crown attempt in living memory, first woman to win a Triple Crown if we can keep Cozee on him, first dual-licence trainers, the list goes on and on. There's way too much against him.'

'The odds are stacked in his favour,' Su argued. 'It's way overdue, he'll redress the balance in one foul swoop!'

'Send him to Seb Churchill in Newmarket and retain Dessaint to ride him and suddenly the media won't hear of him being beat,' Anne pointed out. 'We're the only negatives, not Cozee or his colour or history, and we know we're well capable. The only actual dangers are whoever lines up against him and we've seen no one to be scared of yet. There's no talking horse in Newmarket and he's got to be better than the Dewhurst winner.'

'The old guv'nor always knew when he had a Guineas or Derby horse. They were never jinxed by his confidence, he was bullish about them months in advance,' Chris agreed. 'We knew a year ago he was special. Cozee says he's special. Most of the press think he's special. All we have to do is keep him alive!'

'I'm going out to check on him,' Terry said pointedly.

Anne made a start on the office work, as Chris finished his morning coffee and prepared for the yard work. Half-term meant no students to worry about.

'Hmm, the BHA,' she said aloud, as she picked up an incoming envelope. The ruling body usually just emailed information or included it within The Racing Calendar.

Chris paused to await news on the contents.

'You may sit down again or just head on out,' Anne advised, pulling a fairly thick missive from the envelope, 'this one looks like it'll take a lot of reading.'

He grinned. 'In that case, I'll leave you to it!'

* * *

'You expect me to read all that?!' Joy complained, as Mandy handed her the bursary paperwork in readiness for the new year ahead.

'It's nothing to do with you, you just need to keep it safe somewhere.'

Joy reflected on the peace and freedom they'd enjoyed in the absence of their eldest, now shattered by her return for the half-term break. The small blessing was that even though Jack had become an early bird, Mandy was rarely up before lunch, thus narrowing the time for rows. Although so far the pair had been getting on miraculously well. Maybe university had done Mandy some good. The racing education programme had definitely marked a big improvement in Jack.

Joy wondered when her turn would come. What exciting new career path would fall into her lap to bring cheer and enthusiasm for a bright new future? She and Paul had thought about a fresh start, everyone did; but it was always a case of better the devil you know.

Until the theft, she had enjoyed her job. She liked Maud and the regular customers and even Madam, when she relaxed for a gossip and forgot to play at Boss. It had been a nice place to work, a nice atmosphere, friendly, the sports to watch all day, a bit of banter, the odd bit of excitement. Respect.

Everyone envied the Precinct staff. They'd been together for ten years or more, left alone to run their watertight ship. Anita was a legend. The hours were envied, too. No late nights or Sundays...

Brookhills wasn't the same elsewhere. Joy hated the weekend work and the evening shifts. It wasn't as if she could do much with her morning, on the days she worked late, it just meant her day was longer and she saw less of Paul. And maybe they had all forgotten about the theft, but she still felt the suspicion. They didn't trust her and there was certainly no respect. Even the banter with the customers was reserved for the regular staff. She was still the "new woman" and not to be trusted with personal gossip.

As Jack might say, it sucked. And he did say it, regularly, as he moped about the house for the holidays. He'd asked about getting a lift to the stables and had even looked into buses and taxis, which "hardly cost anything, god! Other people get more than that in pocket money!"

Bully for him, that life at work was better than here at home!

If only.

She had looked at job vacancies. She was really only qualified for cashiering and couldn't face sitting at a supermarket till all day. The Brookhills HR department had made it pretty clear she wouldn't get a reference, either. They weren't allowed to give a bad one, but not obliged to give one at all. A lack of reference pretty much spoke for itself.

She wished she'd taken up Paul on his offer of a few days away, just the two of them. The police had been right, they had managed to save a bit. But when she realised it was safe to spend money, she'd quickly fallen back into her old routine. No chance of a few days away now. Unless you counted Newmarket in May.

The four of them were already booked into a family room in the budget chain hotel for two nights, which apparently Jack and Mandy were paying for as a treat. She wasn't an idiot; that horse of Jack's, Grey Motive, was the one paying for it and it would be Paul's credit card to the rescue if the damned thing lost. She'd seen all the excitement when it had won last October and had seen the ante-post prices flying out the door at work. Fourteens down to tens down to seven to one. Jack and Mandy must have had at least a tenner on to pay for the hotel, the little monkeys.

The loss of a tenner would teach them a lesson. And maybe she and Paul had earned the right to two nights in a hotel. With the kids sharing...

Jack was right, life sucked.

* * *

'So, like, it was like this speed-dating thing, right, and the screenwriting students were all sat there at these tables and us and the directing students had like five minutes with each, going from table to table, right, until the bell rang then you had to move on and we listened to their pitch and then, right, we chose which project and we had to write down on a card our first three project choices in order of choice and the directors as well and then if no one else had your project you got it and if more than one had it you got to sit with the writer again and they got to choose who'd shoot it and who'd direct and then you got your second or third choice, right, so, like, Tisha really *really* wanted to do this thing about Syrian rappers, but so did Baxter and Ivana, so she had to go back, right, and the writer chose Baxter, cos like he's massively hot, that's what Tisha reckons, so like anyway she got her third choice of the community farm project, which she really wanted to do anyway, so then I'm thinking I ONLY want to do the Dignitas thing, it just sounds so good and maybe you might actually get to go to Switzerland and everything, I mean, Switzerland, can you imagine, and I sooo didn't want my second or third choice, even though I'd put them down, like, but then Conor our tutor just says I've got the Dignitas gig and I guess the subject's a bit of a downer really and no one else wanted it, but I'm so psyched to get it, it sounds so cool!'

Jack had got lost round about the third "right", as Mandy told them over dinner about her end-of-year project, and he had no idea what Dignitas was and what Switzerland had to do with anything, but Mum and Dad were as excited as Mandy and hanging on her every word; and it was kind of impressive that his sister was going to shoot a short film that would get produced and everything.

'Are the Dignitas Games in Switzerland this year, then?' Dad asked, thankfully enlightening him.

Judging by the expressions on Mum and Mandy's face, maybe Dad was a bit wide of the mark.

'The what now?' said Mandy.

'You're thinking of those other ones, the Invictus!' Mum laughed.

'OMG! You've got no idea, have you?!' Mandy complained. 'Dignitas – assisted dying? End of life choice. Euthanasia. In Switzerland.'

'Christ, Mands, that's a bit grim, isn't it?' Dad said. 'No wonder no one else wanted it!'

'It's good,' Mum said defensively, 'one of them emotive programmes that get you thinking. That's what you like, isn't it, real stories about real people, like Mr Haydary at the shop. You should ask Jack's teachers if you can go film at the stables, that'd make a good story, too.'

'I just shoot films, Mum, I don't write them or get to choose. Other than choosing an end-of-year project to work on, but that's different. Anyway, I don't wanna hang around filming him all day!'

She pulled a face at Jack, which he ignored. He'd given up trying to perfect a smirk or a sneer, mainly because either way they just looked like he had some sort of facial twitch and besides which, he no longer really needed to smirk or sneer.

Everyone at Sainte Bastien was sound and even Mandy had stopped winding him up, most of the time.

Mandy had used up all her table talk in one humongous sentence and Dad was busy putting away Mum's shepherd's pie like he hadn't eaten in six months and suddenly all was quiet for a while.

Jack tapped his phone, lying politely on mute alongside his plate, and saw he had messages from Mai and Grant. He opened the first, 'wtf ' from Grant, then read Mai's row of exclamation marks, hearing in his head her best impersonation of his over-excited sister.

'Have you seen The RP!!!'

He'd seen it that morning, The Racing Post his homepage on the browser, but Mo hadn't got a mention. The little grey had been figuring quite highly in their features in recent days. He'd checked back in at lunchtime for latest news, but it was all the same and mostly betting guides. Maybe Chris and Terry had announced that media day they'd been planning.

He saw Mum staring at him sternly, daring him to use the phone.

'I was only checking messages, I wasn't gonna reply!'

'And mind you don't, you shouldn't even have it at the table.'

'Mai says there's something in The Racing Post.'

He opened the browser and immediately regretted it.

'NO!' he cried out, unable to contain his emotion.

Dinner, for him, was over. And right then it felt like life was, too.

"Favourite Grey Motive ruled out of Guineas" read the latest headline.

* * *

De Freitas had spent a pleasant enough day with his wife at her sister's in Windsor, his phone on silent and safely at home. The office knew how to get hold of him if it was urgent enough and everyone else of importance to him was present in person. They'd taken a boat out on the river and enjoyed a picnic and spoken in praise of the mild spring weather and lack of rain.

Back home and waiting on the kettle to boil, he checked his messages and was surprised to see several missed calls from Chris, the single text message saying simply, 'please ring, we need your help.'

He looked at his watch, aware it was getting late for habitual early risers.

'I'd better give him a call,' he apologised to his wife.

'Is it work?'

He considered the wording of the text. 'I rather think it might be.'

A few minutes later and he and his wife were climbing back in the car, this time headed for Lambourn. Given the circumstances, there had been little he could do over the phone.

His unerring instinct triumphed again, his wife's presence a soothing balm to ease a fraught atmosphere as Anne and Chris welcomed them into their home. Feeling helpless and full of doubt that de Freitas could be of any use, Su and Terry had already gone home.

'Show me the letter and their grounds for suspending the ownership,' de Freitas asked, as they settled around the large table in the kitchen.

Anne wordlessly pushed across the letter she had received that morning; a lifetime ago. There were no words.

Chris had made a hash of it, trying to tell de Freitas over the phone, and it had been Currid, as Head of Integrity and Regulations at the BHA, who had supplied the official press release. Journalists were left to puzzle over its meaning and question the legality of Ownership head Desprez's statements within it; and the Sainte Bastien phones had been hopping as a result.

De Freitas read through every page in silence and took a moment to mull it over. He passed it over to his wife. Her non-legal, non-equestrian mind might see something they hadn't.

'Have you lawyers?' he asked Anne and Chris.

'We have... but the BHA writes its own Rules.'

'Treated as guilty until you can prove your innocence,' Anne added. 'We've the complete opposite to "beyond reasonable doubt". Ours is if there's the slightest hint of wrongdoing, out the door.'

'That may be so,' Mrs de Freitas reasoned, 'but they point out their own department is completely satisfied there have been no irregularities.'

'They state quite categorically that the ownership licence is currently under investigation,' de Freitas said. 'I'm afraid that although their own department is satisfied, they have the right to suspend the licence until all investigations are complete. The horse is banned from competing in the meantime.'

'Lesley, if the Ownership Department and the Integrity Department are satisfied, who exactly is carrying out the investigation?'

All eyes turned somewhat accusingly to de Freitas.

'It most certainly isn't us!' he protested. 'But if Currid and Desprez are suggesting it's us, then I'm going in with a warrant!'

'You must find out, Lesley! Because the minute the investigation is dropped, the licence can be re-instated. And why is your horse banned? Can you not simply transfer ownership? Lease him to someone else?'

'They're treating him as a potential criminal asset,' Anne explained. 'We tried that immediately, just asked to remove the offending name from the ownership, but they won't give us a name and all assets are frozen. He can't be sold, leased or removed from the yard. And without a licensed owner, he can't race.'

'The Weatherbys account is frozen, so we're not even getting paid, even if he could race! We hold the account for the syndicate, and any bills and entry fees or prize money and training fees that should be going in and out aren't!' Chris told them both. 'The horse isn't allowed to leave the yard and we're the ones supplying bed and board to an owner who isn't allowed to pay for it!'

'Desprez even wanted his entries voided!' Anne said, disbelief still edged in her voice. 'The Trainers Federation came to our aid and have won a temporary stay on that one. The Classic entries were made before he had even entered training or been bought by the current owners and they can't be re-made, even if the ownership licence is approved once more. Of course, he can be supplemented at a late stage, at a significant cost, so there is still every danger Desprez will raise that argument and void his entries.'

'Are the shareholders no longer paying?' de Freitas checked. He could foresee a future problem for Chris and Terry in securing back payments, if and when the problem was resolved.

Chris shook his head. 'No, we're OK there, the share price covered the cost of training fees up front. But Currid and her cronies never even considered that. We're feeding and caring for a horse who isn't allowed to earn his keep. Which isn't the point—the Classics are the point! One shot, that's all, and they've taken it from him. From us. We'll never get another horse like him again.'

Mrs de Freitas looked at her husband. 'Find out who is responsible for the investigation and get it stopped.'

* * *

'We can't go anywhere near this,' McCulloch warned de Freitas, as they sat together over a coffee. Officially they were sitting in traffic en route back from court, but letting the traffic jam abate while in the comfort of a café made more sense.

'I could hardly tell my wife that, with the Marshes looking on. To say their future is at stake is an understatement. The last Triple Crown winner was getting on for a hundred years ago, only one horse has ever tried since. This is a one-off, once in a lifetime.'

'You were under investigation by the IOPC. Imagine how that will look if you call off any investigation into the same horse! And the Super's not exactly going to tell you who and why, even if it is internal. It could be Brookhills' insurance investigators, for all we know.'

'The same horse?' de Freitas frowned. 'But it's not the same horse, is it?'

'The one everyone's backed for The Derby?'

'Yes! But who did we link Fordham to at that open day?'

McCulloch nodded slowly. 'The brown one they sold for a massive profit. So he's no longer linked to any horse, least of all your one.' He drank some coffee. 'Unless he reinvested.'

'No; we're in a group chat, I don't see his name or Heidi Jones appearing.'

'GDPR,' McCulloch reminded him. 'Good old Data Protection. Only those who agreed to join the group chat are in it. How old are you all? What do you use it for, arranging drinks after stable visits?'

'Good point, Will. The actual alerts and updates are to me personally.' De Freitas smiled ruefully. 'And you're right, no young person would want to join our group.'

'He could be in under his own name this time. And definitely using cash, because nothing's showing through his bank.'

'I'll ask Marsh. We were chatting about their children, so it won't seem like business.'

'Does he know about the IOPC?'

'I would imagine so, if they did their job thoroughly.'

'So you haven't actually mentioned it yourself?'

It was true; for all his mild indignation at the weak accusation of any conflict of interest, he had been embarrassed. Technically he hadn't been suspended; in his absence there had been no need. But a November cruise in Norway hadn't only been about the sudden whim to see the Northern Lights.

'I didn't mention it, no. If you're aware you're at risk of saying the wrong thing, then you're much more likely to do so. Marsh and Jones would have responded in all innocence and there was no case to answer.'

'If they're aware of the IOPC, surely they must be suspicious that's the source of any investigation? It couldn't still be, could it?'

De Freitas considered it. 'They were only looking into my own conflict of interest. Done and dusted.'

'Unless it isn't.'

'Seriously? It's a Yes/No question—have I compromised the case investigation. Why would it need to go any further?'

'If Marsh, or particularly Jones, didn't say the right thing. If they believed the IO were investigating them, or Heidi Jones and Fordham, and not you at all?'

'Would the IO even care? They're investigating us, not our case.'

McCulloch tilted his head thoughtfully. 'But what did the IOPC report back to Currid and Desprez? If we were still under investigation, would we know?'

'It would have to be particularly serious to be covert.'

'If established, a conflict of interest is particularly serious. As is the no small point Surveillance could be on our tails as we speak. Instead of heavy traffic as reported, heavy butter on that scone.' McCulloch glanced around the café. 'An intern we wouldn't recognise, such as her, in the window.'

'The window is the perfect spot, but isn't she a tad old for an intern?'

'Haven't you heard of the Actively Retired?!'

De Freitas smiled. 'From Paignton to cruises, I'd be asking questions if I were on the case!'

'In your defence, it's hard to see the Northern Lights from Devon.'

'And harder still to find a destination in November that doesn't involve airports. There's not a lot to do in Paignton in November.'

McCulloch grinned, but de Freitas pre-empted the retort. 'Don't even think about it, Will!'

* * *

'And you think that would work?' Mai said sarcastically as she sat beside Jack, Grant knelt up on the seat in front so he could hang over the back of his seat to join in.

There had been a heavy atmosphere of despondency on the school bus that morning, despite it being first day back in the stables. Jack, however, was determined to lift it.

'Technically,' Grant disagreed. 'If the right documents were left out, his sister could easily zoom in and film them while filming us.'

'Never mind the really big "if" there, why is the BHA even going to accept us on a visit? They know where we're from!'

'They can't refuse us!' Jack insisted. 'Not a class visit with Mandy filming us, then, but what about work placement? We have to do a work placement before the end of term and seeing as how they're the ones responsible, they have to let us do it with them. We can just infiltrate the office and find out all the stuff we need to.' He could see the many benefits unfolding, even as he spoke. 'Whoever finds the suspension form could shred it, by accident!'

'Or delete the only backup copy off the computer using the special password,' suggested Grant.

Jack recognised sarcasm when he heard it, but chose to ignore it. 'Until we're there, you don't know what could be possible! Just cos that Currid knows who we are, doesn't mean anyone else there does! They must get millions of kids coming in.'

'At least work placement gives us a week to nose about,' Mai conceded, 'and "infiltrate"! Even if they do know, they can't watch us every minute, not all of us.'

'You wanted to shadow Cozee Aribo,' Jack remembered, suddenly guilty at standing between Mai and her life's ambition.

'So? Grant wanted to shadow Sebastian Churchill's horse box driver. It's only a week, Mo's more important.'

'They'll probably let us do a proper placement later anyway, if we ask,' Grant assured them. 'No one really knows anything, I bunked off school for a week and worked with Dad in the showroom and he even signed some fake form I made up on the office computer! AND my form tutor accepted the form!'

'It's settled, then,' Mai decided, 'we'll ask and we'll infiltrate!'

They arrived off the bus in better humour, but were soon brought back down by the rest of the team. Even the horses seemed quieter than usual, sad even, as Jack noted. He tried to put on a brave face and whistled cheerfully, hoping the horses couldn't see into his soul.

Somehow he knew this was all Mum's fault.

If she'd only told him she was guilty he would never have asked Les de Freitas for help. And now de Freitas had set the BHA on them and maybe the only way to save Mo's career was to ruin Mum...

CHAPTER 18

April

Mum always said the worst that could happen was they could only say no. But the worst had already happened and still they said no. Worse than that, they'd said yes. The whole Sainte Bastien class was booked into unwanted work placements at the BHA sometime at the end of May, while some other stupid students who prob'ly didn't even want to be there were getting to have the run of the place now, when they needed it.

Grant had said they should just turn up anyway, 'they won't know one kid from another and I bet they don't know how many they're meant to have anyway.' The simple logistics and train fares had put paid to that.

Which left them all helpless, drifting around the stable-yard without enthusiasm, the afternoon's lessons barely holding their attention. As Chris and Terry reminded them, there were other horses in the yard, other races to dream of, and Mo had a four-year-old career to come, even if he missed this season.

'It's a big lesson to learn and better now than later,' Chris told them, as they finished up the yard work. Some sort of pep talk was needed, even if he didn't have the heart for it himself. 'Horses break your heart. Racing has highs and lows, with more lows than highs, you just have to ride out the lows and enjoy the highs. This is your first major disappointment, but it won't be your last.'

As pep talks go, he realised it was one of the worst. The row of faces, if anything, looked even more crestfallen.

'It's only the Guineas,' he said, more cheerfully than he felt. 'The Triple Crown was never more than a pipe dream, but he might still make it to The Derby, the Arc, who knows?'

'It's just the way he can't run that's so sucky, not because it's his fault or anything normal,' Grant complained.

'It'd be more sucky to go out to the paddock and find him injured so he'll never race again! Or suckier if any of you got hurt and couldn't follow your dream! Come on, guys, no one's died! Mo's alive and well and ready to run the minute he's allowed to again!'

Maybe he imagined it, but Chris felt the despondent faces had begun to look a little more hopeful. If only he could say the same. The ban on Grey Motive would always haunt him, always tarnish the lustre of any achievements that lay ahead. A Derby and St Leger win would forever be clouded by what might have been. In fact, without a Triple Crown at stake, would it even be worth running in the St Leger if Mo won The Derby? Far better to aim for the Arc instead... unless the BHA ruled out his whole season.

He watched the students disperse, headed for the classroom. While there were worse problems out there, his own was the only one that mattered to him right now.

He was aware of Jack lingering beside him, not yet ready for maths. The boy looked to have problems of his own and Chris gave him the space to talk. It wasn't used.

'Between you and me, we've not ruled out the Guineas,' Chris said, after time. 'One of Mo's part-owners is a policeman. There's a chance he can get this put to bed long before May.'

Jack's anxiety seemed to increase, if anything.

'How do you and Terry ride out the lows?' Jack asked. 'Like... how can you ever get past them, when they're always there? How can the highs still be highs?'

Chris thought of Anne's concerns and suspected the boy's lows weren't only connected to Grey Motive.

'Shall we go and get a cup of tea? They won't miss you in maths.'

'No; it's OK. I just wondered, is all.'

'Well, I could use a chat even if you can't,' Chris pressed, 'we'll both play hooky for a bit!'

Jack hesitated. He'd thought of what he'd wanted to say, but then it had just seemed a bit pointless. Missing maths seemed pointless, too, but he didn't often get Chris or Terry to himself. He and Mai loved hearing their stories of when they raced and were apprentices. He came to a decision and nodded, walking with Chris to the house and into the kitchen.

'Orange? Cola? Milk? Tea?' Chris offered, standing at the fridge and surveying the contents.

'Orange, thanks.'

Chris put the coffee-maker on and tossed a chocolate biscuit bar onto the table in front of Jack. Jack unwrapped it and made a start.

After a mouthful, he asked, 'When you said you just ride out the lows, how do you? How do you make them go away?'

Chris sat down with his coffee and considered the question. And his answer.

'You don't,' he said, finally. 'You can't. They never go away. You just have to learn to accept that. You learn to live with it and move forward.'

Jack thought of Mum and the money.

'What if it won't let you move forward? It's just always there, waiting for you?'

'And you can't learn to live with it?' Chris shook his head. 'You just have to. You have to get used to it always being there. You can't give in and let it grind you down.'

Mum had. She'd stopped going out and just hid away, cooking and cleaning. Even going back to work didn't help. She never came in and talked about the people at work and things that'd happened. Him and Mandy and Dad always did. He knew Maud and Rhys and Madam, Ann or something? Anita. He knew their names. And old Vinnie with his coin purse and that one who fetched in cakes every time he won. But he didn't know anyone Mum worked with now.

And what she was and what she'd done would never go away.

'I killed someone once, out on the racecourse; an apprentice, not much older than you.'

Jack had been lost in his own thoughts, but looked up immediately in disbelief at Chris, the last bit of chocolate bar halted temporarily on its passage to his mouth.

'It was a fall, in a race. He went down in front of me. Nothing I could do to avoid him. His horse was on the floor and he was down beside it, out cold already, and I had the choice of trying to jump one or the other. One of those split-second decisions you call wrong and have to live with for the rest of your life.'

Chris took a sip of coffee and set the small cup carefully back down, turning it to get the handle just so, before continuing.

'My filly called it for me, really; she shied away from his horse. She reacted and I didn't. Or I reacted too late. Or I made the wrong call. I've gone back over it, over and over again. I still keep thinking, maybe if I'd done this, maybe if I'd done that...

'The reality is, it happened and there's nothing I can do about it. I was told it wasn't my fault; but I feel it was, I'll always feel that. I live with it every day. But the thing is, when we got that letter from the BHA, that memory didn't make it any less bad. And when our twins were born, it didn't stop it being just the best moment ever. Trudie's graduating in June and I'm just so excited and proud. And Lucy's on a fantastic course in Ireland, at the National Stud there, and I couldn't be prouder or more chuffed for her.

'I relive that race every single day, it will never ever leave me; but life just keeps going and the good things still feel good and the bad things still hurt. You don't have to learn to cope, you just have to continue. Just get up every morning and live.'

Jack nodded slowly, digesting every word. Chris was right, he didn't need to learn how to wake up and just do stuff.

'The BHA banning Grey Motive? It's nothing in the scheme of things, don't let it haunt you and eat you up. It's not life or death, no one died. Anything bad, learn from it and move on.' Chris smiled, every line on his face joining in. 'Do you know what else, Jack?

'It's not Fate or anything, unless you believe in some guiding hand, but had that race never happened, had I not called it wrong, who knows, we wouldn't be sitting here now. Twenty years later and this place got left to the BHA because of that race, that death. No one left to inherit, but so many people left to benefit.

'But for a really bad thing, something really good might never have happened.'

Chris had often reflected on that, maybe in Fate truly steering his path. No one at the BHA had even remembered the fatality or were aware he had ridden in the same race. It hadn't made any difference; except to him, personally. Not really redemption; just... just something. Something to take the sting out of the perpetual "if only...".

Jack allowed the remaining bar to reach his lips and chewed it thoughtfully.

'I don't think Mr de Freitas will help us,' he admitted. 'I'm really sorry, Chris, but I think I got us into big trouble. It's Mr de Freitas and me who got Mo investigated.'

* * *

Jack hadn't really minded missing yesterday's maths, but missing the morning's practical sessions made him as uncomfortable as the reason for his absence. He sat now in the Sainte Bastien House sitting room, a place he had only been in once, when first introduced to the stables.

It still felt like a less clean and tidy museum or stately home. Everything was old and a bit grand, but tired and lived in. It had the atmosphere of the headmaster's office, for all its homeliness; he didn't fit in and didn't want to be there.

Chris had been good about it and had taken the news surprisingly well. And yet here they were this morning, facing the police. There was no pretending he hadn't seen this coming; a restless night had dwelt on the what ifs and maybes. But mostly it had been his own conscience and loyalties, arguing away between themselves. What if he told the police? Supposing he went to the BHA? Mum's future or Mo's? Tussles that he could choose to ignore or think about later.

Arriving in the yard that morning, all freedom of choice had been unexpectedly removed from him. Instead of just accepting that he may have been responsible, Chris had dobbed him in and sent him to their own equivalent of the headmaster's office. He couldn't really blame him; and the way Chris and de Freitas were talking to him, it was like they were trying to help, not reprimand him.

'Can you tell me what you told Chris yesterday?' de Freitas asked gently.

Jack really didn't want to, but withholding evidence and perverting the course of justice made him just as guilty as Mum. He'd seen enough TV to know that much. All he could do was tell the truth. It was only what Mum should've done in the first place.

'When I asked you to help and investigate it, I didn't know my mum had taken the money.'

'And what makes you think she has, Jack?'

'She told my dad. I heard her tell my dad and he didn't seem surprised and he told her it would be alright, not to be scared, and they didn't know I heard them. They had a big argument about it at first, but then my dad was OK about it.'

'Your mum actually told your dad that she had taken the money?'

Jack nodded.

'And do you have any idea why she may have taken it?'

'She didn't tell my dad, but I think it was to help my nan and granddad, in case bailiffs took away their stuff. I think they're in trouble and my mum helped them.'

'What makes you think that, Jack?'

He shrugged. 'They pretended to have a clear out, but all the things they really liked they gave to my sister Mandy and me, so the bailiffs wouldn't take it.'

All the while, the other policeman, the one who'd been to their house, had been tapping away at a tablet, and he now showed it to de Freitas.

'Your grandparents aren't in any trouble, Jack. Do you think you could be mistaken about the bailiffs?'

Jack shrugged again. He felt nervous and was anxious about the consequences of not answering the questions correctly. 'Well, I was only guessing, like. I don't really know why my mum needs money, my dad said they'd needed it loads've times before but she'd never stolen any then.'

De Freitas glanced at McCulloch. The money-lending theory suddenly sounded more promising. Several small payday loans accumulating to breaking point. But where was the trail? They'd gone over it enough times, for each of the suspects, to no avail.

'For a caravan, maybe? My mum's always wanted a caravan,' Jack suggested, having thought hard. He felt a little more confident now. 'My mum says we can't save up for it anymore, because when my dad writes a cheque you'll arrest him.' He thought of the caravan money entrusted to Mo, who might have been their saviour but for him blabbing to de Freitas. And now here he was, blabbing again.

'Look, Jack, we're all anxious about Mo and this suspension,' de Freitas said gently. 'You have been incredibly honest with us and we really appreciate that.'

That incredible honesty was part of the problem, de Freitas reflected. The Reids were a good family, Joy and her husband intrinsically honest, which showed in their children. Years of experience and trusted instinct told de Freitas that, whatever Jack told him now. This revelation made no sense.

They went over it formally, though, McCulloch noting every detail and Jack signing it as accurate.

'Are you going to arrest my mum?'

De Freitas shook his head. 'Not for the moment, no. We'll just let Will, here, concentrate on resolving the BHA issue first. I've a vested interest, so my hands are tied.'

'But if my mum tells you where the money is, the BHA won't have to investigate Mo anymore!'

De Freitas leaned forward thoughtfully. 'It's not quite that simple. They're investigating the ownership licence, not the theft. They want to be assured there's no criminal activity linked with Mo.' He paused. 'I think the investigation might be one involving me. I'm linked to both the case and the horse, you see. So for the moment, we just need Will to quash that BHA ban. One step at a time.'

Jack wasn't so sure. If Mum handed herself in and gave back all the money, how could there still be any criminal link to Mo? Unless they counted his bet? He and Mandy were too young to be gambling and maybe they'd say the bet was Mum's, from stolen money? But they'd need to find out about it first, though.

The talk had come to an end and the two policemen asked Chris for a minute or two alone. Jack was relieved to escape back to the yard, particularly when Chris apologised to him as they left the house. Like him, Chris had hoped de Freitas might help and that having an actual guilty party might see Mo reinstated, but they had both been wrong.

'Do you think he's lying, just to protect the horse?' McCulloch asked de Freitas, as they sat alone in the house.

'I think he believes what he's told us.'

'But you don't?'

'I'm not so sure. For a first-time criminal opportunist, Reid is managing to cover her tracks remarkably well.' He sighed wearily. 'They all are. What are we missing?'

'No stone unturned, it's hard to imagine. But if neither of the Reids crack this time, I'll agree Joy is definitely off the list.'

* * *

A betting office was an environment of calms and storms. Sporadically, customers would rush to place last-minute bets as a race went off and queues at the pay-out window would quickly follow. Then came the lulls.

Unlike any other office, there were no personal phone calls or visits. The lulls were too unpredictable and the sudden rush too demanding. So the arrival of a smartly-dressed woman looking to speak to Joy Reid raised immediate alarm bells.

Like her colleagues, Joy feared the worst, her first thought of Mandy, all by herself in the middle of London. The disruption of being left one cashier short never once crossed her mind as the woman flashed an official ID and asked her to gather her things and step outside. At which point she realised that it wasn't Mandy who worked in a dangerous environment.

'It's Jack, isn't it? What's happened? Oh, god! Paul! There's been an accident!'

The plain clothes officer assured her everyone was safe, but requested her presence at the police station. Joy's heart sank. An accident suddenly sounded more appealing.

She sat silently in the back of an unmarked car, the concerns she had once taken for granted furthest now from her mind. There might have been a time when she would have refused to leave her colleagues one short and would have fretted about how they would cope. Right now, she didn't give a damn.

This was it. They'd found whatever evidence was needed to tie her to the theft. A one-way ride. Because she was the only one who needed money. Because money goes to money and Rhys or Anita knew what it was like to have it and couldn't get enough of it. Maud had more than enough and couldn't get rid of it. Gareth had just helped himself and screamed thief.

She was going to serve time for someone else's crime and no one would care except Paul and the kids and her mum and dad, who'd be so humiliated.

Her mind raced, her heart pounded and she felt a sudden rush of fear as she entered the station and was shown to an interview room. She had thought she had resigned herself to this, accepting her fate as just one more cross to bear until it was all over. But now it was actually happening she felt nothing but panic.

It wasn't either of the detectives she knew. The two men introduced themselves but it was a pointless exercise; she couldn't remember her own name, never mind theirs. Did she want her lawyer present? Why? Could he answer on her behalf, did he know anything she didn't?

'No,' she said, more calmly than she felt. 'I've done nothing wrong. I don't need a lawyer.' Oh god.

The questions were always bewildering. Trying to explain how you didn't do something you hadn't done was just repetitive and futile. It was wrong to point an accusing finger elsewhere, but maybe if they hadn't thought about it or searched...

'You did pull the shop apart, that morning?' she checked. 'All of us have always had the same opportunity, but we've never once touched any money. Gareth is the only odd one out, he could've hidden it, then screamed theft, then gone back for it later.' Oh god, listen to herself, desperately throwing someone else to the lions so she could run away.

'We did, Mrs Reid. And Mr Rogers has been equally under surveillance.'

And then came the question—or was it a statement?—that made her laugh.

'A witness has come forward stating you were heard admitting to the theft.'

It was ridiculous, of course it was, but to actually laugh? Was she losing it altogether? What must they be thinking? The Mafia Godfather would laugh in the face of the police, not a mother, not an innocent mother and cashier who'd been pinning up newspapers to a wall as the world shattered. It was nerves. Nerves. She knew that now, but couldn't stop laughing. Heard admitting to a crime she had never stopped denying!

She'd thrown Gareth to the lions to try to get her own life back. Now someone had done it to her. Only better.

Someone had an arm around her shoulder and was offering her a box of tissues. She realised she was no longer laughing. She wasn't sure when or how, but great choking sobs had taken over. Maybe she'd been crying from the start? You have to laugh or else you cry... Laughing hadn't helped any more than being innocent. Innocent 'til proved guilty. That was something to laugh at, alright. Was she thinking or talking?

'Paul?'

She hadn't been aware of voices or of the owner of the comforting arm; but she was suddenly aware of Paul's voice and of his unmistakable arms around her. Her eyes were too wet to see and she really needed to wipe her soaked and sticky face, but she was holding him so tight and didn't want to let go.

'They fetched you off the bus?! Jeez, I must've been in some state!'

Joy sat alone with Paul in the interview room, a tray of tea and biscuits in front of them; Joy's mind in a turmoil as she wondered how long she'd been sobbing? Long enough to fetch Paul and alarmingly enough to need to. Now all she felt was embarrassed.

'I was already here,' Paul told her, his hand hovering over the plate as he tried to choose between a bourbon or a custard cream.

Bourbon, she thought absently; he'll go back for the custard cream.

He plumped for the bourbon and dunked it into his tea.

'They arrested us both at the same time, so's we couldn't get our stories straight, I even had a good cop, bad cop, 'cept they were both really nice, actually.' He finished his biscuit and grinned at her horrified face, as he helped himself to a custard cream. 'You got the two bad cops, I'm guessing?!'

How could he even joke at a time like this?

'They arrested you too?! Pulled you off a bus?'

'Technically we've not been arrested, we came in voluntarily, cos they asked us nicely. Mine did, anyway. Anything to help them sort this bloody mess out. And I was in the depot at the time, which was lucky. What do they do, just leave the bus and passengers sat there 'til the relief bus turns up?'

'It's all you ever do when it breaks down,' Joy pointed out. Why was she even having this conversation?

'I sold poor Gareth down the river!' she said hotly, angry at herself and at Paul for being so bloody cheerful and at the police for making her believe her own guilt! She'd done nothing wrong and couldn't prove it, which was just as good as being guilty.

'I sold Gareth down the river and I don't even know the poor guy, other than a couple of times a year when he covers Lee's day off if Madam's on holiday. All he did was come in and do his job. Which we should've been doing in the first place. And I sold him down the river, pointed a dirty finger and blamed him. Anita's prob'ly had it all along. I bet she just uses it like a piggy bank, taking a bit out, putting a bit back.'

'You're doing it again, pointing your dirty finger.'

'Well, why shouldn't I? Someone pointed it at me. That's why they hauled us in. Someone heard me admit it! Can you imagine!'

Now she was angry. Not flabbergasted or amused in disbelief or blubbing her heart out. Just plain self-righteously annoyed. And about bloody time, too! She should be self-righteous, she deserved to be! All this time she'd been sneaking around in a state of fear and dread, obliged to help, feeling guilty just for being asked questions!

But if they asked, they suspected. And that suspicion was a slur, it was saying she wasn't seen as the good person she thought she was. And that was definitely something to feel guilty about.

She felt her eyes well up again and leaned forward into her teacup, head bowed, hoping Paul wouldn't notice.

'I can imagine,' he said lightly. 'More than that, I can even tell you who.'

'Rhys! Bloody Rhys! I bet he said it was at Jack's open day! We all sat around talking about how we were gonna divvy it up!' Oh god, it had become a compulsion—accusing everyone and anyone.

Paul grinned. He couldn't help himself, it was his natural state of expression.

'It was Jack. Didn't you twig the conversation? You must remember, last summer, you got so upset with me, you thought I thought you was guilty? I dunno, I said something stupid and you jumped on it and I remember trying to calm you down. And all the while Jack was earwigging! I said something about all the years we struggled, crappy cars and furniture, child support payments crippling us, and you never once complained or dipped into the till. So why do it when we're finally OK?'

'Christ, I can't remember that. And I said I took it?! What? Was I being sarcastic or something?'

'I said you took it; well, not exactly, I said why take it now or something. You know, like why would the police think that, it made no sense. But Jack remembered it. He remembered it word for word, as far as I could make out. They read his statement out and I realised then what he'd heard. Poor kid; that's been haunting him all this time. That you were holding out on the latest X-Box and Emirates season ticket!'

Joy smiled, despite herself. 'You and your bloody season ticket! Are you serious—he dobbed me in to save his bloody horse?!'

'No; I guess the pressure just got to him. That horse business has really upset him. And then thinking your Mum's got fifty grand stashed away somewhere.'

'Forty. And thinking I'm a thief, don't forget that!'

'Yeah, well, we'll ground him or something when we get in.'

Joy sipped her tea. She hadn't realised how much she needed it.

'You remembered all that? Us arguing? Me accusing you of thinking I was guilty?'

'Yeah, well, it kind've hurt at the time. That I'd let you down. I said something wrong when I should've just been supportive.'

Jack had remembered it word for word. How hurt must he have felt? Joy had thought she was the only one carrying all this. She felt selfish not to realise they were all just as scared.

'We won't tick him off just for doing the right thing,' she said. 'I mean, thinking your mum's a criminal and turning her in, that's the right thing to do, right?'

'A bit of a grey area if you ask me, but I get your point.' He took the last biscuit and his broad grin crinkled his eyes mischievously.

'You would've gotten away with it, too, but for that pesky kid!'

CHAPTER 19

'The BHA's under pressure,' Chris reported, as he drew first dibs on The Racing Post, by dint of being the first to pick it up, and relayed the lead story. Terry and Su were already reading it on their phone apps, but he read out snippets anyway.

'The bookies' association's making a big noise now, as well as the owners' association and ours. No one's sitting back and accepting this.'

'Except us,' Terry pointed out.

'There's nothing we can do until the appeal's heard. But everyone's on our side. Even The Racing Post!'

'Too late to be worrying about a jinx, anyway,' Terry accepted, almost every page of the racing paper using the first Triple Crown attempt in recent history as its starting point for shock and outrage at the ban on Grey Motive. Most of the national dailies had followed suit.

It was in many cases described as a direct attack on the punter and deliberate move to undermine ante-post markets, which lacked reason but instantly won over the readership. The words "denying the chance" were a common denominator, be it about the punter, the horse or sports fans in general. Never before had there been a news story like this, uniting the industry rather than dividing it.

'If he does get to run, he'll have to win after all this!' Chris said. 'No pressure, but the big firms have introduced a "with a run" market—you get your money back if he doesn't run because of the ban!'

'Isn't that meant to be the whole point—non-runner, losing bet?' Terry complained. 'With a run is surely just "A Bet"!'

'You get nowt for owt, as they say. With a run, he's only three to one.'

'He'll probably start longer than that on the day! If he starts.'

'Whether he's odds-on or a hundred to one makes no difference to him or his chances, but the public's behind us and the BHA knows it,' Chris acknowledged.

It was a valid point. The BHA was very conscious of public image and pleasing its audience. The adverse publicity would be ruffling feathers higher up than the Integrity Department, with any luck. And it was higher up the chain that McCulloch had taken his own investigation into what exactly was being investigated. He'd intended to play his "withholding evidence" card and had hoped not to be trumped by a demand for a warrant.

Chris and Terry could only pray for his success and hope to any and all gods that he wouldn't run into Currid first. She would be an insurmountable brick wall and Desprez neatly topped it with broken glass and barbed wire for good measure.

'It's like they're gunning for us personally,' Anne had complained, but Currid's personal crusade was clearly the stain-free reputation of a racing industry that held "no place for undesirables with criminal inclinations", as she had been repeatedly quoted as stating, saying, commenting, remarking, averring, intoning, opining and even, in one of the dailies, "smiling".

'She will not be happy,' Su predicted now, putting away her phone to start the morning's work. 'The kids will be, though. It's a boost to know other people are behind you.'

'Until he gets reinstated, runs and gets beat,' Terry said.

* * *

For all her daydreams of changing jobs, Joy was actually happy to be reinstated in the Precinct shop, working alongside Maud once more. Going back there, while others were still notably elsewhere, was a visible endorsement of her innocence and trustworthiness.

The regular customers were just as happy to see her back, complaining amiably about the relief staff and dredging up every minor error they could think of as evidence of how much better it was to have her back. And she was happy to believe them, nodding and tutting earnestly, while exchanging a sideways glance and a wink with Maud.

'Did they try to dig about what happened?' Joy asked quietly, when the shop was near-empty during a lengthy lull.

Maud shook her head. 'Old Vinnie's crafty, he'd checked out the other shops, knew we weren't in them. I dare say they were rumour-mongering out there. Not one of them had the bare-face to ask, though. They asked after you, mind you. She's on extended leave, I told them, exam year and you know what that young Mandy of hers is!'

Joy smiled.

'So how is your Mandy? Did she sit her exams in the end? Jack must be taking his now?'

'No, his are next year. He's on a scholarship, in the racing industry. You know that horse Grey Motive? That's his one!'

'You don't say! We need that to lose if we want to keep our shop bonus! And your Jack's looking after it, eh?'

And Joy chatted away, filling Maud in on the dramatic turnaround of her once unsalvageable offspring. Maud had always said they'd come good, that she was over-critical and had forgotten what being young was like.

And for that afternoon, she forgot what feeling guilty was like.

* * *

Officially, McCulloch had reported back to the Superintendent, just as officially they were still in court, without time to return to the station before five. De Freitas buttered a warm scone as he listened to McCulloch's account of his BHA visit, no-shows having bumped their court appearances forward.

'I don't think they've an investigation to cite,' McCulloch revealed. 'The CEO seemed a bit embarrassed about it. She's got a bit of egg on her face thanks to the media frenzy over your horse. I suspect the so-called investigation was just us, rocking up and rocking the boat. Currid made a pre-emptive strike to maintain her squeaky-clean house. If there's any more to it than that, they're playing their cards close to their chest.'

'Could it still be pre-emptive?'

'It is still possible, but—and this is a really good big "but"—my side-step past Currid and Desprez happened to pay a very handsome dividend.'

'You saw the Weatherbys account!'

McCulloch smiled. 'As good as. We'd need to go to Weatherbys for the full entry, but Ellen Mead gave me the full ownership listing and account numbers. No one from All Things Pass bought back into Grey Motive. Seemingly the shares are all gone on him, Chris Marsh and Terry Jones retain a heavy controlling interest. Heidi Jones still holds a Weatherbys account and Mead gave me that number.'

'But no connection?'

'Not with Fordham.'

De Freitas added jam to his scone. 'Oh well. Chris said a few of the college friends chipped in a small bit with Heidi, as she assured them a good dividend. Terry was not best happy about it, but the gamble paid off for them and they had the good sense to quit while ahead. Even so, there was the glimmer of hope Fordham might have seen an opportunity to safely hide away cash.'

'Well, now, there's the thing,' McCulloch added, 'Mead suggested our targets – I gave her the list—could invest in any one of fourteen-thousand horses currently in training.'

'That's very helpful,' de Freitas quipped.

'That's exactly what I thought! But Mead was actually very helpful; she just ran our names through a database and drew a blank.'

De Freitas sat back in his seat in exasperation. 'For Christ sake, that's all we needed from Desprez in the first place! Why couldn't he have done that?'

They finished their tea in comfortable silence.

'We're never going to put a line under this Brookhills case,' McCulloch remarked, as they settled their bill and returned to their cars. 'It doesn't usually matter, after all this time. But the state Joy Reid got herself in, you'd hate to see that of any of the others. They'll never get a clear name and return to normality.'

'We should just put a line through them, too. Lack of evidence,' de Freitas agreed. 'If we can't find anything by now, we never will. And who's to say we didn't already eliminate our culprit? People get away with murder. Someone's got away with a year's salary that was insured anyway and they won't be able to spend for the foreseeable future, forever looking over their shoulder.'

'Punishment enough?'

'No. But does it matter? When innocent parties alike have to endure the punishment too?'

Five percent of their cases never made it to court, de Freitas reflected. Unsolved, filed away, forever pending. How many lives were forever pending? It didn't take a lot to declare that a suspect had been eliminated from enquiries. The Brookhills CEO would be the only one annoyed if that included every suspect.

In the end, people would move on, it would simply pass into history. And the Precinct staff had been taught a valuable lesson in procedural compliance and complacency.

'We'll put a line through it in the morning,' de Freitas said in farewell.

* * *

Mornings were meant to be spent in the company of horses, not under duress in the centre of London. Being given a date for their appeal against the BHA ban did nothing to lighten the mood of the two Sainte Bastien trainers.

They stood together by their jeep, watching the older horses approaching at speed. Mai was poised beautifully on a very good handicapper, a mile specialist kindly loaned to them by the trainer of Grey Motive's older brother. It was in all their best interests for Grey Motive to become a Classic winner.

Alongside Mai, on Mo himself, was Cozee Aribo. Neither rider had to do a great deal. Mai's experienced veteran set a good standard and Mai had only to concentrate on travelling at the correct speed. Cozee had only to sit still and gauge the effort needed to stay with the handicapper. And, indeed, go past him.

From where Chris and Terry stood, it didn't look like any effort at all.

There were many expletives and superlatives they could have used and all ran through their head, but in the end it was the simple silence that said it all.

'Are you sure that's the Hunt Cup winner?' was all Cozee quipped, as they drove alongside the two horses.

'As easy as it looked?' Chris checked.

Cozee simply nodded.

'OK, so he's spot on for the Guineas and if the appeal is delayed or denied, we can keep him ticking over for the Dante. That should put him spot on for Epsom. Or Chantilly. Or Royal Ascot.' Chris bashed his forehead off the steering wheel in frustration. 'Fuck it, Terry, I could cry! We can't even make entries for him! There is no plan B or plan C or D!'

Silence was again the only response.

Back in the yard, Terry took Cozee and Mai into the office, to run through their thoughts on Grey Motive and Mai's progression as a budding jockey. Mai would be spending the six weeks of the summer break at the Racing School in Newmarket and hopefully returning to them as a licensed apprentice jockey. If not, their loss would be another lucky trainer's gain. It was at least one future they could plan.

'The appeal is set for Wednesday the twenty-eighth,' Terry told Cozee as she readied to leave. 'If it goes our way, we'll still have time to declare him as a runner for Newmarket by ten the next morning.' It almost sounded reasonable, as though final declarations were not less than twenty-four hours after the appeal.

'I can't leave it that late. I'm already getting offers.'

'Come on, Cozee – you know he'll win if he runs.'

She grimaced. Her heart and her head were telling her two different things, as Terry well knew.

'Whoever rides him at Newmarket keeps the ride,' he pressed.

'And if the appeal goes against you? I want to ride him, but I don't want to be left without a ride.' She shook her head. 'I can't leave other owners hanging until the day before the race.'

She smiled awkwardly and left.

'Everyone decent will be booked by the Thursday,' Mai observed grimly, 'the appeal's way too late. Whoever rides him in the Guineas, if he were my horse I'd book Cozee again for The Derby. I'm just saying, is all.'

Terry smiled ruefully. 'Even if we get to run, we won't have a jockey.'

'I'll ride him!' Mai volunteered, grinning broadly.

Her smile was contagious, even though Terry's broad grin quite definitely dashed any hopes she might have held.

He marvelled at the ridiculous optimism of the younger people around him and wondered at what age it wore off? He vaguely remembered such optimism, but life just bashed it out of him. A run, but no jockey... was that really the most he could hope for?

At this stage, he'd be happy to settle for that.

* * *

'What's happening with this horse of your Jack's?'

Grey Motive had been causing more of a stir than usual since the shop regulars had realised Joy's son was among the connections. The betting market was in turmoil, with punters afraid to back another listed horse in case Grey Motive ran, and equally afraid to back Grey Motive in case he didn't run.

Betting on the race had been suspended for a while, but now, like most, Brookhills was running a "without Grey Motive" book alongside the opportunity to back the horse "with a run".

'The problem is,' Maud complained now, 'a lot of punters had good ante-post odds on the Irish horse and if Grey Motive doesn't run, they'll clean out our bonus. And if he does run and win, he'll clean it out anyway.'

Joy never understood why Maud was so protective of the shop bonus. All the shops were given an average target figure for turnover and profit and any shop that exceeded that earned a small bonus for the staff. It usually paid for the extra Christmas shopping or toward replacing the car or an aged appliance. But Maud wanted for nothing, it was just brownie points, a point of honour on her shop out-performing the others in the chain. Anita had been fiercely competitive and it rubbed off.

'Yeah, well, Jack's still moping about, so you may just put a curse on the Irish horse!'

'That BHA woman's front page news again.'

Joy smiled ruefully. 'Save me the page, I'll give it to Jack for the student dart board!'

'She's not so bad, only doing her job,' Maud pointed out.

'I wouldn't have the confidence to bet if I thought the racing was bent,' a punter agreed, pushing a slip under the window to Maud. 'But banning a horse! That's going too far.' He paid for his bet and got his slip back. 'Currid's backed something else in the race, mark my words!'

'My brother Harold served with her father, you know,' Maud told Joy, as the rush on the next race ended.

'What, Carmel Currid? Were they in the army, then?'

'No, the police. Old Currid was a Commissioner. You'd never hear a bad word said of him.'

Joy pulled a face. 'The apple does bounce a long way from the tree, then.'

'I wouldn't say that. Like the old chap just said, she's only doing her job. And doing it well.' Maud paused to take a bet. 'Her old dad was good at what he did, but he let too many of the rotten eggs away with things. Half of them he didn't even know were rotten eggs. In the end, that's what did for him. A corrupt department, they said. Poor old devil never even knew the half of it, but he ended up dismissed. And he didn't last long after. Harold always said that caused his heart attack. Harold was offered his job, you know. Very well thought of, our Harold always was. Too near retirement, though.'

Maud got up to put the kettle on. 'You can't blame Carmel Currid for running a tight ship. We all know what happens when you don't. But they drove her off the force. She'd turn her own granny in, they used to say.'

'It's a small world,' Joy reflected.

'Not when you've got as many brothers as I have! And Cardi – well! Don't even ask how many are in his family! I doubt he knows himself! You name a name and the chances are I know them!'

Joy laughed. 'How are his folks, by the way? Didn't you say his mum had dementia?'

'No, that's one of his sisters back home. We lost his parents.'

'That's a shame.'

Joy smiled sympathetically as Maud departed for the kitchen, and settled back to enjoy the quiet spell. Even hearing bad news was good, in its own way. It was part and parcel of the normal comradely banter and being part of a shared family. She understood why Maud wouldn't retire and give up a job she didn't even need.

She was happy to keep going, at least until retirement, herself. It seemed a shame that now things were good and her life was back to normal, and Mandy's dreams were being fulfilled, poor Jack was now so miserable. Why couldn't they all just be left alone to be happy for once?

* * *

'Cozee said she won't wait for the appeal,' Mai revealed, as she and Jack ate lunch together.

'She's mad, we'll win for sure!' Jack said adamantly. He had decided a positive attitude might yield a positive result. He hadn't convinced his heart yet, but his mouth was fairly on board and happy to play along.

'The appeal or the Guineas?!'

'Both, obviously.'

'Even without Cozee?'

'He's straightforward, anyone can ride him. There'll be a good jockey available on the day, there might be a small field.'

'Or the maximum.' Mai clearly hadn't heard about positive vibes.

'Will you stay here, as an apprentice?' Jack asked, changing the subject.

'Maybe. Chris and Terry will be my employers when I apply for my licence. It wouldn't be fair to move on straight away. Maybe one or two seasons. What about you?'

Jack had given it plenty of thought already. 'I'll stay 'til Mo retires, anyway. Maybe the yard will have a lot more horses by then and I can stay on and work my way up to Yard Manager.'

'Travelling Head Groom would be good,' Mai suggested. 'You'd get to saddle and help lead up every runner.'

'Yeah... maybe.' Jack wasn't so sure. He'd miss the daily routine of the yard.

Travelling in the horsebox up to Doncaster had been an adventure, but he couldn't imagine doing it every day. He wasn't even sure if Yard Manager was what he wanted. Everyone kept telling him about career advancement, but what was the point if you were happy already?

Mum was happy back in the same job and same shop she'd been in forever and his friend Les de Freitas, who often came down to the yard just to hang out with Mo, had told him when you find something you enjoy stick with it until you don't.

Which was all well and good until something happened to force you to stop. Or you went past the point of return and then found you weren't happy after all and it was too late to change. He thought of Mo, fit and ready to run and doing nothing but ticking over in readiness for something that might never happen.

Win or lose the appeal, he decided to do that BHA placement after all. Even if he couldn't sabotage Mo's suspension, it couldn't hurt to see how things worked behind the scenes.

'Is your sister still shooting?!' Mai asked, the usual tease in her tone.

He pulled a face. 'Still shooting.'

'She should come and shoot here, even if we're not going to need her for High Holborn now.'

God, why did everyone always say that? 'She's doing a thing about people going to Switzerland to die,' he said, by way of an excuse. She most prob'ly couldn't do two things at once anyway.

'I read about that in the local paper,' Mai said. 'It's like way expensive and this old couple who are too old to look after each other anymore wanted to get their trip paid on the National Health because their son is religious and wouldn't pay for them to go, but obviously the NH won't, so they'll just have to die alone or in a care home. I can message you a picture of it, if you like? It's an old one from last year, my mum had a vase wrapped in it.' She grinned. 'I was meant to be helping her sort out things for the church fete, but I got engrossed in last year's news! Someone from my estate won "Britain's Best Dancer" and I didn't even know! Did you know? Mind you, I never watch it. My mum does, but she never mentioned it. Or maybe she did at the time.'

Jack shook his head. 'My dad hates all those shows. Any old vinyl records?'

Mai smiled. 'I did look, but we only had old CDs in the attic. You should go to the fete, though, you never know, loads of old people giving things away.' She messaged him the poster with the details.

'We will win the appeal,' Jack insisted, as they returned to classes.

'That's the easy one,' Mai agreed. 'It's the Guineas I'm worried about.'

It was the Guineas that Jack worried about, later that evening as he tried to listen to "Five Live Yardbirds" and forget about High Holborn and Cozee Aribo deserting Mo. Les de Freitas had promised him faithfully the BHA CEO would overturn the suspension and allow his horse to run, and Les was something of a miracle worker, a good friend to have in a high place after all. But until it happened, Jack wasn't so sure. Unlike Mai, however, he was certain Mo would win at Newmarket, if only he could get there.

His phone lit up and he glanced at the message.

'Tnx freak'.

Any form of written thanks from Mandy was a first and he smiled to himself as he read her whole message. Mai's Dignitas article had been a year out of date, after all, but at least Mandy appreciated the thought in forwarding it to her.

'The writer already knew about them good call tho kiddo'. She'd signed off with a smiley face. Maybe there wasn't a one-finger salute in her emoji range.

He chose, then discarded, various emoji options.

'Hope you've got my betting slip safe' he tapped instead, as the album came to an end, the needle crackling endlessly in the final groove. He dragged himself from the comfort of bed to lift the arm and return the record reverently to its sleeve.

He returned to bed and switched off the lamp, ready to dream of the weekend's pay-out and Mum's face when they told her. Les had to be right about the BHA, he just had to.

CHAPTER 20

'This isn't going to go well,' Terry said, as he and Chris entered the BHA offices in High Holborn.

'Everyone's on our side,' Chris reminded him.

'Exactly! Currid and Desprez will want to save face. If we're guilty, they're not.'

'We're not guilty, we're not even accused!'

Terry said nothing in response, but glowered around reception.

'I hate this place, it scares the life out of me,' he complained.

'You've never been here before!'

'And that's why. Fear of this place. I made sure I never did a thing wrong to get referred here. Doesn't it give you the creeps?'

Chris looked around, with less pessimism clouding his vision. 'Not really. It's just an office.' And not his licence on the line. Were it he facing suspension and not just their horse, he might have been more inclined to agree with Terry.

Still, Terry had a point. If they couldn't argue innocence, Currid and Desprez had merely to establish the possibility of guilt. Despite the presence of lawyers, they couldn't be any further from a court of law.

The receptionist took their details and told them someone would be with them shortly; and shortly someone was – Carmel Currid, no less, chilling even in her pleasant welcome.

Terry shot Chris a told-you-so glance as any optimism vanished.

'This shouldn't take long,' Currid informed them, escorting them into the Stewards' Office. 'A formality.'

And she was right.

It didn't take long to establish that Currid and Desprez had been given a list of suspects in connection with the only remaining Sainte Bastien Racing Syndicate. An earlier dissolved syndicate had profited appreciably following the sale of All Things Pass. Until criminal investigations ceased, the horse Grey Motive was to be considered a criminal asset.

Nor did it take long for the Sainte Bastien legal team to produce a file showing all those listed had been eliminated from police investigations, together with the holy grail—a supporting document stamped by Ellen Mead herself, showing that none of the names had ever been registered with Weatherbys.

Chris and Terry hoped that would be sufficient, but were made to suffer a twenty-minute deliberation by the panel, during which all but the panel were asked to leave the room.

The two opposing sides stood outside the door.

'Have you any idea how many of my department were related to licence holders, when I first took over?' Currid asked conversationally, as Chris and Terry maintained an awkward silence.

'Sixty percent?' Terry hazarded. Most people with any professional interest in racing came from a racing family, in his experience.

She arched her brows. 'Nearer eighty. But that doesn't surprise you?'

'Isn't that exactly why the BHA set up Racing Futures? To give kids from a non-racing background a foot in the door?'

'Then doesn't it worry you,' she countered, 'that those policing you were not unbiased?'

Terry considered it. 'You banned our horse because my daughter had a share?'

Currid pursed her lips, clearly exasperated. 'Your daughter has nothing to do with it! I spent five years alongside Guillaume, carefully cleansing our department, ensuring we had nothing to hide and full transparency. My predecessor had left a mess, but I know my department can stand up to full public and government scrutiny.

'And then the police drop in! Not just money laundering, oh no—money laundering via a potential Classic winner, a horse that could headline in every national paper and generate unwelcome headlines globally! Can your legal team and CEO-signed "pardon" truly prevent that? Are you happy to let that horse run, confident the owners are who they say they are?'

She glared at them piercingly.

'You stand on the threshold of the biggest success story to hit racing in nearly a century, and we all stand on the precipice of the biggest scandal to ever rock our sport in consequence,' she warned. 'I mean to prevent that. To send a clear message.'

'From day one the police were barking up the wrong tree,' Chris assured her. 'Our pardon, as you call it, proves that. There never was any money laundering.'

'Really? I don't see any arrests elsewhere. Certainly not by your DI de Freitas, registered owner.' Her unspoken accusation soured the air.

Guillaume Desprez put a gentle hand on her shoulder, betraying more than a mere office relationship, had Terry and Chris noticed. Their de Freitas would most certainly have. Currid shrugged him off impatiently.

'If your little sheet of paper from Above gets you off today, you'd better make damn sure your stable, your horses and your students are as clean as my office.'

She ended the conversation, but not the chilling stare. Desprez only doubled its intensity.

Chris avoided Terry's eyes; High Holborn was beginning to scare the hell out of him, too.

The ensuing cold silence was broken by a steward inviting them back in.

It was made immediately clear which way the decision had gone.

'Mr Jones, Mr Marsh, you'll be relieved to know we have reached a decision,' announced the smiling Senior Steward, chairing the panel. 'Ms Currid, Mr Desprez, we thank you wholeheartedly for your diligence and for your lightning reaction that would undoubtedly have saved us a good deal of embarrassment under different circumstances. However, we have agreed to overturn the ban on the Sainte Bastien Racing Syndicate and request that the licence be restored with immediate effect. We can see no further need for concern over the registered parties. Thank you gentlemen, Ms Currid, for your time and input.'

Currid smiled politely and nodded her head in acknowledgement before her immediate departure, followed out quickly by Desprez. It took Terry and Chris slightly longer to recover their breath and composure.

Once outside, they took a moment to exhale and look each other in the eye, even Terry's expression breaking into a broad smile.

'Phew or what! We've a horse to declare for the Guineas tomorrow!'

Terry simply nodded, not yet finding his voice.

'We'll sit quietly in reception and ring the girls.'

'Two miracles in one morning?' Terry ventured.

Chris looked at him quizzically, before remembering the press representatives who would already be gathered there. He took out his phone and made the call.

'We won!' He hung up, unnoticed amid the audible squeals of delight from the other end.

'Cozee,' Terry reminded him.

Chris nodded and repeated the simple call.

'She's on the gallops, I left a message.'

'Text her!'

In the hope there might still be time before accepting a booking elsewhere, Chris text the two magic words. He noticed his hand was shaking.

'Christ! This is really happening! Our first Classic runner!'

He was suddenly grateful for the build-up forced upon them. He wondered how many sleepless nights he would have been able to cope with. No more than three now awaited.

In reception, they dealt with the handful of reporters as best they could, promising a media morning in the yard on Monday, should Grey Motive win on Saturday. Maybe by Monday the whole circus would have moved on, decamping to one of the big Newmarket yards. Or maybe this was going to be their life for the rest of the year, or at least until June. Chris exchanged a glance with Terry.

They'd known from the outset Grey Motive would be life-changing. And now, like a brick from the sky, a cartoon Acme anvil even, life had changed.

* * *

'This is the life!'

Paul had completed the tour of the hotel room, far from budget in his opinion, and Joy was trying out the tea-making things, while he sat in an armchair with his feet on the window-sill. A view of part of the many expanses of Newmarket gallops was just discernible from his angle.

The only thing currently missing from the family room was Mandy, who would be arriving in Newmarket on the coach from Victoria later that evening. The free toiletries had been earmarked to go missing on Sunday, when they checked out.

'A step up from self-catering in the caravan!' Joy agreed, passing Paul a mug of free coffee. A good brand, no less. The room-only rate hadn't even been that dear, considering there were four of them.

'Mandy's having the zed-bed!' Jack announced, laying back on the single.

'You need a good night's rest,' Joy agreed, 'we're depending on you to get your horse to the start in good order! Mind you, Maud, Anita and Rhys want him and the Irish horse beat, to save the shop bonus!'

Jack smiled to himself knowingly, their winnings far outweighing any bonus, if only he could keep from ruining the surprise before tomorrow afternoon.

Free teas and coffees and biscuits duly taken advantage of, they ventured down the town to meet Mandy off the London coach and find somewhere for dinner, opting for The Golden Lion. Jack promised himself he'd treat them to somewhere nicer the following evening, although Dad had already booked them a table in the hotel. 'Guineas weekend, you won't be able to walk in off the street anywhere,' Mum had pre-warned.

She and Dad remained in the pub, giving a key to Jack and Mandy to walk back after dinner.

'It's nice to see Mum out again and happy,' Mandy remarked, as they headed to the hotel with little complaint. Mandy had pushed her luck by asking if the room had a mini-bar and Jack hadn't been altogether sure if she was joking.

'I can't wait for tomorrow, this is just massive!' Jack shared.

'Mum said you're dragging us round a museum in the morning.'

'Not a boring one, it's a racing one, Chris said we can't miss it, they've got real horses and everything!'

'Alright nerd boy, take a cold shower!' She smiled affectionately.

'Did those old people die in the end?' Jack asked her, as they sat on the double bed and flicked through the TV channels.

'What old people?'

'The ones I sent you, that Mai found.'

'Ah, them—yeah, safely on their way and departed. That was good, actually, our only couple. Like, couples went, but only one of them had the one-way trip. Must be a bummer, coming back home on your own. Can you imagine Dad coping with that?! I'd pay the extra to have him put down too!'

'Is it dear, then?'

'Jeez, I'd have to watch the film, I only shot it! I think it's about ten grand. You needn't start saving up to bump me off, though—they need the full signed consent of the client! We're just editing now, it needs to go in for our year-end marks the end of next week.'

'Will it be a real movie?'

'It is a real movie, bell-end! A docu-short. But it'll only go on general release if it gets passed by the Met, and then maybe indie festivals. You should see Tisha's, it's well good from what she says, you'd love it with all the animals!'

The talk of the cinematography course moved to Jack's course instead.

'*Totemo tanoshinde imasu*,' he told her in Japanese, adding in his weaker French, '*c'est bon*.'

'If you say so!'

By the time Mum and Dad got back in he was ready for bed, happy to drift comfortably off to sleep as he listened to Mandy repeat everything again. His confidence banished all nerves and he thought only of the satisfaction of the day ahead.

* * *

The Two Thousand Guineas had first been run in 1809 and de Freitas wondered why, of all the winners since, Brigadier

Gerard alone had been sculpted to stand in the Newmarket pre-parade ring, in front of the saddling boxes? How special was the 1971 winner? Would a bronze or marble of Grey Motive one day grace the paddock area? The enormity of it all suddenly engulfed him. He hadn't thought of the gentle little grey colt in terms of historical icon. It hardly seemed real.

He had arrived at the designated spot a little too early; some horses were already walking round, but the majority of the fourteen runners were yet to make their entrance. He could see Chris and Terry standing quietly within a saddling box and knew better than to disturb them. A few of the other syndicate members were beginning to file in and he joined them, nodding politely but on the whole silent. This, then, was what pressure felt like.

He studied the horses circling the pre-parade ring. His wife wondered how anyone could tell the difference between them all, but for him they were no different to the people he encountered daily, with a wealth of individuality shining from each pair of eyes. He could recognise meanness, kindness, nerves and excitement. Alas, not ability. Any one of these might presumably have the beating of Mo.

Chris had told him to look for a rock star or a Hollywood legend. He hadn't been quite sure what that meant, surrounded now by nothing but equine rock stars with Classic credentials. But when Mo walked in, it fell into place. Not a brash front man, but a modest superstar who owned the very ground he walked upon. The grey wasn't the biggest and lacked the heavy muscles and swagger of some; but when they caught his eye they shrank somewhat. There was an imperceptible pecking order among the three-year-old colts and it was clear to de Freitas that Mo was near the top in most of their estimations.

He smiled at Danno and Jack, walking either side of the colt, Danno looking no more than professional, his feelings masked. Jack, on the other hand, could hardly stop beaming, his step light and bouncing. God, the confidence of the young! Teenagers were invincible, life held no consequences for them. Sometimes in his line of work that was bad news, but here in the spring sunshine it just felt good to behold.

He watched Grey Motive getting saddled, a television camera obscuring part of the process. The horse with a big reputation from a tiny unknown stable, albeit one steeped in history, was at the centre of media interest and had become public property. Millions on their settees at home wanted to see their horse in that intimate setting, the closest they were likely to ever get. De Freitas didn't begrudge them and counted his blessings.

The Reids had secured a spot on the parade ring rail and waited with anticipation, Joy with her phone poised for photographic duty.

'Quick! There he is!' Paul nudged her, hastily retrieving his own phone as the sudden urge to click away took hold.

'Don't you dare show him up and call out!' Mandy warned.

Videos and snapshots duly secured, Joy and Paul exchanged a little kiss on the cheek and squeeze of the arm, as pride and the thrill of the moment overcame them.

'I don't give a damn about Maud and Anita's bloody bonus!' Joy said, 'I just want him to win, bless him!'

Joy watched Jack's progress around the vast parade ring, until he was obscured by the groups of owners and trainers in the centre. She recognised Chris and Terry and their wives and would have pointed them out instantly to Paul and Mandy, but for two other familiar faces standing with them. She felt her blood run cold.

'That's him! And with that nice woman who was at Jack's open day! Well, of all the lowdown, sneaky, spying...' she paused to think of another recrimination to hurl at the traitor DI de Freitas.

'Who?' Paul asked innocently.

'My nice policeman! There! I trusted him. He frightened the life out of me, but I thought he was the only one who believed me.'

'That's Jack's high up policeman friend,' Mandy said. 'He owns Mo. Jack was convinced he was helping him!'

'Owns Mo!' Joy scoffed. 'Like policemen can own racehorses! Jack told us how much it costs! And all along he was just spying on us and getting inside information!'

'Still?' Mandy wondered. It seemed more likely the policeman actually did own the horse.

'Still?' Joy repeated. 'You mean he's still investigating me, undercover?!'

'No! More like he's pots of money and does own Mo!'

For the sake of enjoying the race, Joy tried to believe her, but all the old guilt had already flooded back. As cunning as it seemed, it also made so much sense, the police lulling her into a false sense of security so she'd slip up and reveal the money. She felt the blanket of stress drop oppressively across her shoulders once more. Just when life was good and Jack needed all the good luck going.

It had deserted them.

The bell rang to signal time for the jockeys to mount, although most of the connections were still talking. Jack prepared the saddle and stirrups for Cozee, glad she could still share in this experience with Mo. She had, after all, delayed until the last possible moment to take another booking and the partnership remained unbroken.

Terry and Cozee came over and crossed in front of Mo, Terry legging the jockey up at the usual unbroken walk. Cozee leaned forward and gave Mo a pat, then asked Jack how he was. Just normal small talk belying the big occasion.

Jack and Danno led the horse and jockey round a couple more laps of the parade ring, as the grooms tried to get the runners in race-card order for the parade. The horses then filed out onto the track and paraded at a walk in front of the grandstand, before turning back and released by their grooms to canter to post.

For some, it was a step too far, jig-jogging, sweating, boiling over at the added delay. Mo was unconcerned, happy to do anything asked of him. Even when a couple of horses broke parade and cantered past him, he took no cue from them and remained calm. Others in the parade, however, were set alight by the miscreants and the parade soon dissolved.

Jack had told his family to wait at the winner's enclosure to secure the best spot and watch the race on the big screen. He and Danno joined the other grooms by their own viewing spot, ready to run out and greet their charges in what would be a very long five minutes' time.

The connections watched the horses leave the parade ring and then dispersed. Chris, Anne and Su went out to the grandstand to watch the race; Terry found a quiet spot within the parade ring, to listen alone to the commentary. He wasn't the only trainer doing the same.

'And they're off!'

From Jack's perspective, on the running rail some way out from the winning post, the race over the straight mile track was a cavalry charge. For much of it he could see only the colourful pack, no individual discernible. As they did come into full view, they looked to be in a line, the almost head-on perspective deceptive. But there was Mo, Cozee working away where she'd never had to work before. She was wasting her time, Jack could see.

Mo was clear of the pack, maybe by three lengths as the replay later showed. Cozee was taking no chances, driving him out for the line, ensuring he wouldn't ease down and get caught by a flying late finisher. But Mo was barely doing any work at all. Just as at Doncaster, he didn't need to find top gear.

The winning margin of two lengths didn't tell the full story, a flying late finish from the French raider just nudging out the Irish horse on the line, the Precinct Shop bonus depleted but not bust.

The Triple Crown dream was now a reality.

The scenes in the winner's enclosure were joyous. Jack retained his composure, the result never in doubt in his mind, but all around him were laughing and crying in equal measure. Terry covered his face with his hand as Chris fielded all congratulations and media onslaught, the girls hugging Mo rapturously.

Mo loved it all, of course. He posed for the photographers and gazed into the crowd, ears pricked, accepting the cheers and applause as his reward for winning. He didn't know what it was to lose, but he could see the second and third home were not getting the attention. Jack was confident Mo understood the connection. Horses wanted to win, just as the disappointment of those beaten was obvious. They would need a 'confidence booster', an easy race to restore their self-belief. Mo's confidence knew no bounds.

He was already a very short-price Derby favourite, before even walking out of the Newmarket winner's enclosure.

Officially speaking, Jack didn't work for Sainte Bastien and hadn't been on duty that afternoon. Leading up was a work experience reward and he was able to re-join his family as soon as Mo had supplied the necessary post-race veterinary samples and was safely back in a stable under the care of Danno, ready for the drive home.

'They're all watching back in the shop, and you got interviewed and everything!' Joy said proudly, giving him a hug. 'Your Nan and Grandad will be going nuts! You know he's the six-to-four Derby favourite now? There's even a Triple Crown book! No one's ever run an actual Triple Crown book before! He's twenty-to-one! We were stood right next to that one off the telly and he was saying even that was too long a price!'

Jack beamed broadly. 'Mum, I've got some really *really* good news.' He was aware of Mandy shaking her head frantically behind Joy. He frowned, but continued. 'Mandy and I put a bet on Mo last year, when the odds were like really really long, hundreds to one!'

Mandy still shook her head, but was far less animated.

Jack felt his voice lose its excited momentum. He looked at Mandy doubtfully. 'We had thirteen pounds on at a-hundred-and-fifty to one.' Surely she hadn't lost the slip? 'And we've won one-thousand-nine-hundred-and-sixty-three pounds. Haven't we?'

Mandy wouldn't meet his eye. She slowly shook her head.

'See, the thing is,' she admitted, 'you were like so determined to win forty-thousand. For the caravan. And we only had half that, right. And you were so certain he'd win the Triple Crown. So instead of the six bets...' She stopped. 'I'm sorry. Instead of all the individual bets, I just put all of it on the Triple Crown. Seventy-eight pounds on at five-hundred to one. We'll win thirty-nine-thousand pounds, though.'

Despite his confidence, right at that moment Jack felt he'd been robbed of nearly two-thousand pounds. Well, Mum had. He didn't know what to say.

'I don't believe the pair of you!' Joy admonished. 'What have I always told you about gambling?! Unreal!'

Paul had been smiling broadly throughout, nothing his kids ever did a surprise or a disappointment to him.

'Thirty-nine-thousand pounds! Wow.' He slowly took out his wallet. 'So until September, I guess I'm paying for the hotel then, am I?'

Jack and Mandy looked shame-faced.

Paul's grin never wavered. He opened his wallet and removed a pink betting slip. 'I guess I'll have to use this, then!'

He handed it to Joy. 'A tenner at eighty to one. Not quite two-grand, but it'll do. I couldn't be listening to Mo this and Mo that and not take advantage, could I?' He winked at Joy.

'Is this it? No losing bets you're gonna conveniently forget?' Joy demanded; but she looked incredibly happy.

'Anything less than those odds isn't worth the risk, and I doubt we'll ever get that kind've inside info again! I had two bets. The other's on The Derby, one-hundred-and-fifty to one, a tenner again. I'm not so daft to have anything on the Triple Crown or St Leger a year before the event and it's too late for that now! We'll have to rely on this pair of geniuses!'

'Seventy-eight pounds!' Joy laughed. 'You really scraped the sides of the piggy banks, didn't you!'

'But forty-thousand, though. Nearly,' Jack reminded her, coming around to the fact that Mandy had actually done them a favour. Thirty-nine-thousand. Mum's caravan money.

'Until September, it's just a worthless bit of pink paper,' Joy pointed out.

'You have one of those, too?' de Freitas said jovially. He and Mrs de Freitas had come over and stood beside them, unnoticed. 'It seemed like a good idea at the time, but apparently we can't collect until September and have to endure this excitement at least twice more.' He smiled warmly. 'Excuse us for intruding, but we just wanted to say hello and to thank Jack for his part in Mo's success.'

Jack was delighted to be able to introduce the inspector to his family at long last, but to his consternation Mum looked at de Freitas coldly and muttered, 'We've already met.'

'What's going on? Are you still watching us?' Paul demanded, defensively.

Jack looked from his father to de Freitas anxiously. 'Watching us?'

'Well, you are, aren't you? Pretending to own Jack's horse just so's Jack might give the game away!' Joy said accusingly. 'Did you tell the poor kid that's why you hauled us both in the last time, did you?'

Both Jack and de Freitas looked horrified.

'I think we should go and avail of one of those picnic benches over there,' Mrs de Freitas suggested firmly. She opened her handbag and took out a twenty pound note, handing it to Mandy. 'Perhaps you wouldn't mind fetching over six teas for us all, dear.'

She led them to the furthest bench.

'Now then, Lesley, perhaps you would like to explain how you came to be involved in Grey Motive, and let these good people know you are most assuredly not on duty.'

CHAPTER 21

June

'So, a Derby-winning owner—how does it feel?'

De Freitas looked at McCulloch thoughtfully, still trying to work that one out himself, as he settled at his desk on the Monday morning after Epsom. 'Surreal,' he said, after consideration.

And it had been surreal. Like Royal Ascot condensed into a single day. Top hats and pomp and cameras following him and the other Sainte Bastien connections at every step. He had seen the media circus swamp missing children cases, never giving the families involved a moment's peace, but he had not before been on the receiving end. Until the Guineas, he had successfully avoided stress altogether, even side-stepping promotion to maintain a comfortable existence.

The Guineas had changed all that. It was true, he had managed to remain anonymous, the Sainte Bastien team itself bearing the brunt. There had been a private party for the staff and connections on the Sunday after the race; and a media day on the Monday, which simply overran non-stop into the first Saturday of June, four weeks later. But wearing the Grey Motive Owner's Badge at Epsom was anything but the height of discretion and he had been picked out by sniper cameras from arrival to departure; as had every partner in the syndicate.

Grey Motive, now simply Mo to the millions who had taken ownership via their newspapers and TV screens, was public property. Chris and Terry and Cozee were good material, but Danno and Jack and the rest of the staff and students were a media goldmine. It wasn't just a Cinderella story, but every happy-ending fairytale rolled into one. Providing he and McCulloch and his team hadn't missed something and messed up, it must be their old friends Currid and Desprez's perfect wet dream.

'You watched on TV?'

McCulloch nodded. It had been quite the talk of the office since that heady first Saturday of May. 'Kept seeing you. And Mrs de Freitas getting value from The Hat. They showed the horse arriving in a lorry and being led off it. Arriving in his stable. Getting washed, getting brushed, getting dressed, pretty much every intimate detail of a horse I'd never considered as primetime viewing before. They did some pre-recorded features on the stable and staff. I hope you recorded it all?'

'Mrs de Freitas' sister has it all saved and ready for a viewing party at the weekend.'

'You'll enjoy it. Especially the experts who said the track wouldn't suit him. I'm surprised it suited any of them, it's like a rollercoaster, they showed the gradients! A drop the height of the Eiffel Tower, or ten double-deckers, a football pitch and two-and-a-half blue whales in layman's terms!' McCulloch joked. 'And the experts were good value, they listed one or two better chances in the race. Apparently, yours wasn't good enough odds to bet on. The one who finished four lengths behind your horse in second, seemingly he was the value horse of the race. Go figure, eh?'

'I have to admit to believing them, Will. It just seemed too much to hope for.'

Jack and, indeed, Mo had never once showed any doubt, lapping the Epsom pre-parade and parade rings as cool as cucumbers, the contagious beam on the boy's face buoying their step. The pressure, not to mention warmth, of Derby day had been greater on the horses than at Newmarket, with most of them sweating foam and some straining the strength and patience of their handlers.

It was true that the race could be lost before the start, but Chris affirmed it would make no difference to the good ones. 'In this company,' he'd revealed, 'it only affects the horses who probably shouldn't be here. The good ones will still be at the top of their game, upset or not.'

That had hardly quelled his nerves. He had been resigned to defeat right up until the point Mo and Cozee had cruised into the lead shortly after straightening for home and it became obvious nothing would catch them.

After that, the afternoon had been nothing but tears and hugs. Not to mention copious amounts of champagne and congratulations from people he didn't even know. Nothing in his life to date even compared. As his wife succinctly put it, twice the bubbly and kisses of their wedding day.

The largely desk job of detecting hardly compared, but was kinder on the heart.

'Were you thinking of opening one of those files? Or just thinking?'

De Freitas looked up, miles away. 'Just thinking you're a bit slow with the coffee this morning!'

'Fair enough, you are supplying the whole department with cream cakes at lunchtime, after all!'

'I am?'

'Derby-winning tradition. All our owners of Derby winners do it.'

De Freitas laughed and began to open the files in his in-tray. He studied the contents, but with none of his usual enthusiasm. New cases; new information on cases in progress; and nothing to report on cases about to be set aside. Since meeting the Reid family at Newmarket, it was the latter that played on his mind.

It had been easy to put a line through POIs, rendering them no longer of interest and free to return to normality. As far as he'd known, they had. Meeting the Reid family socially had changed that view.

Not for the first time since Guineas day, he fetched up the Brookhills case on screen and read through the summary, trying to find something they'd missed. He didn't need to; but the Reids, the Fordhams, the Baxters, the Rogers, Simmons and Wallises needed him to. Until one of them was convicted, a shadow hung over all of them.

His team had eliminated three of them almost immediately. He'd double-checked and triple-checked the validity of that, but the Saturday girl Tracey Pattinson had no way of accessing the floor safe. Gareth Rogers' movements had been wholly recorded on camera on his only day in the shop during the period of the theft. And Maud Simmons was still innocently adding to her accumulated wealth, their joint account rarely touched by her and her husband.

Baxter and Fordham hadn't been shy to spend money and de Freitas was still haunted by the memory of McCulloch showing Pritchard the procedural alternative to habitual shortcuts. He didn't like coincidences and, by coincidence, Joy Reid wasn't the only one connected to a forty-thousand pound equine investment opportunity. So far, Baxter was still legitimately paying a mortgage on a holiday apartment and Fordham wasn't linked with anything tangible, but the longer the period of time, the more careless they were likely to become.

Or, they were simply innocent.

But the money hadn't crumbled to dust or left of its own accord.

* * *

Jack had become accustomed to cameras over the past month and the media training, designed to help the prospective jockeys and trainers among the students speak comfortably in front of journalists and TV crews, had stood him in good stead. The week-long Student Showcase at the MetFilm School would be an interesting opportunity to see how others handled the sharp end of a camera. And how his sister handled the business end.

'Will we get to see the film?' he asked Mandy, as he sat on her bed, looking through the leaflet she'd fetched home. There seemed to be lots of activities and events, including exclusive screenings.

'Of course! That's the whole idea! And industry professionals are on the guest list!'

'Sweet!' He handed her back the leaflet. 'I'll get to see the old couple I found you!'

'Steady on, Stephen King, Louisa had already found them!' She gave him a friendly hug. 'But if she hadn't, you would have saved the project and been responsible for the highlight of the whole film!'

She put the leaflet up on her dressing table.

'You won't actually get to see them, we had to pixelate their faces, so's their son doesn't find out. But I videoed our pre-edit on my phone, so if you're very good I'll let you see it.'

Jack considered her words. 'How is her son not gonna find out? They're dead, aren't they!'

'Yeah, but he won't know how they did it. Could've saved up, like, or found some sponsor or something. But definitely not their daughter-in-law! She's meant to be Orthodox whatever as well. They reckoned it was lip-service, though, just to marry him and keep him happy. When push comes to shove, kiddo, family comes first above some may-or-may-not exist deity. The old pair believed firmly, but they also believed firmly God would forgive them.'

Jack watched the video on Mandy's phone and came to the same conclusion himself. Any god who wouldn't forgive them would have to be a seriously callous bastard. It was sad that their son couldn't see that, and him a Cardinal and everything.

They were dead old and had been married for more than fifty years. The wife was so frail she was in a wheelchair and couldn't lift herself or do anything. The husband had to do everything for her, like everything. It was pretty gross, but he knew Dad would do the same for Mum and they'd only been married half that. He felt pretty sure they had a twentieth anniversary coming up. And then the husband got cancer. Terminal. And neither of them wanted some stranger to be bathing her and stuff. Jeez, who would! She was scared and didn't want to be on her own and he was scared and didn't want to die on his own.

It didn't make him cry or anything, but Jack just found the whole thing really sad.

'Is the whole thing like this, cos you'd better not let Mum and Dad see it, they'll be bawling their eyes out!'

'Yeah, it's powerful filming, right? But some of the others are really like upbeat and happy, right, and had the holiday of a lifetime and created brilliant memories and then died really really happy and their family never even got to see them sick and only remembered them happy, so it was a real feel-good film in the end.'

'If you say so.' Jack couldn't imagine it himself. 'You sure none of the animals die or anything in Tisha's film?' he checked.

'Cross my heart and hope to die,' she said solemnly, doing the actions.

He thought of the people who died in Mandy's film. It seemed like a really good idea. But how did you know when? He'd hate to go too soon or leave it too late. Not that he would ever afford it anyway.

And then another thought occurred to him.

'Would you say Maud was a common name?' he asked Mandy.

She shrugged. 'Dunno…'

'Well, d'you know anyone called Maud?'

'No, doesn't mean it's unusual, though.'

'S'pose not,' But still, it bothered him. 'Mum's friend at work is called Maud.'

'Oh yeah, there you go, then.' She looked across at him. 'Don't worry, we edited out the names.'

'Their Maud did something very brave and dangerous to pay for them to go to Switzerland. They said God would forgive her, too.'

The girl interviewing them had then asked them what she'd done. They'd said it was very wrong, she shouldn't have done it, but they would be eternally grateful she had and God knew that. God would forgive her.

'So? She paid for them to go when her husband said no.'

'What with, Mandy? You said it cost loads.'

'Shit! You think it's Mum's Maud! That's where the shop money went!' Mandy sat up on the edge of the bed. 'Think about it for a minute. She can't be the only Maud in Reading. And I don't think her husband's a Cardinal. Mum would've mentioned it, surely? And Mum said no one else in the shop needed any money. Isn't it Maud who goes to Barbados every Christmas? Or is that Madam?'

'I think Maud's the one they call the wealthy widow.'

'Well, then she definitely doesn't have a husband, either. She's the wrong Maud. It was too much of a coincidence anyway.'

They sat quietly, feeling crestfallen. They both knew how much it would mean to Mum to be truly cleared of guilt.

* * *

Grey Motive's next race had been decided as the King George VI and Queen Elizabeth Stakes, run over The Derby distance of a mile and a half at Ascot on the last Saturday of July. It had not been an easy choice and the Eclipse Stakes over a mile and a quarter on the first Saturday of July had been tempting. They were conscious that speed counted for everything at stud and a Derby winner coming back in distance would be far more commercial than a Derby winner adding the mile and three-quarter St Leger to its CV. But Ascot gave their horse longer to recover from Epsom and was a better stepping-stone to Doncaster.

'He'll stay in training next year anyway, he'll be a much better four-year-old,' Chris reasoned, 'we can have a crack at the Eclipse then.'

Their controlling ownership had held sway when the offers flooded in. They might have become several million pounds richer had the vote gone the other way, but Grey Motive would have been heading for the Prix de l'Arc de Triomphe instead of the St Leger, and off to stud instead of an extra year on the racecourse. In the stallion stakes, millions were invested, not risked. New owners would reap their returns through stud fees, but for Chris and Terry every race only brought with it the risk of defeat and devaluation.

They had, of course, considered running in both the Eclipse and the King George; but the Triple Crown was their focus. The plan had been mapped backwards from the St Leger and only one race now stood between The Derby and their fateful day at Doncaster.

The doubters came out in force. Grey Motive would be taking on his elders for the first time. Four-year-old colts were stronger and more experienced. There would be the previous year's top filly to contend with as well. Not as physically strong as the colts, perhaps, but receiving a favourable weight allowance to make up for it. Was this year's Classic form as strong as last year's?

Mo had everything to prove and a big reputation to lose.

The Reid family had missed Epsom, one of the busiest days of the year for Mum in the shop and too expensive, even if it hadn't been sold out in advance. Although Mum still couldn't get a Saturday off to go to Ascot, Nan and Grandad were going and the house was filled with excitement as they dressed up for the occasion.

'It's not Royal Ascot,' Jack pointed out.

'But it's Ascot! Nan and me have fascinators!' Mandy insisted.

'Maud's got today off and she's planning to go,' Joy told them, as she gave the outfits a final approval before leaving for work. 'She reckons it's not every day you get to see a Triple Crown winner!'

'That's a first, isn't it?' Paul remarked. 'I didn't think the pair of them ever went anywhere.'

'Cardi's not going. He only leaves the house to go shopping. Still, I know the feeling,' Joy sympathised.

'We'll fetch you back a souvenir!' Paul teased.

By four o'clock, in the vast amphitheatre of Ascot's parade ring, Jack was feeling the pressure. Maybe it was because until now he'd been the only one certain of Mo's Triple Crown ability. Now everyone shared his belief and shared his horse and, in return, shared with him their doubts.

For Mo's sake, he tried to maintain his usual positive vibe, but when he looked around at last year's Oaks winner, the fillies-only equivalent of The Derby, and last year's Arc winner and that year's Eclipse winner, all so much bigger and stronger than Mo, he realised the enormity of the race ahead. The weight of an unbeaten record didn't help, either.

Nan and Grandad waved and called out good luck each time he passed them, much to Mandy's embarrassment. To make matters worse, they were stood on the rail right in front of the TV camera focused on him, so Mum and the entire shop would see them. Except Maud, who was somewhere out there, watching in person. Without Cardi.

Jack wasn't sure why his mind was wandering, trying to think of anything but his precious Mo finishing last of the five runners. Only five. Only four horses brave enough to take him on.

He gave Mo a confident and hearty pat on the neck.

The bell rang, he pulled down the stirrups and freed the reins, aware of Cozee being legged up, before he led the pair out under the grandstand and onto the track.

He desperately wanted to watch the race with his family and wished Mum could be here too. Instead, he waited with Chris, Anne and Su in the parade ring, watching on the big screen in the company of the gathered owners. Terry, as usual, stood alone somewhere and Danno remained out in the chute, from where they'd released Mo onto the track.

Anne had told his family where to stand for the race and Jack glanced up at them. Mai and her family were up there with them, and Grant and his dad. Nan spotted him and waved and Grandad gave him a thumbs up. They had the best seats in the house to watch the first four home get led back into the winner's enclosure beneath them and to see the trophy presentations after, by a member of the Royal party. The winning groom would also get a prize. But, for the fifth home, there was nothing but prize money and an empty unsaddling enclosure for one.

A silence fell over the racecourse as the last of the five runners was led into the stalls. Jack realised he'd never actually seen any of Mo's races from the very start, other than watching the recordings later. Maybe he shouldn't watch, maybe it would be bad luck to watch... but his eyes were drawn to the big screen and the five horses jumping out perfectly in a line.

He felt a heavy hand on his shoulder and glanced behind him. De Freitas smiled reassuringly. Mrs de Freitas was clutching her husband's arm tightly. The air was heavy with silent prayers.

And up on the giant screen, the five horses had fallen into a conga line, the filly leading them in single file, bowling along with her ears pricked and loving every minute. The colts behind were settled, no one pulling hard, the jockeys all sitting tight, no movement from the saddle.

They remained that way, the order unchanged, as they ran down into Swinley Bottom, the sweeping turn that would bring them onto the straight for home. And still no one moved. Jack felt the grip on his shoulder tighten.

A bell rang in the distance. The runners had rounded the turn and were on the straight.

The crowd started to roar. The procession of horses fell apart as the filly tried to pull away further and the colts swallowed her up. It was the Eclipse hero now going forward, his jockey barely moving, hands and heels. Two others hot on his tail, one rider motionless still, the other already throwing everything at his mount to reel in and pass the leader.

They were shouting for Mo now. Jack could hear them on the other side of the grandstand, a universal cry of 'Go Mo! Go Mo!', echoing the familiar voices now screaming the same beneath the giant screen. Was his among them? He realised he was only mouthing the words silently, his mouth too dry to speak. His lips formed the words over and over, as the Arc winner finally got the better of the Eclipse winner in a head-for-head battle. And at last Cozee lowered her hands and began to pump and urge and drive, as Mo swept up alongside the two lead horses and hovered with them for a while.

For one desperate, heart-stopping moment Jack thought that was it. His beloved grey was stretched and couldn't go by. Third was brilliant, an honour, a crushing, crushing blow. He stopped mouthing the words, just stood in silence and watched, as Mo quickened again and put one, two, three strides between him and the tiring lead horse. The other fought back, snatched second, but the race was already over.

Grey Motive had won by a length.

The small group of people erupted. Terry came racing over from nowhere and jumped on Chris, nearly knocking him over. There were no tears, only hugs and joy and utter, utter relief. The expectation of losing was so much easier to brush off than the expectation of winning, it seemed.

Jack sprinted back out under the grandstand to jump on Danno and do his best Premiership goal scorer impression. The pair danced around in an animated hug, screaming into the television crew's mic as the cameraman ran out for the money shot.

Mo took an eternity to pull up and canter back, but at last there he was, Cozee leaning over his neck hugging him. Danno and Jack ran either side of him and added their own hugs and kisses. A TV presenter walked alongside and thrust a mic on a pole up at Cozee to gain her on the spot thoughts, then those of the two ecstatic grooms.

It had been a bit of a shock to Mo to have to dig deeper and find an extra gear, Cozee said, but there was still plenty more in the tank if needed. A horse of a lifetime, said Jack, aware that a very big lifetime still stretched ahead of him and that it really didn't matter if he never felt this magic again. It would never, ever leave him.

At some point in the winner's enclosure, as the 'horses away, please' was announced, it was decided Danno would take Mo back to the stables and Jack would go up for the prize. Jack promised to only collect it on Danno's behalf. It was Danno's trophy and Jack's moment.

The drive home was quiet. Mandy and Dad and Grandad never stopped talking and Nan kept repeating softly to Jack how proud she was, how well he'd done for himself. But to Jack, it was a sea of silence. He relived the race again and again, blocking out the inane chatter.

Then it really was silence, just him and Dad and Mandy parked outside the house.

'Maud has got a husband, then,' Mandy said, as they climbed out and followed Dad up the front steps.

'What?'

'I was thinking about it, Mum watching in the shop and Maud being there today. D'you think Cardi could be short for something? Like, maybe Cardinal's an actual name?'

CHAPTER 22

It was, as Mandy said, a moral dilemma.

'We have signed contracts and everything, we agreed to pixel out their faces and not use their names.'

'You're not a priest or something, though! If you think it's evidence, you have to go to the police,' Jack argued.

'If it is Maud, she did a nice thing. We can't send her to prison for it. What about her Cardi? Those were his parents. It's not like Mum's going to prison. Your Mr de Freitas promised her it was all over.'

Jack remembered Newmarket and the look on Mum's face. He'd felt betrayed by Les. But that was nothing to how Mum had felt. No matter Les' assurances to the contrary, Mum would be looking over her shoulder every day of her life.

'That's it!' Jack declared. 'We'll show it to Les, he'll help us, he'll know what to do.'

'He's just a normal detective, Jack – he was on Mum's case, not some high up bigwig helping you.'

'Well, he was helping me. He helped Mum, didn't he? And he'll help us still. It can't hurt to show him.'

Mandy wasn't so sure. 'I don't even think I'm allowed to.'

'What if he'd gone to the screening, then? He could've watched it if he'd wanted. Nothing to say he couldn't.'

'I wish I'd never shown you it now or said anything.'

'Yeah, but you did. We have to show it to Les. Then everyone will know Mum's innocent.' He stopped and thought about it. 'Then Mum will know that everyone knows she's innocent.'

'What do we do, wait for him to be at your stables?'

'He gave me his card. It has an office address, we'll go there.'

'What about Mum?'

Jack shook his head. 'She'd never let us rat out Maud. And then she'd have even more to carry round on her shoulders.'

'OK, then. First thing Monday.'

'First thing Monday,' Jack agreed.

* * *

'I fetched cakes!' de Freitas announced, as he hung up his jacket and sat down at his desk.

'How many more races will the horse have, I could get used to these monthly treats.'

'Just the one more, Will. We need to watch our waistline. Not to mention my wallet. Cakes aren't cheap, you know, and I'm an owner in name only, remember.'

'I read his prize money stands at just over three million. Not bad for a twenty-grand investment.'

'I never had twenty-thousand to invest and that three million is split between the shareholders. No sour grapes.' De Freitas leaned back in his chair. 'You know what, Will? I wouldn't give up this experience for any of that money. Being around that horse has just been... well, priceless.'

'Same for all the office, a good bit of fun. Pritchard's putting together a racing club, if he gets fifty members it's only a tenner a week.'

'You're forgetting the cakes.'

Pritchard himself interrupted them, to inform them of visitors.

'They say they've evidence you need to see and they've refused to talk to anyone else,' he said, popping the desk slip in front of de Freitas.

'Mandy and Jack Reid! Good Lord! Show them up.'

Mandy and Jack were given a quick tour of the large single-floor office, with many different desks and work-stations but generally open plan. Jack was still unconvinced that most of the work was done there and privately noted the many empty desks, imagining the usual occupants out investigating crimes, like the proper detectives on the telly.

'So, what do you have for us?' de Freitas asked. 'You don't mind if Will sits in, do you?'

Jack explained about Mandy's film and Mandy passed de Freitas her phone, cued up ready for the unedited Simmons segment. McCulloch pulled a seat up alongside and watched over his shoulder.

'OK,' de Freitas said slowly, as the clip ended. 'And this was when?'

'March,' Mandy said.

'This March?'

'But the newspaper feature was last year, January,' Jack added.

De Freitas looked at the clipping Mandy had received from Jack, and McCulloch instantly googled it, finding the full paper and date.

'December, the year before,' he noted, 'but, still...'

'I'm afraid the dates don't add up,' de Freitas told them, knowing he was crushing their hopes. He and McCulloch had been crushed often enough themselves by this bloody case. 'Sorry to disappoint, but the theft pre-dates this by at the very least three months.'

Mandy confidently took charge.

'You need to watch the whole film. I've only the unedited copy on my phone, fifty-minutes, but these people don't wake up in the morning and decide today's the day, it doesn't work like that. It's all pre-booked and they get to enjoy their last year or eighteen months, even. The Simmons knew. They had their date booked. Maud took the money to pay for it.'

'But why? She has so much more than that in her bank.'

Mandy smiled. 'Mr de Freitas, could you withdraw nine-thousand pounds without your wife knowing about it?'

'Good point,' McCulloch agreed.

'Her hands were tied, Mr de Freitas,' Mandy insisted. 'You have to at least ask her.'

'But don't arrest her,' Jack added hastily. 'From something really bad can come something really good, that's what Chris once told me and that's what old Mr and Mrs Simmons would say if they were still here. She did a little bad thing for a massive good thing.'

'It's theft, Jack. You know that.' De Freitas sighed. 'We'll talk to her.'

'What about my film?' Mandy asked. 'It's confidential.'

McCulloch smiled. 'It is, but this newspaper feature isn't. And it's now the basis of our enquiry.'

'Wow, Mai found that, just by chance,' Jack told them. 'It could help my mum and her brother.' Just in time he stopped himself from continuing 'even if he is an arsehole'.

'I certainly hope so, Jack, we'll do our best. And for Maud, of course.'

De Freitas wondered how. His job was complicated by innocent guilty parties, which seemed to be a trait with Sainte Bastien.

He looked at the two children before him, technically two young adults, which in turn complicated his immediate thought.

'Would you like a ride home in a squad car?' he offered hesitantly.

He and McCulloch dropped the Reid offspring at their home and continued in their unmarked car to the home of Maud Simmons.

'You can come in, if you like, Cardi's only just gone out. He's shopping and picking up the dry cleaning as well, he won't be back for at least an hour.'

They accepted the offer of a pot of tea and settled down in the living room, where many an interview had already been carried out before. Maud's bank balance had repeatedly been a Get Out Of Jail card.

'So, what's the story? Have you caught him yet?'

By way of reply, McCulloch handed her the print-out of the newspaper feature. Maud studied it briefly.

'Oh.'

De Freitas had already gleaned much from her expression.

'I take it the surname is no mere coincidence?'

Maud shook her head. 'You're a bit late in finding it.'

'Google,' McCulloch told her truthfully.

'Would you like to tell us about it?' de Freitas asked gently.

'I suppose I better had.'

There had, of course, been arguments. She could always win with Cardi, but not when he fetched in The Big Guy Upstairs. Two against one, so to speak. And in the meantime his parents were frightened and desperate and seeking help elsewhere, to no avail.

'And there was the float,' she told them. 'I knew it wouldn't get checked or changed for at least six weeks. Initially I planned to put back whatever we didn't use, and then try to build it back up again before it was checked. But realistically, I'd only be narrowing your search, wouldn't I? Why so precise an amount missing?'

So she had taken it all and spent it as quickly and thoroughly as possible. Dignitas had been booked and paid. A week's holiday in Switzerland for Beryl and Clive next door, neighbours of her in-laws for most of their lives.

'Someone had to go with them and it couldn't be me, could it?'

She took her in-laws to the funeral home and let them choose a nice burial plot together and whatever coffins they wanted, 'money no object!'

'Funny how you can actually have a good laugh and enjoy yourself, choosing your final resting place,' she recalled. 'It took them a while to agree on the music, mind you.' She smiled fondly, her eyes misting.

She had made a reasonable dent by now in the shop float and realised she hadn't a hope of replacing it without raising Cardi's suspicion.

'I'm a widow, not a divorcee, and that's how my heart would like it to remain.'

De Freitas and McCulloch hadn't been able to trace the bulk of the money simply because they hadn't known where to look. In the age-old question of why would you steal, the answer to give to charity had never been put forward.

Maud carefully folded up notes to the value of five-hundred at a time and posted them into every collection box she found. She slipped the remainder into an envelope and handed it in to the local hospice.

'By the time they knew it was gone, it was gone,' she concluded.

She held her hands straight out in front of her. 'You'd better cuff me and bring me in, before Cardi gets home. I wouldn't want him to see.' She dabbed her glistening eyes with her sleeve. 'I wouldn't want him to know, but there's no avoiding that now. They came home to the chapel of rest and he forgave them. I cleaned out their savings and left them overdrawn, that all went to charity, too, so he assumed they'd managed it all on their own, in the end. God's will, in a converse way. It wouldn't have been, had we interfered.'

She jiggled her wrists, hurrying them along.

'Hands by your side,' de Freitas insisted, 'I'm sure there's no need for force.'

He walked with her out to the car, feeling as reluctant as she no doubt felt. If only catching the bad guys was only about catching the bad guys.

She sat quietly in the back, looking relieved, if anything. Maybe the weight of guilt wasn't only oppressive on the innocent.

De Freitas climbed into the passenger seat, assigning the executioner role to his sergeant.

'Which way are you going?' he checked finally, after several missed turns and wrong roundabouts.

'The right way,' McCulloch assured him. 'Mrs Simmons, would you be able to list the charities and amounts involved, including Dignitas? I checked, they're a not-for-profit organisation.'

'Yes, I think so. It was a while ago now, but I won't forget all those collection boxes in a hurry.'

McCulloch pulled his notebook from his pocket and passed it back to her.

'Make a start, would you. Who got what, until the full amount is accounted for.'

By the time she'd finished, they were parking in the Brookhills head office car park.

'Are you going to make me give it all back?' she asked McCulloch, looking anxiously to de Freitas, who simply shrugged, just as confused.

McCulloch shook his head. 'Work with the best and learn from the best,' he said, with a nod to de Freitas. 'I think I can get us out of this, if you don't mind taking retirement?'

'But I love Brookhills!' Maud protested. 'And Cardi will go potty having me under his feet all day!'

'What did you do during your suspension?'

'Volunteered at the food bank.'

'There you go, then. And it's better than prison, surely?'

Maud made no further protest.

'Are you sure about this?' de Freitas asked McCulloch quietly, as they waited in reception for the CEO to see them.

'Isn't our job about judgement of character? You even use it on horses!'

'Fair point. I just hope you're right about this chap. People tend to progress up the company ladder by stepping on people.'

The Brookhills CEO made no secret of his delight that they had finally arrested the culprit.

'Long overdue! Not sure what you were doing all this time.' He looked doubtfully at the sad elderly woman accompanying them.

'Who's this?'

'Maud Simmons, Sir, the cashier responsible,' McCulloch explained. 'It took us so long because we were looking for a motive, one of personal gain. Mrs Simmons simply had a momentary crisis of conscience. She gave some money to a poppy seller on the way to work, then removed the cash from the floor safe and gave it to a number of other charities.'

McCulloch handed his notebook to the CEO, who solemnly read through the list.

'Is she...' he wasn't sure of the politically correct way of phrasing it, conscious that "she" was present. 'Are you, um, aware of your actions? Is there any medical background we should know about?'

Maud shook her head. 'The money was there and I took it.'

'And this is how you spent it?'

'As best as I can remember.'

The CEO returned the notebook. He could think of nothing further to say. Well, done seemed inappropriate. 'Well, thank you for letting me know, gentlemen. I shall issue a letter to those involved, exonerating them. Should you need me in court, I will of course be available. I assume it's a guilty plea?'

'Actually, Sir, we wondered if we might make a request?'

With Maud out of the room, watched by a secretary, it was easy to persuade Brookhills to drop all charges. The embarrassment of charging an elderly cashier, long past retirement age, of misappropriating funds to charity was smoothed by the alternative of accepting her resignation and publicly acknowledging the company's substantial contribution to local charities, list provided.

They dropped Maud back home and stopped in at a favoured cafe to pass their lunch break.

'I think the lunch is on me,' de Freitas decided. 'You played a blinder there, Will. I might even relieve you of coffee duty for the foreseeable future.'

'Oh, I don't know, I probably owe you the odd tea run for training supplied.' He grinned.

They finished their lunch in amiable silence.

'It was something the Reid boy said, actually,' McCulloch revealed, as they returned to the office. 'A bad thing leading to a good thing. I thought we may as well be forgiven for trying the theory out.'

* * *

The first Saturday in September

'You want to know my theory on whether he'll stay or not?' Terry expounded as they set aside the day's Racing Post, cover to cover a lesson in pedigrees and thoroughbred DNA as experts argued over Grey Motive's St Leger chances. An extra quarter of a mile was unknown territory for the horse.

'Genetics is a can of soup. You stick a spoon in and slurp up a bowl of vegetables and lentils, you stick the same spoon back in the same can and slurp up a second bowl of nothing but liquid. We don't know what way the mix went. If he only got the bare minimum from his dam, did that include her stamina?'

Typically, he was a can half-empty sort of guy.

'We knew when we bought him he'd stay,' Chris argued. 'You were the one who said he was a Triple Crown horse! St Leger day is not the time to doubt it! Even if he didn't inherit her stamina, he'll have inherited her guts. He's not going down without a fight.'

They'd had their moment of fear and doubt at Ascot, but confidence had since returned, despite the odds stacked against them. There had only ever been fifteen Triple Crown winners, the first in 1853, the last in 1970. Only one horse had even attempted it since then. Could they be the ones to finally achieve it and restore the Triple Crown to a legitimate target for Classic generations to come? A small stable still in its infancy with a bargain-basement colt?

Chris began to see the half-empty soup can, but wasn't about to admit it.

'Try telling your theory to Jack!' he laughed.

Together they walked down to the racecourse rails and looked across at the Doncaster winning post. It alone held the answer.

Joy had secured a rare Saturday off. Her colleagues had been more than supportive; the Triple Crown was the biggest event in racing's modern history and her shop the epicentre, thanks to Jack. The customers had doubled in numbers and the walls were filled with private photos of "their" horse, supplied weekly by Jack.

For Joy, there was more at stake than just Mo's Triple Crown. A stake of seventy-eight pounds at five-hundred to one, to be precise. The original money had been long-forgotten—they had spent so many weeks dreaming of their thirty-nine-thousand pound pay-out that that had now become the sum of money they were about to lose.

'How long does it take to run this one?' Joy asked, wondering if she could stand the strain.

'About three minutes and four seconds,' Paul informed her, looking at last year's result in the race-card.

'Christ! Have you ever watched the clock waiting for an egg to boil?! Can't he do it any quicker?!'

There were again only five runners, Mo frightening away all but those hoping he would fizzle out of steam before the end. Chancers more than challengers. It didn't take much of a pre-race discussion of tactics in the parade ring.

'Cozee, we've only one instruction—ride him like he stays,' Chris told their jockey. 'Don't nurse him or hold him up to save him for the finish. If something goes on to try to test him, for god's sake go with it and stay up there. Seriously, if you're rowing up the straight trying to reel in the leader, I'm not going to be there to welcome you back in.' He smiled at her frown. 'The medics will be using one of those defibrillator things on me!'

Ten minutes later she thought of his words, pictured their faces, saw in her mind the expression on Jack's face, knowing they were up there, a furlong ahead, leaning over the rail adding their voices to the now-familiar chant of 'Go Mo!'

She wasn't rowing; not yet. She was nursing him along, holding him together, feeling him running on fumes for the first time in his life. Her view of the winning post was framed by his ears, still pricked, his nose straining forward, pushing himself all out for the line he knew so well.

She could see no other horses, but she could hear them. The slaps of the Pro-Cush whips, the heavy breaths, the beating hooves, behind her. Alongside her. The change in the roar of the crowd. Desperation.

She dared not turn her head, lose her rhythm, cost him his. She could only keep going, nursing him, nursing him, inexorably to the line.

* * *

Yourtopia Caravan Park, Tenby

The second week of September had always been the cheapest option for the family holiday, denied them last year. This one was long overdue. Joy sat in the car for a moment, not quite believing it had finally come, as Paul took the bags in and came back out for her.

'Take your time, there's enough of it ahead of us,' Paul said, holding her hand tightly as they walked up the freshly-painted white-railed steps.

Joy opened the door and looked at the photo Paul had fetched, standing in pride of place on the kitchen worktop, of a beaming Jack leading in the victorious Grey Motive. She really didn't need to look at much else in the pristine ex-holiday rental.

'It's perfect,' she said.

END

Acknowledgements

Thank you to...

My ever patient and encouraging family, Tony, Samantha and Susan.

The wonderful team at Maverick House, Liosa for her eagle eye and attention to detail, and particularly to John Mooney, who has been so hugely supportive and encouraging with every book and unimaginably patient between titles.

Booklovers and racing experts Alastair Nicolson (and his wonderful Mother), David Carr, Andrew Speedy, Anne McGann and John Scanlon who were kind enough to say very nice things to encourage me to keep going. Similarly my fellow authors Michael Tanner, Peter Corbett, Brendan Lynch, Roy Hunt, Paul Wright and Gabriel Woods and to my inspiring group of Carlow ETB writers.

To our very dear friends from Cork, the nicest super villains you will ever meet (and you meet them here in their BHA alter-egos!) and to my good friends Maggie, Sue, Diana and Hilda.

The trainers who continue to inspire, support and share their passion, Ilka Gansera-Lévèque, Gina Rarick, Conny Whitfield, Dick Brabazon and Takashi Kodama, not to mention

John McConnell, who took such great care of my very own "Grey Motive", Leitmotif.

And no thanks to...

The pets Amber, Gary, Leitmotif and assortment of ducks and hens and elderly goldfish, who keep me sane and bring such joy, but make so many demands on my time it's a wonder I ever got anything more than the Dedications written...